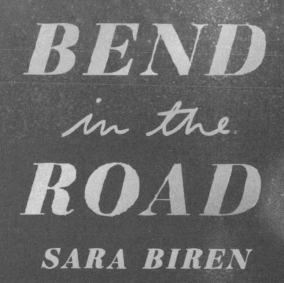

BEND
in the
ROAD

SARA BIREN

BEND

in the

ROAD

AMULET BOOKS
NEW YORK

Cataloging-in-Publication Data has been applied for and may be obtained from the Library of Congress.

ISBN 978-1-4197-4873-8

Text © 2021 Sara Biren
Book design by Hana Anouk Nakamura

Published in 2021 by Amulet Books, an imprint of ABRAMS. All rights reserved. No portion of this book may be reproduced, stored in a retrieval system, or transmitted in any form or by any means, mechanical, electronic, photocopying, recording, or otherwise, without written permission from the publisher.

Printed and bound in U.S.A.
10 9 8 7 6 5 4 3 2 1

Amulet Books are available at special discounts when purchased in quantity for premiums and promotions as well as fundraising or educational use. Special editions can also be created to specification. For details, contact specialsales@abramsbooks.com or the address below.

Amulet Books® is a registered trademark of Harry N. Abrams, Inc.

ABRAMS The Art of Books
195 Broadway, New York, NY 10007
abramsbooks.com

To my parents—thank you for always believing in me.
Mom, you are the strongest woman I know.
Dad, I miss you every day.

Chapter One

GABE

WELCOME TO STONE & WOOL FARM.

The sign hangs from a stone pillar at the main entrance to the farm. Tall, sprawling pines hug one side of the long driveway. Cones of light from lampposts on the opposite side scatter across the gravel, some of them dim, some out altogether. Frank's pickup bumps along ruts in the long road to the main house.

"Place looks better in the daylight," he says.

Frank hasn't talked much since he met me at the baggage claim at Minneapolis–St. Paul International a couple of hours ago. A gruff, "You hanging in there all right, kid?" along with a tight, bone-crushing hug. A few comments like, "No fancy limo, then, huh?" and "You hungry? I could go for a burger myself."

I've always liked that my uncle Frank is a man of few words. A man who recognizes that you don't have to fill every moment of silence with meaningless conversation. This whole ride up from the airport, he didn't ask about the album or my very recent ex, Marley, or even Chris. He's smart, too. Knows how to read a room. Or the passenger seat of a pickup truck, as it were.

We continue down the gravel road until Frank turns in to the driveway at Gran's, a big white house with a wraparound porch and stone columns. The porch lights are on, as though someone knew I was coming.

"I asked you to keep this to yourself," I say, my words hard and cold. My pulse races and I can feel that familiar weight of dread settling in, a brick low in my gut.

"I told Laurel," he says. "That's it. I had to make sure the place was livable, Gabe. She won't call the paparazzi, if that's what you're worried about."

I shake my head. "I don't give a fuck about the paparazzi." It's not exactly true, but I'm running out of fucks to give.

"I didn't tell your dad, either, so you don't need to worry about that." He sighs.

"Laurel will if she hasn't already. It's her job."

"I asked her not to. Come on, kid, give me a little credit."

He's right. I know I can trust Frank. That's why I called him in the first place. I take a deep breath, try to break up that brick of dread. I'll need to talk to Chris at some point while I work my way out of this mess. But I'm not ready yet.

"Thanks," I murmur. "Bet you never expected so much drama when you married into this family."

He shrugs and turns off the ignition. "It's not so bad. Besides, a little drama is worth it for the free concert tickets and backstage passes, am I right? Let's do this. I'm beat, and those cows won't milk themselves in the morning."

I probably should have gotten a car instead of calling a guy who's up every day before dawn to milk cows and whatever the hell else he does. Busts his butt to keep a farm and a family above water. Helps with this farm, too. But I called him, and he dropped everything and drove two and a half hours one way to meet my sorry, incognito ass at the airport so I could pretend to be nobody special, getting picked up at MSP by a regular guy with a beard wearing a Minnesota Wild ball cap and a rust-orange Carhartt jacket.

Truth is, I'm not pretending. I'm nobody special after all.

Leaves crunch beneath my feet as we walk up the driveway and sidewalk to the porch, the paint grayed and chipping. I tighten my hold on my guitar, swing the duffel bag onto one shoulder, and grab the wooden railing, which wobbles under my grip. My memories of this place are few and far between and, to be honest, hazy. After Gran died—five, six years ago now?—so did our main reason to come back. Chris spends a few weeks here every summer, a couple of days here and there, but otherwise the farmhouse sits empty. Empty and exactly the way Gran left it when she died. Laurel runs the farm. She asks Chris every now and then if he wants her to clean out the closets or pack up Gran's belongings. He'll say something like, "That's my problem, not yours. I'll worry about it when the time comes." I asked him once, not long after Gran died, if he planned to sell someday since he wasn't there much, anyway. He shrugged and said, "We'll see."

Frank holds out the key ring. "Take good care of the place." When I wait a beat longer than I should to reply, he says, "You sure about this? You know you're always welcome at our house."

"Nah, I'm good." I shake my head and grab the key ring.

"So, there's one for the round barn. Big barn. Garage, but don't get any ideas about the Mustang. Laurel and Chris are the only ones with keys." He skims over this like it's not a big deal, but I wouldn't mind getting behind the wheel of Chris's vintage Mustang. "Coupla other sheds. You'll figure it out."

I shrug. No reason to figure out any of it. It's not like I'm going to be here more than a few days. "Which one is for the house?"

He takes the keys back and flips through them, stops at one in the middle, gold with a broad, square head. "Look here," he says, placing his calloused thumb on the surface. "This one's old."

I take the key back and hold it close. An engraving, worn almost completely off: *Stone & Wool Farm 7-20-1964.*

"Your grandparents' wedding day. Your great-grandpa gave them the farm as a wedding gift and moved to the cabin on Halcyon Lake the next day. The place has been in the family since 1907, but it's a lot older than that."

I never met my great-grandfather or my grandfather, who died when I was a baby. "Thanks for the family history lesson." I can't help the undercurrent of sarcasm. I'm tired and need to sit my ass down again before I collapse, and what difference does any of it make, anyway? The farm's past means nothing to my present.

He ignores me. "Last chance," he says.

"For what?" I know exactly for what.

"Gabe, come on. You're seventeen years old. You're still a kid. You shouldn't be alone right now. Come to our place and hang out with Ted. Janie would love to have you over. She'll feed you, make all your favorites."

My favorites? Even I don't know what my favorites are anymore, although I do remember from short visits and summer weekends at the cabin that my aunt Janie is an amazing cook.

I shake my head. "Thanks, but I need some time to myself. To figure shit out, you know?"

He nods. "I get it. How long are you planning to stay?"

"A few days. Week at the most."

"I'll call you in the morning, kid," Frank says. "Come over for supper tomorrow night. Ted will pick you up."

"Sounds good."

For long seconds, he looks at me, nodding. "You sure you're OK, then? Janie thinks—"

I cut him off. "I'm good. I swear."

Obviously, he's seen the pictures. There might even be video. Fuck. I blow out a heavy breath.

"Right. Call if you need anything."

Frank leaves me standing on the porch, the bright light of the LEDs in the sconces a direct contrast to the chipped paint and loose railing. For what feels like endless minutes, I stand there and will myself to go in. What other option do I have? Frank's gone, his taillights long faded into the darkness of the farm. I shiver. It's cold here in northern Minnesota, even though it's only mid-September. Temps were in the high seventies when I left LA this afternoon. I'm glad I thought to bring a jacket, although it's buried at the bottom of my duffel and I'm sure it won't be warm enough for this level of cold.

I tell myself again: *Go inside.* Still, I stand at the door, paralyzed by uncertainty and my own disappointment, until I hear a howl in the not-so-far distance. Like in the woods at the edge of the property, maybe a hundred yards away. Wolves? Coyotes? I have no idea, but I'd rather not find out.

I unlock the door, not sure what to expect when I step into this other world, this farmhouse I hardly remember. I take my first steps into the hall, barely illuminated from a light that's been turned on in the kitchen at the back of the house. I reach for the banister of the staircase to steady myself and toe off my Vans.

I'm not expecting to be hit with a memory so visceral, so absolute; it's like Gran's standing in front of me, wiping her hands on a green plaid dish towel, chiding Chris for being late and holding her arms open to me.

"Who is this boy?" she cried. "That can't be my Gabey. You've gotten so tall! Come into the kitchen. The cinnamon rolls are ready for the maple icing, and you can help me."

This house, somehow, still smells like it did that day, cinnamon rolls and pecans and maple syrup. I couldn't have been more than six or seven. We were here for Gran's birthday. Late that night, I heard Gran and Chris arguing. *You need help, Christopher. Leave Gabe with me. I hardly get to see him. He needs his family. You both do.*

I think about Gran's funeral, the last time I was here. The day she died, Chris called from the road to tell me the news. I remember how I handed the phone back to my tutor, Persephone, wiped tears and snot onto my sleeve. Chris and Elise were still together. Elise was shooting on location somewhere overseas but came back for the funeral. She swept in, tall and too thin and probably high, and consumed all the air in the little white church by the river. She wore a sleek black dress and mile-high heels, a fancy black hat with feathers, and a short veil that sat at an angle over her glossy platinum blonde hair. Back then, I thought she looked beautiful, glamorous, so important and special, my movie star mother. Perfect. What did I know? I was a stupid kid who thought the world revolved around me and my famous family. Now, as I stand at the threshold of a history of hard work and hardships, the memory of her that day feels ridiculous, pretentious.

I pull the front door closed behind me and turn the deadbolt against the darkness and the tremulous howls. I set my duffel and guitar on the hardwood floor. The house is warm, a hiss of air moving through the registers. I should sleep in one of the bedrooms upstairs, but suddenly I'm so exhausted and wrecked that the thought of climbing those steps seems like an insurmountable task. Fuck it. I take a leak in the tiny bathroom next to the kitchen and wash my hands. There's a fresh towel and a brand-new bottle of hand soap that smells like pine needles. I drink a glass of water from the kitchen tap and then crash on the living room sofa, pulling a handmade afghan over me.

But as tired as I am, as long as this day has been, sleep doesn't come. When I was with Frank, driving through the lively, bright night of the Twin Cities and then the quiet, deep black of northern Minnesota ("Help me watch for deer," he said, and I did, even though I wasn't sure what to watch for), I could focus on my surroundings. I took in what little of the scenery I could distinguish in the headlights' beams. I didn't have to think about Marley or the money. The album. That goddamn brick of dread.

Now, in my dead grandmother's living room—under an afghan she crocheted decades ago, vintage photographs of family members I don't recognize on the wall above me— everything comes rushing back. All of it. Marley crashing the strangers' wedding reception on the beach, drunk and shouting. The staring, open-mouthed guests. The paparazzi who arrived out of nowhere as they always do. The restaurant manager standing with his hands outstretched, not sure if he should touch Marley or not. A bouncer who finally carried her over his shoulder while she beat on his back with her fists, to the lot where I'd parked her dad's Bentley. I pulled the key fob out of my pocket and clicked *unlock*, but she wouldn't get in the car, screamed that she didn't want to go anywhere with me ever again.

Horrible things shot from her mouth like arrows.

I hate you. You think you're so much better than the rest of us. You think you're so above it all. But your album is shit, Gabe. You're *shit. We're done. You'll never come back from this without me. And you want to know something else? I* never *loved you. I never wanted to be with you. It was all fake, all of it.*

The bouncer tossed her in the back seat, and somehow I locked the vehicle, hoping she was too wasted to figure out how to unlock it. She pounded on the window, screaming, but I couldn't move, couldn't open the door to simply get in and drive away. I crouched down against the driver's door, gasping for air, my head in my hands, sharp steel flames slicing my lungs.

Get in the car. All I had to do was get in the car and I would be able to breathe again.

I never loved you. I never wanted to be with you. It was fake, all of it.

How could I have been so stupid to not know she was with me for the publicity?

Two days. She'd waited a whole two days to dump me after I'd given her the money she'd begged for. She wouldn't quit, not even after I said I was broke, that the money from the first album was gone. She wouldn't quit when I told her I couldn't ask Chris for the money. I couldn't ask him for anything.

"Please, Gabe," she sobbed. "I'm in trouble. Don't let me down. I need you. You're the only person who can help me."

Her hands were shaking, so I clasped them between mine to still them. "Hey," I said, "whatever it is, we'll fix it." She looked up at me then, her warm brown eyes so lost, distraught, and I was filled with a wave of devotion for her. My oldest friend, my star, my Marley.

I didn't want to know why she needed it, but I did what I had to do to get her that fucking money.

Now, I take in a few gasping breaths and push away the swirling sick in my gut when I think about the money and her meltdown; close my eyes against the raw footage in my mind, the clip that's played on repeat for nearly twenty-four hours.

It's after nine o'clock in LA now. I've avoided social media and the tabloids and the bloggers who've followed and speculated about my relationship with Marley Green for two years like we were the royal family or something. I ignored calls from Chris and my manager and that sleazebag from the record label. As soon as I got on the plane, I powered off my phone, and I haven't turned it back on.

We had a deal, me and Marley, both of us the product of rock stars and Hollywood royalty. We'd always have each other's backs, protect each other from the backstabbers. I trusted her. I have *feelings* for her, despite all the back-and-forth Hollywood drama and attention that she craved. I never said the words, but I felt *something*, a softness for only her. When the drugs became more than the occasional party favor, I defended her, I lied for her. I stole for her.

I held up my end of the bargain. Guess somewhere along the way, she let go of hers.

I had to get away from LA, a place I knew, a place where I thought I knew who I was. A place where I'd worked to make a name for myself, where I tried so fucking hard to be more than Chris Hudson and Elise Benson-Beckett's son or Marley Green's on-again, off-again rock star boyfriend.

Tonight, I'm none of those things. I'm alone, I'm broke, I'm fooled.

And here, in this farmhouse in northern Minnesota that feels both familiar and unknown, I'm something else I've never been: I'm in hiding.

Chapter Two

JUNIPER

THIS IS MY FAVORITE TIME OF DAY, MY FAVORITE TIME OF YEAR, MY absolute favorite place: a calm, cool morning at the park reserve overlook. I came up here early for the sunrise, a swash of pink and orange and deep blue, watercolors spilled across the sky. This hike always energizes me, my muscles warm and loose. Nothing has yet tarnished the day, and in this crisp, smoky autumn air, I feel as though nothing could.

Life slows down for us on the farm in the fall, the world quiets, and we prepare for the stillness of winter. This time every year, I feel content and at peace. Everything is moving at the right pace. That's what I feel today as I look out over the fast-moving river, across the water to where the farmland meets the shoreline.

We had a good summer. We're good, Mom and me. We've got this.

I glance at my watch. It's nearly nine, time to go. Mom's waiting for my help in the big barn. Leaves crunch beneath my feet as I follow the trail down the hill and around the southern side of the park reserve, where the river takes a gentle curve to the west and meets the Hudson property.

Our house, the red house, stands guard, closest to the main road, an early-seventies rambler with redwood siding. At one time, the place belonged to an old hippie beekeeper and his wife, an artist. When they moved to New Mexico to be closer to family, Chris bought it. He's always called it the Beehive. My parents had been running the family farm for him for a couple of years at that point, living in a rental in town, and it made more sense for them to live on the farm, he said. I was born three years later, and it's the only home I've ever known.

Some people call our place the caretaker's house, even though Mom doesn't call herself the caretaker, and neither does Chris nor any of his family. Her official title is a mouthful: Hudson Family Farms Property Manager, Stone & Wool Farm. Ask her, and she'll call herself a farmer and a fiber artist, plain and simple.

I turn in to the farm from the park trail and start to count the trees along the main road like I always do. Fifty-two norway pines from the county road to the farmhouse. The number never varies, a constant as the seasons change. I walk past our house toward the big barn.

I don't get that far. Mom's on the porch at the farmhouse, talking to someone in an old-fashioned black wool peacoat, the collar turned up. My breath catches. Not just someone. Chris's son. He's wearing dark sunglasses, hiding what I know are striking, earthy green eyes like his dad's. He's not very tall but stands a good few inches over Mom, on the backs of his heels as though he's trying to lean away from her. A shaggy mess of curls, black as the coat, tumbles down almost to his broad shoulders. His square jaw, high cheekbones, and long, stately nose give him a serious look. Older than his seventeen years. Classically handsome, if a bit scruffy. And he must be roasting in that heavy coat.

He's frowning at whatever Mom's saying, her hand upturned and moving in emphasis and in rhythm to her words, a gesture I know well as she makes her point. He shakes his head. Somehow, I recognize that look of disappointment and frustration, that worried crease between his eyes, and something low in my stomach flips. Something's not right.

Not that I care.

I don't know him, not really, but I'd know him anywhere, the son of the town's favorite—and sometimes wayward— son. Gabe Hudson. *The* Gabe Hudson, celebrity. A musician, like his dad. His music's fine—the first album, anyway, which reminds me of Dig Me Under, Chris's band. A broody, deep, grungy sound, some of it heavy, some of it pensive, some of it loud. I haven't heard Gabe's latest album.

He's the last person I'd ever expect to see here again. It's been years since his grandma Leona's funeral, the only time we've ever spoken, and after that day, after he'd proven that all the rumors were true—he was conceited, pretentious, rude—I wouldn't have been disappointed if he'd never come back.

Why is he here now? I take a step toward them, and a branch cracks below my feet. Gabe's head snaps in my direction, and Mom turns, too. "Juniper!" she calls. "Look who it is!"

He lifts his sunglasses and rests them on top of his curls as I approach, then looks away.

"Here's Juniper," Mom says with a huge smile. "You've both grown up so much."

He shoves his hands in his pockets and nods curtly but doesn't say hello.

"You remember Gabe, don't you?" Mom prompts.

"Oh, how could I possibly forget?" I ask, and I'm sure that she doesn't miss the sharpness in my tone. "And of course I recognize you from, you know, the Internet?"

I mean for that to sound snarky, too, but it comes out more like I'm a twelve-year-old girl who searches for images of him online and downloads them as her phone wallpaper. Crushing on him like everyone else in middle school. And still crushing on him in high school, thinking that if he ever comes to town, he'll fall madly in love with a local girl, as if everyone here has a special claim to him.

That will never be me.

"From the Internet," he repeats, shakes his head slowly, and looks down at his shoes, a pair of solid black Vans. "Of course."

There's an uncomfortable beat where no one says a word. Mom looks from Gabe to me and back to Gabe before she says, "We're so happy that you've come home." She puts a hand on his shoulder and squeezes once before releasing it.

But this isn't his home. This will never be his home.

"Whatever you need, let us know," Mom continues.

"I need keys," he says, "to the Twister. Do you know where Chris keeps them?"

Right to the point.

I can't help it. I laugh, a quiet *ha* that I try to swallow down. If Gabe notices, he doesn't give it away.

"Oh, honey, I'll have to ask him." She smiles, her eyes kind and soft. "I'm sure you know that." Of course Mom isn't simply going to hand over the keys to Chris's Mustang, a rare, restored, mint condition model from the early seventies. After he bought it a few years ago—after the Grammy win, after Leona died—he had the garage completely refurbished. He's also got a newer-model Mustang, and a teal Chevy short-box pickup that reminded him of his grandpa's truck, and a garage full of classic cars in LA, too.

"Fine," Gabe says. "I don't need the car. I'll get my groceries delivered."

I snort. "By whom?"

Now he turns to me. "A service?"

"A service," I repeat, shaking my head. Typical pretentious LA child celebrity.

"Make a list," Mom says gently. "Juniper can shop for you this morning while you get settled."

"Me?" I blurt. "What am I, his personal assistant?"

"Juniper," she says with warning in her tone, "Gabe's our guest."

Well, that's closer to the truth than welcoming him *home*.

"I'll figure it out," Gabe says as he takes a step backward

toward the front door. He looks directly at me, and I'm struck by those deep green eyes. "I'm not here to make friends," he says so sadly, so quietly, I almost believe he didn't say it. He opens the door and disappears behind it, closing it with a quiet *snick.*

"Juniper!" Mom hisses. She's short with long, straw-colored waves of hair—streaked with more gray strands than she'd like—pulled back into her usual ponytail, her tanned face lined with worry and hard work and laughter crinkling at the corners of her eyes. *Work hard, love hard.* I've heard her say it a million times. We don't take any single day for granted. "I can't believe how rude you were to him just now."

"Me? How about how rude *he* was?"

I never told Mom what happened the day of Leona's funeral. Dad had died the year before, but I still cried for him every day, clinging to the words Mom had said to me the day that we lost him: "I know that the pain is sharp now. It will still be sharp tomorrow. But it won't always be so sharp, I prom-ise." I said that to Gabe then, when he was hurting, too, but he said nothing. He turned and walked away without looking at me, without thanking me, without acting in any way how a person should. I wish I hadn't shared those words with him, words that were so special to me. Words that he tossed aside like trash, which felt like a slight to my father, to his memory.

"What's he doing here, anyway?" I ask. "I mean, *obviously* he's not here to make friends."

"What difference does it make?" She puts her hands on her hips. "That's not how we treat people."

"And how could you offer me up like that without talking to me about it first?" I snap. "Last I checked, *grocery delivery service* wasn't listed in my job description."

"You don't have a job description," Mom counters. "You do as I ask."

"Well, there's your first mistake. You didn't *ask*. I'll be in the greenhouse if you need me for anything. Anything except buying groceries for Gabe Hudson."

"This conversation isn't over," she calls after me as I walk back up the driveway toward our house. "Far from it. And don't forget, it's your turn to make lunch, and I'm inviting Gabe."

If there's anyone as stubborn as me, it's my mother, and I know she won't let this one go. But I won't back down, either.

Chapter Three

GABE

No way am I letting Juniper Blue buy groceries for me or even drive me to a store and wait for me in the parking lot while I shop. Do *anything* for me. I'm not staying in Harper's Mill long, and like I told her, I'm not here to make friends.

I have two memories of Juniper Bell. The first, watching her on TV the night she walked the red carpet with Chris at the Grammys, overwhelmed and shell-shocked and starstruck and awkward in her floofy pale pink dress and high-tops. Her last name is Bell, but Juniper Blue is the name that made her famous for all of thirty seconds at the Grammy Awards years ago, when Dig Me Under performed the song Chris had written for her.

I watched the show live from Elise's New York City penthouse—she and Chris had split up again but of course would reunite after he brought home the hardware—and then watched clips from it a million more times on YouTube. Every time I watched, I thought, *It should have been me*, even though I'd gone to countless awards ceremonies with one or the other of my parents, sometimes both. Now I've been invited to some on my own, performed my first single, "Burden," at the Radio KidCo Awards when it was up for Song of the Year. It didn't win, too heavy for that crowd, but dating the KidCo princess earned me a courtesy nod, I think.

My second memory of Juniper, a few months later, is hazier, a moment in Gran's living room after the funeral, the last time I was here. Back then, she was a little scrap of a thing, her curls more a cold white-blonde than warm, golden sunshine. She walked up to me, practically shaking, the only time she'd ever spoken to me. I don't remember what she said or if I said anything back. I only remember that I was so tired of people telling me they were sorry for my loss. I was tired of Minnesota and the thick, humid air and the ugly brown river that ran through town and Gran's backyard. I wanted to go home, or the closest thing I had to one.

It no longer bothers me that "Juniper Blue" launched Dig Me Under's comeback. I don't care that Chris wrote a song for her and took her to the Grammys. I don't care that he probably spent more "quality time" with her in that one weekend than he's ever spent with me. Juniper's a girl who happens to live on the farm, that's all.

I can admit, though, that Juniper surprised me today. I wasn't expecting someone so short, for one, or so . . . I don't know. Sharp. Captivating. She packs a lot of attitude into that Yoda-sized package. Hair in two loose blonde braids past the small of her back. Army green cargo pants rolled at the ankles, a long-sleeved gray T-shirt with the words *Hike More, Worry Less* in flowery script, battered hiking boots. Cheeks flushed and glowing from the crisp autumn air. Ice-blue eyes that flashed in indignation.

I'm standing in Gran's kitchen, scanning the small supply of food Chris keeps on hand. Tuna packets. Cans of tomato soup. Some sort of microwavable rice dish. None of it seems very appealing, but for the first time in days, I've got something of an appetite. For the first time in days, I slept through the night, even though the living room sofa wasn't comfortable. This morning I found a fresh can of Folger's, and the coffeemaker worked, so I'm calling that a win.

But I have to eat.

As much as it kills me, I'm going to have to call in reinforcements. I find my duffel bag where I dropped it in the living room, its contents spilling across the floor. My phone's in the side pocket. When I power it back up, it buzzes with notifications and texts: Chris. Elise. My manager. Rocky.

My stomach lurches. I can't think about Rocky right now. I swipe them all away, pull up a conversation with my cousin Ted, and type: Hey, you probably heard I'm in town. I could use a favor.

It's not thirty seconds before I see that he's texting back. Then: What do you need I can be there in 15.

He's over in ten. He pounds up the porch steps, blows through the front door without knocking, and scares the everloving piss out of me even more than the probable coyotes last night.

"Gabey baby," he barks as he crosses the living room. "Your chariot awaits and all that, Prince Charming. Let's keep 'er moving. I've got shit to do."

Who needs Juniper or a grocery service when I've got this guy?

I stand up and grab my grandfather's wool coat from where I'd tossed it over the back of an overstuffed, floral monstrosity of a recliner. The jacket I brought with me isn't going to cut it in this cold. The peacoat's too big, musty from the mothballs in the cedar closet upstairs where I found it along with clothes spanning the last fifty-plus years, but it'll have to do for now.

"Nice to see you, too, Theodore," I say. "How's things?"

"Blah-blah-blah. How's things with *you*? You finally got rid of the psycho, huh? Now *that* was entertainment. Much better than her last KidCo series."

I shrug. I'm sure our very public, very spectacular breakup made for good TV, but it hurts. "I didn't know you were such a KidCo fan. Do you like the cartoons or the live-action stuff?"

Ted ignores me. "Was the sex good?" he asks, grinning. "Nah, don't answer that. I mean, who wants to hump bones?"

Ted was born without a filter, the exact opposite of his reticent dad. He's your classic Midwestern farm boy/high school running back hero who wants to grow up to teach history and coach three sports at his former high school, the same three at which he himself excelled: football, basketball, baseball. He's one of the nicest guys on the planet, too, always ready to lend a hand, no questions asked, which *is* like his dad. He's tall, broad, muscular, with a ruddy complexion, wearing a flannel shirt, dirty jeans, and an Allis-Chalmers trucker cap. My guess is that he's been helping his dad around the farm today. *Shit to do* might mean something to do with actual cow shit.

We don't see each other or talk much. But we used to hang out together those weeks at the cabin when we were younger, and we text once in a while. Chris flew the family out to LA a few times, and we did all the tourist stuff. The Hollywood Walk of Fame, the beach, Universal Studios, Disneyland. Last year, he asked if I would introduce him to Ariana Grande and told me to fuck off when I said I didn't know her. He's a good one.

I blow out a long breath. "Much as I'm enjoying our little catch-up," I say, "I could really use some groceries."

He bursts out a laugh. "*That's* the favor you need? A ride to the grocery store? Why don't you just drive one of Chris's cars?"

"I asked for the Mustang and was denied."

Ted laughs. "Chris would shit himself if something happened to the 1970 Ford Mustang Mach 1 Twister Special." Chris always refers to his baby with its "full name," which Ted mocks whenever possible. "Oh, cripes, I just remembered about that time you and Marley took the Beamer up the coast and—"

I put up my hand to stop him from telling the story of how the hardtop had malfunctioned and we had to drive back in a rainstorm. Marley didn't speak to me for days because naturally someone took photos of us, drenched and frustrated and angry with each other. Chris was worse, though. Made this big deal of taking away the keys, threatened to buy me a used piece of shit. He did, too, an ugly orange first-generation RAV4 that surprisingly passed the emissions test and was impossible to ignore in the Barlow-Winston Academy parking lot.

"I remember."

He laughs again. "OK, why can't Laurel take you? Or Juniper?"

"Don't ask." I'm not going there. I know that Ted and Juniper are close.

"Alllll righty then, let's roll."

Ted rambles the whole ride into town. On and on about last night's football game (they won 17–14, and *by the way, it was the first game my dad has ever missed because he had to pick up your sorry ass from the airport*), the farm, major league baseball, the Minnesota Vikings.

In town, he pulls his truck into a space at Bjerke's Super-Valu and shifts into park. Most of the spaces are empty, which gives me a small amount of relief that the entire population of Harper's Mill won't see me shopping for groceries.

Ted reaches for the door handle but pauses. "Look," he says. "I'm going to guess that you haven't exactly been scouring social media for the latest gossip, but you should probably know that your girl Marley threw you under the bus."

I shrug and open the door, step out onto the cracked asphalt, and slam the door shut. "You follow something other than sports?"

"Her parents sent her to Betty Ford again." We walk across the lot into the store. "Some reporter is claiming an exclusive from her that she got the smack from you and you shot up together."

I scowl and yank a metal cart from the corral. "It's bullshit. You know it's bullshit."

If Marley's in rehab—because she *should* be in rehab—how is she going to get me the money? Twenty-eight days—or more—and then what? She owes me a shit ton of cash, but if she lied to me about—well, everything—then chances are good that she lied to me about that, too, and she always planned to screw me over. God, I'm such an idiot.

"Maybe it's bullshit," Ted says, "but if you don't come clean—pun intended—about where you are or what you're doing, people will assume you're in rehab, too. Like father, like son, you know? Rumor is that you're at Hazelden. Somebody got pictures of you at the airport."

Of course. Why else would I fly to Minnesota if not for an extended stay at the famous treatment center that saved Chris's life not once, but twice?

When I don't say anything, he continues, "Gabe. I've seen the video."

I huff out a laugh. "You're going to have to be more specific. Which video?"

He sighs. "The one of the bouncer tossing Marley into the back seat of a Bentley and you freaking the fuck out."

"Ah. So there *is* a video."

"Yeah. Doesn't do much for your claim that you weren't on something."

Before I can think about it, I say, "A panic attack does

not look like a bad trip." I don't think so, anyway. I've never watched myself when it happens. Maybe I should take a look at the video.

"Panic attack, huh? Well, this one looked like a bad trip."

"What do I care? Let them think I was tweaking." I turn the cart down the first aisle and head toward the small, dismal-looking produce section. The back wheel on the left is wonky, so I lean in and force it to follow a straight path. I stop at a display of bananas, spotted brown, all too ripe.

"Not your best idea," Ted says. "What's your plan, then?"

What's my plan? My stomach lets out a low, rumbling growl. The tabloid situation is familiar but I'm in new territory here, shopping for my own food. My plan, at least right now, is to make my way through this dump of a grocery store and figure out what the hell I'm going to eat for the next few days.

"Frozen pizzas, I guess," I tell Ted. "I can probably manage a box of mac and cheese."

Ted's phone rings and my stomach drops. He barely glances at the name on the display before he answers. "Yep, I got him," he says in greeting. Then he hands me the phone. "I'm just gonna . . . I'll meet you outside. Uncle Chris wants to talk to you."

Chapter Four

JUNIPER

THE GREENHOUSE WAS AN EXCUSE, AND MOM KNOWS IT. I NEEDED to be alone. Seeing Gabe made me feel unsettled, like something has shifted, having him here. He might look like Chris, but they seem so different. Yes, Chris is a world-famous rock star, but to me he's always been a regular guy, my dad's best friend. He doesn't act like he's better than the rest of us. His son should take a lesson from it.

I putz around, watering, checking on the tea plant that's beginning to flower, harvesting some arugula and basil. The greenhouse was Dad's baby, his special project. Shortly after my parents moved here, he worked with the University of Minnesota extension service on the sustainable design and then ran studies for them. He and I spent a lot of time together here, and I'll never feel like it was enough. He taught me the basics, but I still have so much to learn. For a long time after he died, I couldn't set foot inside without crying, so I avoided it.

The spring before Leona died, she convinced me it was time to try again. "You've got your dad's green thumb," she said. "Don't let that talent go to waste, Juniper. He'd be disappointed. Get in there and cry it out and start growing things again, because life is short, and you've got to live in the sunshine." She was reminding me of the farm's rules for living, rules that had been painted onto the wall in the round barn by her father-in-law. *Live in the sunshine, swim the sea, drink the wild air,* a quote from Ralph Waldo Emerson. She was already sick, and the prognosis wasn't good.

So I went to the greenhouse, cried it out, and planted a few simple things: basil, chives, mint. I worked through my grief here. Well, here and with a therapist in Fred Lake, who I saw regularly for a couple of years after Dad died.

Frank Sr. helps maintain the building now. Most of the space is for growing—herbs, salad greens, a few flowering plants for teas—and the rest is my work space for drying plants and experimenting with teas. I even put in a small desk area for when inspiration strikes, the small shelf above the simple structure filled with notebooks of recipes and ideas, old copies of *Mother Earth News* and *Old Farmer's Almanac,* and a seed catalog I found in a wooden crate, marked up with Dad's notes.

I work for an hour or so, then walk across the lawn to the house to start lunch. Lunch for *three,* apparently. In the kitchen, I unplug my phone from the charging station at Mom's desk and open messages.

Amelia: Am I hearing rumors Gabe's in town? And I don't have a text from you?
Amelia: Have you seen him yet? Is he as hot in real life?

She's sent me a photo of Gabe onstage, shirtless, singing into the microphone, eyes closed, dark curls gleaming in the spotlight. Honestly. She's ridiculous.

I type a reply: I've seen him. He's rude. Also he was wearing what I suspect was his gpa's coat, which smelled like mothballs. Super hot.

I open the thread from Ted, one of my oldest friends, Amelia's longtime crush, and, as it happens, Gabe Hudson's cousin.

Ted: Whatcha doin? I'm hanging out with my notorious cousin. Ma says I'm supposed to invite you and Laurel to supper tonight. Lee Lee too. You can meet him then.

Ted's mom is the nicest woman on the planet, so it's no surprise that she wants us to join them for supper. To Janie—to all the Hudsons, actually—we're family. I switch back to my conversation with Amelia: Ted invited us to supper. Us as in YOU, too, LEE LEE. 😍

That should take her mind off the shirtless rock star staying in the farmhouse. For as long as Amelia and I have been friends—since the beginning of middle school, when she and her mom and little sister, Kat, moved to Harper's Mill after her parents divorced—she's had a crush on Ted. Someday, she says, she'll get up the nerve to tell him. "Today *is* someday," I've told her a hundred times.

I reply to Ted: I met your notorious cousin this morning. He seemed hangry.

Ted: rofl

A notification pops up with another text from Amelia:

Amelia: I'm in luv I'm in luv & I don't care who knows it! 😍😍😍😍😍
YESSSSS to supper. Can u pick me up? Mom needs car.
Me: Today is someday. TELL HIM.
Amelia: In my dreams.
Amelia: Will GABE be there? Is the rumor abt him true?
Me: Which one?
Amelia: He's in MN for rehab ???? 😳

Gabe looked tired, yes, and like he could make short work of a burger and a milkshake, but he did not look like a drug addict. At least not like the drug addicts I've been exposed to, mostly fictional. And Chris. I only saw him strung out or high a couple of times. He looked sick, his face a pale gray and the skin under his eyes a smudgy purple. He spoke too loudly and lost his balance. Mom reamed him out for coming over to the house. I asked Dad what was wrong with Chris, and he didn't sugarcoat it. I spent a long afternoon reading online articles about addiction after that conversation and swore I'd never touch the stuff. Mostly, though, Chris wasn't around when things were really bad.

Me: Probably not, if he's here?

I don't tell her how I made a complete fool of myself in front of him, how quiet and withdrawn he seemed.

Amelia: Why aren't you more excited about this? If I had a hot rock star living down the road from me, I'd totally make a play for him.
Me: Oh, like you've totally made a play for T? That's some pretty big talk.
Amelia: That's different.
Me: How so?
Amelia: Because it would mean something with T.
Me: But it wouldn't with Gabe? Are you objectifying him?
Amelia: Hell yes I'm objectifying him. Also y not? PS It's been like a year since Ty.

I sigh. Not going there. I open up a different conversation to message Chris: Everything OK?

Not that I'm expecting an answer right away. He is a rock star, after all. But I wonder if he knows that Gabe's here and not in LA. I don't even know that *Chris* is in LA. He hasn't been to the farm since June. He could be anywhere, although I know Dig Me Under's not on tour right now.

I take a container of potato soup out of the freezer and heat it on the stove while I set out bread and leftover roasted turkey for sandwiches. Mom comes in, washes her hands, and sets the table for three. Gabe doesn't show, but we both pretend to ignore the empty place setting.

After lunch, I walk down the hall to my bedroom, close

the door behind me, and flip open my laptop. I've got homework, but I convince myself that a few minutes of detective work won't set me back too much. I type *Gabe Hudson musician* in the search bar, and the screen fills with headlines within seconds.

Broken record: Is Gabe Hudson following famous dad's footsteps to rehab?

Marley Green and Gabe Hudson crash (and burn) random beach wedding

Green and Hudson on the rocks again

Gabe Hudson's sophomore effort: Embrace the Suck lives up to its name and then some

Rocket Launcher bassist Parker Green checks daughter Marley into rehab for a third time, Gabe Hudson not far behind? Exclusive videos from wild night.

I click on the last link and read about Marley Green, KidCo Channel superstar, recording artist, and Gabe's on-again, off-again girlfriend. The first paragraphs describe the "wild night" at some wedding they crashed, and then the article delves into their relationship:

Marley has once again been dating Gabe Hudson, son of Dig Me Under lead singer Chris Hudson and himself a recording artist. Hollywood's latest teen "It Couple," Marley and Gabe were born six days apart and have broken up and reunited several times since they officially began dating eighteen months ago. Although Marley has claimed that Gabe's drug use has been the young couple's biggest challenge, reminiscent of the issues Gabe's parents have faced in their volatile twenty-year relationship, sources close to both deny these allegations.

However, exclusive photos and video footage obtained by *Celebrity Insider* suggest otherwise. Less than twenty-four hours after the incident Friday night, photographs show Gabe Hudson at the Minneapolis–St. Paul airport, fueling rumors that he checked himself into Hazelden Betty Ford, the addiction treatment center where both his parents, Chris Hudson and Elise Benson-Beckett, one of Hollywood's highest-paid actresses, have sought help.

After a short time apart last spring, Marley and Gabe reconciled in June. A recent Instagram post showed the two embracing at an unknown nightclub, Gabe kissing Marley's cheek. In the caption, Marley wrote, "I met my soulmate when I was six days old. Not many people can say that. This is it for me. He's the one. I can't wait for forever with you, Gabe." The post has since been deleted.

My stomach flip-flops as I hit play on the first of two embedded videos, taken by a wedding guest. It's shaky at first, with lots of background noise, the bride and groom in the background with their mouths open in shock as they realize what's happening. Gabe tries to reason with a red-faced Marley, who screams at him to stop touching her, to get the hell away from her, *you goddamn loser*. Ouch. So much for soulmates. Another shaky section shows a bouncer lifting Marley over his shoulder, and whoever's filming follows them out to the street. Marley's still screaming, now with tears blackened from mascara. The bouncer tosses her in the back seat of a car. I half expect him to brush his hands together, done with that dirty task. The recording ends.

The second video is shorter, not even twenty seconds, steady and zoomed in on Gabe, who is now crouched against the gunmetal-gray vehicle, his face in his hands, shaking, his chest rising and falling heavily. There's a conversation happening between whoever's filming and someone else. The first voice, more in the background, says, "What the hell is happening?" and the closer voice responds, "Dude's gotta be on something. He's hardcore into the same shit his dad did."

This recording ends abruptly.

So this must be what sent Gabe running to Minnesota. Is it true? Was he on something? Or was this something else?

I go back to the search results to read the article about the new album, riddled with insults meant to be clever but that, honestly, are just plain mean.

I can't imagine what living in the spotlight, so exposed,

must be like for him. And while I'll never forget my trip to the Grammys with Chris and the thrill I felt when he wrote a song for me, I would never want to live that life.

I close the laptop, shutting out the tabloids and the speculation, grateful for quiet days on the farm.

Chapter Five

GABE

"So." That's Chris's loaded opening line. "Want to tell me what the hell you're doing in Minnesota?"

When I don't answer, he continues. "Let's start with this, then. Are you OK?"

"Don't you think you should have opened with that?"

"Haven't you had enough theatrics this week? Well? Are you OK?"

Define OK, I think. I roll the cart back and forth in front of a cardboard display of Halloween Oreos with orange filling. I grab two packages and set them in the cart. "Right as rain."

He blows out a breath like he's fighting for patience. "Why Minnesota? Why not your mom's?"

"New York seemed like—I don't know—too much, maybe? I don't want to deal with Elise's disappointment. Plus, she's filming in Australia."

"She's not disappointed in you," Chris says.

"She is. She wants everything to be perfect, and if it can't *be* perfect, then it should at least *look* perfect on the surface. You know that more than anyone."

"Well, I can't argue with that," he says.

Since the divorce, Elise has transformed. Like Chris, she eventually got clean and then took clean next level. No cigarettes, no caffeine, no sugar. She went on a seven-day silent retreat, she sees a naturopath, she meditates for hours at a time when she's not filming her new series of yoga videos. She wrote a vegan cookbook filled with snippets about resetting her body with real food and releasing the toxins from her life—including Chris and me, it would seem.

"Look. Let's take a step back," Chris continues. "We don't have to overanalyze your whole thought process with the album if you don't want to, but I think you owe me a little something at least. Something to explain why you thought cutting that deal behind my back, working with a second-rate wannabe producer, and releasing a crap album was a good idea."

"Why don't you tell me how you really feel?" I mutter.

"I *am* telling you how I really feel. We produced a fucking awesome album together when you were *sixteen* years old. 'Burden' is a killer tune. You've got a shit ton of talent, more than me, if I'm being honest about it. But even with that success, you couldn't wait for me. What the hell were you thinking?"

"How long did you expect me to wait? Chances were better for Oasis to get back together and tour before you got around to it."

"Three months," he says. "You couldn't wait three fucking months."

"You said three months six months ago."

"Poor you," he says. *"Embrace the Suck.* Whose brilliant idea was that? Talk about a self-fulfilling prophecy."

"Oh, clever," I say. "Haven't heard that one yet. You know, I'm not sure this is a conversation I want to be having in the bread aisle at SuperValu."

"Don't buy bread at SuperValu. Go to Hartman's Bakery downtown."

"Now we're discussing bread?" So like him to change the subject when things get a little uncomfortable.

"No. Now we're going to discuss the video and Marley and why the hell you're in Minnesota," he says. "Let people say what they will about the album. If it's a shit sandwich, it's a shit sandwich. Move on. But what you can't ignore are the rumors about the drug use. You can't pretend people aren't talking about it, especially with that stunt Marley pulled the other night and that video of you freaking out. You know I gotta ask, Gabe. We live under the same roof, but I've barely seen you the last few months. Is any of it true? Are you using?"

Growing up, I watched both my parents struggle with addiction. Elise hurt her back filming the Devil's Tower scene in *Child of Reckoning* and got hooked on pain pills. Most of her life, she's struggled with an eating disorder, and the pills didn't help. Chris has done it all—booze, coke, heroin, whatever you put in front of him. He finally got clean for good after Gran died. So that's one thing I'm crystal fucking clear about. I don't touch the shit, any of it, not even alcohol, and I had to put up with Marley and her friends in my face about it for years, even before we were together.

"Nope." That's all I'm going to give him. "Where are you?" I ask, even though I know the answer. He's not in Minnesota.

"LA. I'm going to try to get there in the next couple of weeks. I've got a lot of shit going on right now."

"I'm not sure how long I'll be here, anyway," I say.

"Look, Gabe," he says slowly, "I've got something to tell you. I'd rather tell you in person, but I don't think it can wait. No sense in waiting until your birthday, either, especially since you're there and if you have questions, you can talk to the attorney."

My stomach drops at the word. I switch the phone to my other ear, clench it tighter. "Did you say attorney?" I try to keep my voice steady. "Why do I need an attorney?"

"Hang on a sec," he says. "Hey, Wheeler, what are you doing? Careful with that. Gabe, I'll be right back. Don't go anywhere."

Shit. An attorney. Did he find out about the money? Maybe I *should* have read that text from Rocky. I pull the phone away from my ear and swipe to find the message.

Rocky: This is Rocky checking in. I heard about what went down and want to make sure you're still on top of it.

Everybody knows a guy like Rocky who begins every text by telling you who he is in case he's not in your contacts. I type a quick response, one word: Yeah.

Getting the money was easier than I thought it would be. Chris's accountant, Rocky—now my accountant, too—has worked for Chris since around the time of Dig Me Under's first album. Rocky's cool, even if he's never moved past the long stringy hair, flannel shirt, Chuck Taylors look. He's loyal to Chris and, by extension, me. But the guy lives for the weekends, when he can get out of the office and jam with his buddies and reminisce about the Seattle days and that time he was an extra in *Singles*, so if you want anything, catch him on Fridays around three o'clock.

"You know this isn't exactly legal, right?" he asked me the day I surprised him at his downtown LA office. "At best, it's not, y'know, ethical."

"Rock," I said with as much sincerity as I could drop into one syllable, "you know I wouldn't ask you to do this if I didn't truly need it."

He sighed, long and heavy and put out. "I've seen your financials, Gabe. Obviously. It's bad, but it's not like you're in dire straits. Not *yet*. Are you in trouble?"

I paused, not sure how much to tell him. "Not me."

He nodded. "Aha. Say no more. Look, I've known you since the day you came out scowling and howling at everybody in the room. I'll do this for you one time. *One*. That's it."

"I swear, I'll put the money back. It should only be a few days."

Rocky shook his head as though he couldn't believe what he was doing. "Yeah, you'll put the money back. Chris really digs into the books a couple of times a year. Year-end's coming up late December. The clock's ticking, so don't dick around. This could cost me my job or worse."

"I know," I said.

"Do not fuck this up," Rocky said, pointing his index finger at me almost violently, then sighed heavily and turned back toward his computer. "I'm counting on you, Gabe."

Only eight days ago.

"You still there?" Chris huffs into the phone. "Damn, I'm getting old. I shouldn't have to haul equipment like that."

"Yeah, I'm still here."

"Gabe." He says my name like it's a complete sentence. "I'm going to cut to the chase here because I've got some shit I need to take care of. After Dad died, Mom updated the will. She got it into her head that we should both get the farm. You and me, and she split it forty-nine, fifty-one. She named you majority owner of Stone & Wool, and when you turn eighteen, you'll inherit fifty-one percent of the farm."

Holy *shit*.

When I turn eighteen. In four weeks.

I stand here, mouth hanging open, one hand gripping the phone, the other tight around the cart handle. "You're kidding me," I choke out. That familiar brick of dread increases in size tenfold. He can't be serious. Now, on top of everything else, I'm responsible for a farm, for part of my family's history? A family—let's be honest here—I barely know? In Nowhere, Minnesota? "Why would she do that? What the fuck am I going to do with a *farm*?"

"Well, looks like you've got plenty of time on your hands now to figure it out."

The brick presses against my chest. My hands shake. I

pull at the collar of my T-shirt, hot, too restricting. Tightness. Panic. The video was bad enough. This can't happen in a grocery store. I have to get out of here.

"Gotta go," I say, my voice scratchy, my breath coming fast. I pull the phone away from my ear and hit *end*.

Calm the fuck down, I tell myself. *Calm down.* I take a few deep breaths, think about what I'm going to do next. I'm going to wheel this shitty cart to the cash registers at the front of the store, put the groceries on the belt, hope to hell my card doesn't get declined, find Ted, and go back to a farm I don't want. Or deserve.

Chapter Six

JUNIPER

Mom and I pick Amelia up on our way to Ted's. She's straightened her long, dark hair and applied about twelve coats of mascara. She climbs into the back seat and fans herself, her nails flashing a glittery copper.

"Do I look all right?" she asks, her voice thin and shaky.

"Gorgeous," Mom says. Considering the time that Amelia's spent at our house over the years, and that Amelia feels as comfortable around her as she does her own mom, her gigantic crush on Ted is no secret. "Absolutely gorgeous."

Amelia *is* absolutely gorgeous, even without the excessive mascara. Her tawny skin practically glows, especially after the summer months, and she's got a broad, friendly smile. She's what I like to call an extreme extrovert. Her dad is Hmong, a filmmaker best known for a documentary about the history of the Hmong in Minnesota. Her mom was the white nurse who cared for him after he'd gotten jumped and beaten in a shady area of Duluth, all his equipment stolen. Amelia got her movie obsession from her dad, not to mention her need to be around people all the time and the desire to know their stories. She seems to find something in common with every person she meets. She never feels awkward meeting new people or going to new places. And what she calls her "unrequited love" for Ted hasn't stopped her from dating other guys.

I, on the other hand, have had only one boyfriend, if you can call it that. Tyler and I worked together at the park reserve the summer before eleventh grade. On paper, he was perfect— he'd achieved the highest rank as a Wilderness Trek Youth. He loved to camp and hike and explore the park. He flirted with me at work, we held hands in the break room at the nature center, he kissed me sweetly in stolen moments on the trail, we texted late into the night.

We went on one movie date that summer, and he insisted we drive all the way to Duluth.

"I don't want to see any of the movies playing in Fred Lake," he said.

Amelia thought it was strange that Tyler and I rarely saw each other outside of work. I didn't think much of it, but what did I know about dating and boys? I found out our relationship was less than I thought on the first day of school, when he barely glanced my way as I said hello.

"Oh, hey," he said. My stomach dropped at his casual, disaffected tone. "I'll see you at work later, June."

He was the only person who'd ever shortened my name. I didn't like it, but because it was Tyler and I wanted things to work out between us so badly, I hadn't said anything.

"Something's not right," Amelia said.

Later, at lunch, Tyler walked in, hand in hand with class president and swim team captain Lily Reynolds, crushing my poor, naive heart like a crisp autumn leaf underfoot.

Tyler avoided me at school but couldn't avoid me at the park. Our first shift together, I waited until the group of kids started working on their scavenger hunt and then, shaking, confronted him.

"You had a girlfriend the whole time, didn't you?" I asked, not bothering to ease into it. "That's why we never went out. That's why we drove to a movie theater an hour away. So that no one would see us. Am I right?"

He shrugged. "Sorry, June. I thought you knew. I mean, Lily and me have been a thing since, like, ninth grade. Everyone knows that."

"That's horrible!" I practically shouted. "Of course I didn't know, or none of this would have happened! I really liked you, Tyler!"

"Calm down," he said. "It's not like you and me did anything, anyway."

I throw my hands up. "You and *I*."

"That's what I said."

"You're an ass," I said.

"You're a prude," he shot back.

"Don't call me June. Don't call me *anything*!" I stomped on his foot with my heavy hiking boot, turned quickly, and went back to join the group of kids, now swinging from the low-hanging branches of a nearby tree.

"Stay on the trail!" I snapped at them.

Tyler and I worked together almost every weekend that fall, speaking to each other only if the task absolutely required it, and every minute was torture. I was relieved when he quit to go work at the outdoor outfitters in Fred Lake, and I swore off boys, especially coworkers.

"I don't know why I'm so nervous about this," Amelia says now with a small laugh. "I mean, it's *Teddy*. I've been over to his place a thousand times. And it's Sunday night *supper*. Not a *date* or anything."

When the three of us hang out, which isn't as often during football season, it's usually at Ted's. There's always room at the Thomas table for the kids' friends.

Apparently, there's enough room for the Hudson Family Farms attorney tonight, too, who's already sitting at the long dining room table with a beer when we arrive. Allan's got long, thinning white hair pulled back into a ponytail and a reddish face full of loose, wrinkly skin like a shar-pei. He's wearing one of his signature Minnesota Twins hoodies, this one a faded navy with the TC logo.

"Girls." He greets us with a nod. "Laurel. You all look lovely on this lovely evening."

"Thanks, Allan," Mom says. "It's nice to see you. I didn't know you'd be here."

"Ah, well," he says slowly, then takes a sip of his beer. "Chris called and asked me to stop by in case Gabe has any questions."

He's here for Gabe? I look over to Mom as she sighs and rubs a hand across her forehead.

"I see," she says. "He knows, then? Since when?"

"Chris told him this afternoon," Allan says. "And if I'm being honest, he should have waited until a more appropriate time, and preferably in my office." He tugs at the strings of his hoodie until each side is exactly even.

"What's going on?" I ask.

Allan looks from me to Amelia and back to Mom. "I didn't realize that Jane had invited so many people tonight. We should probably hold off on any discussions."

Janie walks into the dining room carrying a large platter of roast beef, carrots, and red potatoes. She sets the platter in the center of the table. "Good idea. I was just about to call everyone in."

She turns to me, smiling as she takes in my appearance: twin braided buns at the top of my head, a white blouse with puffed sleeves and covered in cherries, a black cardigan tied around my waist, rolled-up jeans, and Mom's hot pink snake-skin loafers from when she was in high school.

"Hey, girls," she says. "Amelia, so glad you were able to join us. Juniper, you look so cute! I remember those shoes. I had that exact pair in navy. Your mom was always so much cooler. Have you seen Teddy and Gabe? They were out on the porch watching football."

"Not yet," Amelia says, looking at me with eyebrows raised.

"What's going on?" I ask, unable to calm the tremor in my voice. "What's wrong?"

"Everything's fine," Mom says. "Allan? I'm not sure what I can or can't say."

"You can't say anything at this point," he says.

"But I can," Gabe says as he walks in from the porch. "Everyone's going to find out soon enough."

There's an awkward moment of silence as we all look at Gabe.

Finally, Allan says, "Maybe you'd like to hold off for a couple of days. Chris was hoping I'd get a chance to talk to you about this privately, Gabe."

"Well, Chris isn't here, is he?" Gabe says, his mouth pulling into a deep frown. He looks at me briefly, then flicks his gaze around the room. "Gran left me the farm."

Allan sighs. "In a nutshell. There's more to it than that, of course."

My mouth drops open and a sick feeling whooshes through me. Leona left *Gabe* the farm? Not Chris or Janie? Not anyone who knows anything at all about farming? My brain kicks into worst-case-scenario mode: Gabe's lack of any sort of agricultural or business knowledge drives us into ruin. Or he sells off the land to some shady developer who builds cheap apartments with astronomically high rents. Either way, that's it for me and Mom and the farm and all the sheep and my greenhouse.

I clamp my mouth shut again. I look at Mom, who has her worried face on, the lines between her eyes deep and creased. She smiles, but it's a half smile, and not a very convincing one.

Leona left Gabe the farm. "But—but—" I sputter, and Mom gives a tiny shake of her head.

Ted bursts through the door. "Let's eat!" he cries. "I'm starving!"

Gabe's announcement is swallowed into the chaos of chairs scraping across the floor, the clatter of dishes, an argument between Frankie and Izzy over whose turn it is to say grace. We're crammed in around the table—Ted's family, me, Mom, Amelia, Allan, and Ted's great-uncle Bud. Gabe sits across from me, squished between Ted and Allan, but never once looks at me.

At one point during what is probably the most uncomfortable meal of my life, Amelia leans over and says in a low voice, "This reminds of that movie *Far from the Madding Crowd*, you know, when—"

"*No*," I cut her off, loudly enough that, finally, Gabe looks up at me. "My life is not a movie," I whisper. "Especially that one. The scene with the sheep . . ."

"I'm not talking about the sheep," she says.

"And this is not Victorian England. This is my *life*," I hiss.

"You're so literal." She scowls.

I can't think about *Far from the Madding Crowd* right now or follow any of the conversations happening at the table. I look around the table, at Mom, at Ted and his parents and little brother and sister, at Amelia. My people.

Gabe upsets the balance.

Chapter Seven

GABE

ONE THING YOU CAN SAY FOR THE HUDSON FAMILY: THEY COME together in a crisis. Even Great-Uncle Bud, Gran's oldest brother and last living sibling, took time off from the restaurant to come to dinner.

"It'll be good to have ya around, kid," Bud says. "How long are you staying? If you need to make some extra cash, let me know. I can always use another busboy."

Ted snorts. "I'd pay money to see that."

I don't think a part-time job at Bud's is going to solve my problems.

Bud's gotta be pushing ninety but swims laps at the Y every morning and hasn't missed a day of work since he got home from serving in Korea in the early fifties and opened Uncle Bud's World Famous, a diner in Fred Lake. It's known for its milkshakes, fries, and the most popular menu item, Uncle Bud's World Famous Blueberry Pancakes, served all day. Janie's roast and vegetables are delicious, and there's probably pie for dessert, but man, I could go for one of Uncle Bud's rocky road sundaes right about now.

In her weird fifties-style outfit with those cherries on her blouse, Juniper looks like the poster child for Uncle Bud's, like she should strap on a pair of roller skates and deliver an order of onion rings and a root beer float. She even smells like cherries. I lean over and reach for another roll to cover up the fact that I'm trying to smell her from across the table. Not just cherries. Vanilla and almond, too.

"Working on any new essential oil blends, Juniper?" Janie asks, and Juniper looks up from her plate. "I gave my last sample of lemon-lavender to Sheryl at church this morning."

Juniper nods. "I've got more of that one if you need it. And I'm working on a eucalyptus blend for flu season."

"You ever think about selling that stuff?" Frank asks. "I don't recognize half of what you've been growing this summer."

"I'm planning on it," she says. "I've got a hundred roller bottles on order. I'm working out a few kinks, but I should have five or six blends ready by spring."

"Will you sell them at the farmers' market?" Frank asks, shoveling a forkful of Janie's roast into his mouth.

"Yes, there, and possibly a natural living store in Fred Lake."

"Guinevere's place?" Janie asks.

Juniper nods again.

"What about your teas?" Janie says. "What was that last one you sent home with Ted? Something fall?"

"Oh, did she give you Fall Fireside?" Laurel asks. "It might be my favorite one yet."

"We could probably sell some of your things at the counter at the restaurant," Uncle Bud says.

"That would be amazing, Bud." Juniper looks up from her plate, which looks untouched except for the one red potato she's been moving around with her fork. When she smiles at him, two deep dimples appear and her eyes glimmer in the light from the chandelier above the table. "Thank you so much."

"You're making quite a name for yourself around here," Janie says, then turns to Allan. "Did you take the boat out at all during this latest stretch of nice weather?"

I glance around the table. It's been a long time since I've been to a family dinner—anyone's family, let alone my own. This reminds me of the weeks we spent at the cabin in the years before Gran died, although those memories have become hazy and distant. Frankie and Izzy are at the opposite end of the table arguing about who knows what. Uncle Bud says he's thinking about hiring someone else to run the place for a few months so he can move down to Arizona for the winter with his lady friend. Frank Sr. gets on Frank Jr.'s case about not refreshing the hens' water. Juniper's friend Amelia tells Ted about the Hitchcock marathon she's watching on some new streaming service. I do my best to ignore the attorney, although he asks about my school in LA and my plans for the future. The future. I'm not sure about my plans for tomorrow.

Finally, Allan pushes back his chair and places his napkin next to his empty plate. "Delicious as usual, Janie," he says. "Gabe, why don't you come over to my office first thing tomorrow and we can talk things over."

I glance over at him, surprised that he'd want to talk to me without Chris. "I'm not exactly well versed in estate planning," I say. "Maybe we should wait for Chris?"

"Not necessary. He's up to speed."

"But what if I have questions that you can't answer?"

Allan chuckles. "Believe me, I've heard it all over the years. I doubt you'd be able to stump me."

I look around the table, at Laurel and Juniper, who are both, it seems, trying to appear as though they aren't paying attention to this conversation. God, my head is spinning. All I wanted was to get away for a few days.

"Look," I tell Allan, "I'd really like to wait until Chris is here."

"Why don't I come with you, Gabe?" Frank says. "We can meet with Allan and then go out for breakfast or something."

I give him a grateful nod. "Yeah, that sounds good."

Allan stands up. "Excellent! I'll have Chickie move a few things around on my calendar and we'll get this out of the way."

"That's not fair!" Izzy cries from the other end of the table. "I want to skip school and get waffles."

"Life's not fair. Get used to it," Ted says. After a few minutes, he pushes up from his chair. "Mama, I know it's my turn to help with the dishes, but Frankie owes me. Gabey, you wanna take a ride with me? Juniper? Amelia?"

Juniper looks at Ted, her eyes wide, then to Amelia, whose cheeks have pinked up.

"Shoot," Amelia says. "I can't. I've got a test on *Brave New World* in English tomorrow."

"Yeah, sorry," Juniper echoes. "I'm—I've got to work on my college essay."

"You do?" Laurel asks. "I thought you finished that."

"I did," she says. "I had another teacher look at it for me, so I want to make some edits."

"Which teacher?" Laurel asks, almost as if she doesn't believe her.

"Marxen," Juniper says and lifts her eyebrows.

"Bummer," Ted says. He turns to me. "Well, what are you waiting for? What else are you going to do tonight?" He's got a point.

"Where are you going?" Janie asks.

"For a drive," Ted says. "Probably to Fred Lake."

"We've got a special on root beer floats this weekend," Bud says.

"Keep an eye out for deer." This, of course, from Frank.

"Well," Ted says as we drive out of the farm, "you survived your first family dinner! Congratulations!"

"Could have been worse."

"What could be more awkward than having an attorney come to Sunday night supper?"

Ted drives into town, past the high school, the drugstore, and the SuperValu, out of town, and about twenty miles east on the main highway into Frederick Lake. All the while, I scan back and forth for deer. Fred Lake seems to be going through a boom—a couple of fast-food restaurants under construction, a bright green GRAND OPENING banner at a food co-op, parcels of farmland with giant FOR DEVELOPMENT signs, thick yellow and black stripes below the words.

We pull into the parking lot at Uncle Bud's, and Ted has to drive around back to find an open spot. He takes out his phone and dials. "You want anything?" he asks me.

"Surprise me," I say.

"Violet, hey, it's Ted. Oh, you were at the game? Yeah? Thanks. Well, I'm in the parking lot and—yeah, I'll take my usual, but make it two. You'll never guess who I have with me. . . . Gabe Hudson, in the flesh." He pauses while Violet yammers on. "Really? You'll do that? Perfect. I'm parked in front of the service door in back, actually."

He ends the call. "On the house tonight *and* Violet's sending somebody out with it."

"Who's Violet?" I ask.

"Bud's great-granddaughter, which makes her a cousin. You've met her. She sang at Gran's funeral."

"Ah," I say, as though I remember.

A few minutes later, a kid wearing a backward baseball cap and a bright green T-shirt with *Uncle Bud's World Famous* embroidered above the pocket brings out a giant white paper bag and two drinks in a carrier. He hands them to Ted through the open window.

"Hey, Ted," the kid says, his voice cracking. "Violet said to tell you to stay out of trouble."

"Tell her thanks." Ted hands me the bag and when I start to open it, says, "Whoa whoa whoa. Hold your horses there, buckaroo. You can't eat that here. This calls for a trip to the park."

We pass the movie theater and a used bookstore and Ted turns in to Riverview Park, home of Big Louie, a twenty-foot-tall wooden voyageur. The sun's gone down and the place is nearly deserted. I follow Ted across the grass to a picnic table by the statue that overlooks the Lone Wolf River, which from here winds around to the west, through Harper's Mill and the Hudson property.

"Now you may open the bag," Ted says reverently.

I do, and with a dramatic flourish pull out two foil-covered paper boats of Bud's Spuds, deep-fried hash brown tots loaded with cheese, bacon, sour cream, and green onions.

"Oh, damn, I haven't had these in years," I say. "How are you hungry already?"

"I'm always hungry." He takes the bag and roots around, pulling out napkins and two plastic sporks. He hands me half of the haul, then lifts his drink and taps it against mine. "Cheers. Welcome to Minnesota."

"Cheers." I lift the lid off my cup and sniff before drinking. Root beer. I replace the lid and take a long sip. "That's good."

"Bet they don't have spuds and root beer like this out in LA," Ted says and laughs. "If you need a reason to stay, this could be it."

"Funny." I stab one of the tots, making sure the distribution of toppings is balanced for maximum flavor, and pop it in my mouth. He's not wrong about these spuds.

"So. What do you think about it all?" he asks tentatively.

"How long have you known?" I ask.

"About Gran's will? 'Bout as long as you, I guess."

"You didn't seem surprised earlier when I told you."

He shrugs. "I'm not surprised. And I'm not mad, if that's what you think. I guess I just assumed she'd left it all to Chris, you know? I never thought I'd inherit, anyway."

"But, I don't know, would you want to?"

He shovels another forkful into his mouth and shakes his head. "Nah," he says as he chews. "I don't mind the work, but I'm not cut out for a lifetime of farming."

"Not even the dairy? When your dad retires?"

"Nope. I want to play football in college and then teach. Coach someday. I'm not a dairy farmer. That's more Frankie's thing."

We eat in silence for a couple of minutes, then Ted asks, "What if you stayed for a while?"

I look up in surprise. "Stay . . . here?"

"Yeah, at the farm. What's keeping you in LA right now? I mean, no offense, but your career's in the shitter—temporarily, of course—your girlfriend dumped you *and* threw you under the bus. Seems like you could use a break."

"Wow, when you put it like that . . ."

He ignores me. "The farm's basically yours now. Why not stay here and be a regular high school kid for once in your life instead of some, I don't know, world-famous, award-winning rock star?"

Ha. A regular high school kid who's about to inherit a farm. Good one. "You're serious, aren't you?"

"Hell, yes, I'm serious. It would get you out of the spotlight for a while, and you'd get to hang out with me. What more could a guy ask for?"

Let's see. I'd start with a briefcase full of cash and/or a time machine to travel back to when I told Marley I'd get her the money she needed and this time tell her to figure it out herself. As an added bonus, maybe she would have dumped me sooner. And, as long as I'm asking, I'd go back even further and not fuck up the album. Easy.

"What have you got to lose?" Ted asks when I don't respond right away. He lifts his drink and sucks through the straw, the loud gurgle of the empty cup filling the cool night air around us.

"Yeah," I murmur. There is nothing left to lose. "Hey, Ted, how much do you think Stone & Wool is worth?"

He chokes a little and sets down the cup. "Why? You wouldn't *sell* the farm, would you? Because that would be a shit thing to do. You know that, right?"

"Yeah, yeah," I say. "I'm only thinking about my assets, you know? To have some idea of what it's worth for my, uh, portfolio?"

"Your assets, huh?" Ted lands me a skeptical glance. "I don't know much about assets, but I do know a thing or two about asses. And only an ass would sell off his family's farm, Gabe."

"I know, I know," I say, putting my hands up in surrender. "Forget I said anything!"

Until he said the words, the thought of selling hadn't

crossed my mind. But he's right. Only an ass would sell. The same kind of ass who would beg a guy to transfer money from his dad's account into his own to give money to his addict girlfriend.

Ex-girlfriend. Who probably won't pay me back even if she does get out of rehab before the end of the year.

I sigh and look past Ted to the river. Chris brought me here once, the summer after he and Elise split up the first time and after his first stay at Hazelden, the one that didn't stick. We sat on a bench not far from this spot and watched the river rush by, the same river that borders the Hudson farmland. He talked about rehab and how sorry he was about the separation.

He went on and on about the river. How he could sit for hours and watch the river pass, how the river changes constantly yet remains the same. He was reading a book called *Siddhartha*, thinking about the idea that you can never step in the same river twice because the river has changed and so have you. Big Louie, he said, has borne witness to a lot of life-changing moments.

I think I might understand what he felt that day.

"You know what?" I say. "I could probably stay for a few weeks."

"Cool," Ted says, nodding. "Mom can probably help with all the school shit."

"Sure," I say. "That would be great."

I take a deep breath of cool air, rich with the scent of pine and river and earth. Tomorrow, I'll get my shit together. I'll talk to the attorney and find out what it means that I'm about to inherit the family farm. I'll get Janie's help to register at the high school. I'll lie low and let the rumors die down.

Tonight, I'll sit by Big Louie with Ted. We'll watch the river together, watch it pass by, watch it constantly change and never change.

Tonight, I am a river.

Chapter Eight

JUNIPER

MONDAY MORNING, I WAKE EARLY, GROGGY AND OUT OF SORTS, SO before I shower, I take a brisk walk to the park and back. I don't have time to go all the way to the overlook, but even so, the sunrise is spectacular: pale blues and pinks that deepen to a rosy orange. This early, the air is brisk, the grass still damp and covered with oak and maple leaves, golden yellow and rich red. I can always count on the trail, no matter the season. I fill my lungs with crisp, clean air.

That's better.

When I get back to the house, Mom is already at the big barn. I work through the rest of my morning routine: Make my bed, shower, dress. I go downstairs to make breakfast, wheat toast with chunky peanut butter and a glass of cranberry juice—my mainstay since I was in preschool. Then I brew a fresh pot of Proper Cuppa, my traditional English breakfast blend with a hint of blackberry and hazelnut. I pour myself a to-go mug, scribble Mom a note that we're almost out of peanut butter, and grab my backpack.

I back out of the garage and wait for the automatic door to close before actually driving away, thinking that everything could change. Today, Gabe meets with Allan. Chris hasn't been here much this year. Maybe he's already decided to sell, and he needs to get Gabe on board when he comes into the inheritance. And why wouldn't Gabe want to sell? He has no ties to this place. But I do. This is the only home I've ever known, the repository of all my best memories, the place where, every day, I honor my dad and the work he did here.

The idea that things might change—because of Gabe—creates a knot of worry in my stomach.

I drive the same route to school every day. Cutting across Walnut Street might save me a couple of minutes, but I prefer staying on the county road, which hugs the river. I listen to public radio for the news and weather. On Wednesdays, I leave a few minutes early to give myself time to stop into Hartman's Bakery for a bear claw because every Wednesday, Hartman's donates all the day's proceeds to a local nonprofit. On Friday mornings, I bring tea samples to the office ladies or the FACS teachers or the media center specialists.

I like my routine, which isn't to say I get flustered or upset if the bear claws are sold out or I need to stop for gas on my way to school. It's more that, if possible, I like to be prepared for the unexpected, which makes no sense, I know.

I've had enough unexpected in my life, thank you.

I want things to be the way they're supposed to be.

I want to drive to school, park in my usual spot, eat my usual lunch, learn the usual things.

No one can fault me for that.

Chapter Nine

GABE

Frank pulls in to a parking spot on Main Street in front of the Law Office of Keen & Clark at five minutes to nine Monday morning. I barely slept and I couldn't eat, so I'm running on caffeine and uncertainty. I have no idea how this meeting's going to go, but I'm glad that Frank's here with me. I open the door into a small lobby, which seems smaller with dark seventies wood paneling on the walls. A window AC unit blasts cold air into the room even though it can't be fifty degrees outside.

"I'm Gabe Hudson, here to meet with Allan Keen," I say to the woman with ash-gray hair who sits behind the reception desk.

"Hi, Gabe Hudson. Hi, Frank," the woman says. I hear the buzz of an electric typewriter, which she switches off before she stands and extends her hand. She smiles as I shake it. "Chickadee. You can call me Chickie. Nice to meet you. You both have a seat, and I'll let Allan know you're here."

Frank and I sit down in orange overstuffed chairs to wait. I lean forward, my hands on my knees, and *whoosh* out a breath.

"You nervous?" Frank asks. "Nothing to be nervous about. Now, singing onstage in front of tens of thousands of people?

That's something to be nervous about, and you've done that often enough. This'll be a piece of cake."

God, I hope he's right.

"You can go on back now, boys," Chickie says as she reappears from a long hallway. I let Frank lead the way to Allan's office. The room is sparse and neat, a desk with a laptop and a few file folders, a round table in one corner, a wide window that looks out into a parking lot. There's a painting of a ship in a storm on the wall behind him with a plaque underneath: *The Wreck of the Edmund Fitzgerald.*

"Young Hudson," Allan says after I sit down. "Frank. Good to see you again. So. Let's jump right in. Tell me how much you know, Gabe, and I'll skip ahead if I need to."

"Considering that I know nothing, why don't you start at the beginning?"

The wrinkles of his face fold onto themselves when he smiles. He leans forward and steeples his fingers. He's clearly thrilled at the prospect and lays out a story that goes back generations, beginning with Finnish immigrants. He tells me how the Hudson family came to own first Gran's farm and then the dairy. Some of it seems familiar, things overheard at the cabin or from Chris.

"Now," Allan says, then pauses. He reaches for a mug on the desk, looks inside, then sets it down again without drinking. "Here's where things get tricky. I know I don't need to tell you about Chris's struggles with addiction."

At my nod, he continues. "Your grandmother had a lot on her plate in those days. Her husband had died, Chris was gallivanting around the world snorting cocaine—apologies for my insensitivity, Gabe—and she had two farms to manage. That's when she sold the dairy business to Frank here—Frank, how are ya?—and thank goodness she had Doug and Laurel running Stone & Wool. She had some decisions to make, and let me tell you, the hours I spent at that kitchen table drinking coffee and eating coffee cake to get there. Did you ever have your gran's sour cream coffee cake, Gabe?"

I smile and shake my head. "Not that I recall."

"Shame, shame. Maybe Janie has the recipe. But I digress."

Much of what Allan explains is over my head, but to boil it down, Gran was worried about Chris (and Elise) overdosing and leaving me a homeless orphan—which, at the time, wasn't far-fetched. She wanted to make sure I had a place to live. He goes on and on with the legal stuff about the inheritance.

"What questions do you have for me, Gabe?" Allan asks finally, sitting back in his chair.

I might as well be the ass and ask the question. I lean forward. "What if I want to sell? How quickly could that happen?"

Frank turns to me in surprise.

"Hypothetically speaking, of course," I add quickly.

"Well, assuming Chris is of a similar frame of mind, a transaction of this nature could wrap up in, oh, two, three months."

"I see." I sit back in my chair, the wheels in my brain turning with *ifs*. If Chris wanted to sell. If I could find a buyer—and fast. If all the moving pieces moved in the right direction at the right time, I could have the money by the end of the year and back in Chris's account before his year-end recap meeting.

"Best piece of advice I can give you right now?" Allan says. "If you ultimately decide to sell, let me know immediately, and I can assist throughout the process."

"Got it," I tell him.

"I've got one more thing and then I'll let you go. You are the first grandchild, Gabe. To hear Leona talk, the sun rose and set with you. When she got sick, I asked her if she wanted to revisit the estate plan, and she said she knew in her heart that this was the right thing to do. She hoped you would see this for the gift that it is. To learn to appreciate your heritage. . . . At the same time, she didn't want you to resent her for it, and she wanted to protect the family legacy. It's a delicate balance."

Gran was a good person. Too good for me. Too good to me. God, she'd be so disappointed if she knew what was going through my head right now.

"I'm on your side, Gabe," Allan says. "I'm here to help you."

He doesn't know me or what I've done. If he knew why I needed the money, I doubt he'd be so quick to offer.

✧ ✧ ✧

"Well," Frank says as we sit down at a booth in a diner across the street from Allan's office, "you've got a pretty big decision in front of you. Pancakes or waffles?" He laughs at his own joke.

"Funny. French toast, actually."

The server brings us coffee, water, and orange juice before we've even opened the menus. We don't speak for a long time as we look over the menu selections.

"So, you get all that?" Frank finally asks after the server takes our orders.

"What?" I ask. "What Allan said?"

"Yeah."

"Yeah, mostly."

"Good."

"Yeah."

"So, Ted said you were thinking about maybe staying, then?" Frank says after he drains a glass of orange juice.

I nod. "For a few weeks." I glance at my watch. I should be in first period at Barlow-Winston right now. I wonder if Chris called me in absent and laugh to myself. "I guess I need to figure out school."

"Why don't I drive you over there after breakfast, and Janie can get you all settled?" he says. I nod. The server brings our plates, and for a few minutes I watch in awe as Frank packs it away—bacon, sausage, eggs, pancakes, hash browns.

I eat half of my French toast and then set my fork down as an idea occurs to me. "Frank, what about you? Would you ever consider buying Stone & Wool?"

He laughs as he sops up egg yolk with a piece of toast. Then he looks up. "You're serious?"

"Well, yeah. Why not?"

"In a perfect world, right? I can't oversee two farms this

size, even if I did keep Laurel on to manage Stone & Wool. And I think I can be honest with you here and say there's no way I'd be able to afford the buyout, anyway."

"Right," I say, trying to hide my disappointment. That would have been too easy.

"Thanks for thinking of me, though," Frank says. "You're a good kid, Gabe. Hang in there. Everything's going to work out the way it's supposed to. That's what Leona always used to say."

My phone buzzes and I pull it out of my pocket.

Chris: I took care of a few things on this end. PR guy from the label made a statement. All good.

There's a link to a video.

Me: You didn't think you should run it past me first?
Chris: What have I always said? Control what you can control. Tell the story you want people to know. You should be thanking me not giving me shit.

I sigh and look up at Frank as I click on the link. "Sorry, I think I need to watch this."

Clear up misconceptions. Experienced an isolated panic attack. Spending time at beloved family farm, focusing on creating new music. Cherishes the time he and Miss Green have spent together, best wishes for her health and recovery, blah-blah-blah.

All the right things. I don't read the comments or look at the reactions on social media.

Suddenly, it all crashes down on me again—the album, the videos, Marley, the money, of course the money—and it's not panic so much as it's nausea, hot and swift and lurching. I stand up, fast, as sour saliva pools in my mouth. "Restroom? Where's the restroom?"

Frank frowns and points to a door behind the bakery counter. "What's wrong?" he asks, but I don't have time to answer.

I make it to the small bathroom with enough time to flip on the light, lock the door, and kneel at the toilet, losing my breakfast in violent spasms. I kneel there for long minutes after there's nothing left, catching my breath, wiping away stinging tears. Finally, I stand, wash my hands and splash my face, and return to the table. The server has cleared our plates, and Frank is signing the receipt.

He looks up. "You look a little green around the gills. You OK?"

"I'll live." I point to the receipt. "I'd like to pay."

"Ah, kid, I appreciate that. Next time?"

I nod and follow Frank toward the front door. He reaches into a bowl by the cash register and hands me a small, wrapped peppermint.

"How about I drop you off at the farm and you can take care of school tomorrow? You can sleep off whatever bug you got."

It's the best idea I've heard all day. Unfortunately, I don't think a nap will cure what ails me.

Chapter Ten

JUNIPER

I LOST THIS BATTLE.

Chris owns a garage full of vehicles. Ted lives less than a mile away. And maybe I came out on the right side of the grocery delivery argument, but no amount of reasoning could sway Mom on this. According to her, it makes the most sense for me to drive Gabe Hudson to school.

"I'm not comfortable with it," I finally said, a last-ditch effort.

"What makes you uncomfortable?" Mom dug in. "The decision itself or the fact that you felt you didn't have a say in the matter? Or does being around Gabe make you feel unsafe in some way?"

That deflates my sense of injustice slightly. "No, it's not that. More of a general discontent."

"I see. Well, here's a tip, Juniper. All your life, things are going to make you feel uncomfortable. That's what it means to step out of your comfort zone. You'll have to get used to it. Who knows, maybe you and Gabe will become friends."

"Don't hold your breath," I snapped. "And I happen to like my comfort zone, OK?"

I sit in the driveway of the main house now and wait,

my fingers tapping against the steering wheel of the Chevy Impala that once belonged to Janie's mom, who sold it to us for a song when she moved into an assisted living facility. Five minutes pass and still, no Gabe. I don't have his number, so I message Ted instead.

Me: Could you please text your notorious cousin to let him know that I'm sitting in the driveway and if he doesn't get his ass out here in the next two minutes, he'll be late for his first day of public education?
Ted: Salty.
Me: Don't test me today, Theodore.
Ted: Here's his contact info. OMW 2 weight room. See ya at lunch.

I glance back up at the house, a second home to me. Ted and I spent a lot of time with Leona, especially during the summers. She taught me to crochet dishcloths, and I helped her can peaches and green beans and pickles. Ted and I played hide-and-seek in the cornfields and hiked up to the overlook in the park reserve and ate Leona's home-made grape popsicles—frozen grape juice in Dixie cups—on her front porch. When she got sick and started chemo, we cleaned the house every Saturday morning, taking special care with the knickknacks and picture frames in the living room while she told stories of the people in the photos. Now, she's a memory, too. A story to pass down.

I save Gabe's contact info and am composing a scathing text about how my time is valuable and I deserve respect (which, of course, I won't actually send, but wasn't it Abraham

Lincoln who said you should write your "hot letter" and get everything off your chest even if you never sign or send it?) when the front door opens and Gabe takes his sweet time making his way across the porch, down the front steps, and across to my vehicle in the driveway. I watch his every move, and I'm not too pissed at him to recognize that his every move is loose and smooth and confident, like he's comfortable in his own skin. He opens the passenger door and slides in.

"Hey," he says. He's wearing a pair of dark jeans and a soft gray T-shirt under a moss-green Army jacket. No ridiculous, oversized wool coat today. He must be adjusting to the cooler temperatures. His curls aren't quite as wild as they were yesterday, and he's got those dark sunglasses on even though the sky is still a dusky pre-sunrise blue.

I barely slept last night, worried about the farm and what Gabe plans to do with it once he turns eighteen, knowing that he met with Allan yesterday morning. I also tortured myself by playing the videos over and over and clicking through photos of Gabe at the airport. This morning, there's a video of the guy from the record label reading Gabe's statement, that he's decided to spend time on the family farm to regroup and recharge and eventually work with Chris on his next album.

I'm irritated with myself that I even care.

"Hey," I say and back out of the driveway. I glance at him and run my eyes over that jacket again. Is that—oh my God, it has to be.

"Um, uh," I stammer, "is that the jacket that Chris wore for

Live in Berlin? European leg, '97? It is, isn't it? He gave that to you?"

"Well, he *is* my dad," Gabe snaps.

"Well, it should be in a museum," I snap back, "or at the very least, a Hard Rock Café."

Gabe huffs out a laugh. "Have you ever even been to a Hard Rock Café?"

This conversation is going about as well as I could expect. "There's one at the Mall of America, which, I will point out, is located in *Minnesota.*"

"Ah, of course. The Mall of America has everything."

"Well, no, the American Girl store closed in March." My cheeks warm at that comment. He probably doesn't even know what American Girls are. I turn onto the county road. Only eight more minutes of this awkwardness to go. "My point, I guess, is that it's pretty cool that Chris gave you the jacket. I've always wondered about Watson. His story. How many tours he served. If he's doing OK." And now I'm rambling.

"Watson?" Gabe asks.

"The name. On the jacket. Watson."

"Oh, right." Gabe runs a finger across the name patch. "That's . . . I guess I've never thought about that."

"That doesn't surprise me."

"What's that supposed to mean?"

I wave my hand around vaguely. "You know. I'm sure you're very busy worrying about your rep or something."

"My rep," he repeats, then falls silent. He doesn't say another word the remainder of the drive.

"Meet me back here at 3:30 if you want a ride home," I say as he gets out. He nods but says nothing, doesn't make eye contact. I watch him walk through the crowd in the parking lot toward the front steps of the school. Everything about him looks out of place here with our cracked and rutted parking lot, rusty pickup trucks, flannel shirts, hiking boots. We are such a cliché.

"Wow," I hear from behind me and I close my eyes, take a deep breath. This is all I need right now. "He's even hotter in person."

Chloe Harland, dubbed Chloe Horrible by Ted after their one "date" to his eighth-grade formal when she ditched him for Deacon Parsons, is your typical almost-mean girl. In a town like this, at our tiny consolidated high school, it doesn't matter much. Everyone's a friend in the most basic form of the word, and the friendships come and go in waves. Chloe looked down on me, though, for being a farmer's daughter (especially because the farmer was a woman and a single mom) and for living in a house that we didn't own on someone else's property, someone who used to be a celebrity and was now a washed-up rock star drug addict. However, when Dig Me Under released "Juniper Blue" and Chris reclaimed both his sobriety and his celebrity, and was Harper Mill's cherished son once again, Chloe welcomed me back into her fold.

The three of us—me and Amelia and Chloe—survived a lot of sleepovers during the middle school years, until we hit high school and Chloe went one way (makeup, boys, drinking) and Amelia and I went another (mostly studying and hanging out with Ted). My association with Gabe, however, no matter how peripheral, is sure to revitalize my friendship with Chloe once again.

"Hey, Chlo," I say as I turn around to face her. Her ivory cheeks are rosy in the brisk morning air, she's curled her strawberry blonde hair into perfect ringlets, and her smoky eye is flawless. She looks gorgeous, as usual. "What's up?"

"Maybe you should tell me what's up. I can't believe you've been holding out on me."

It's all I can do to not roll my eyes. "What do you mean?"

"Gabe Hudson is finally in town, and you've been keeping him all to yourself!"

I start to walk toward the front door and Chloe follows. "I wouldn't say that, exactly," I say. "I've barely seen him. And honestly, if you're trying to find an in with Gabe Hudson, I'm not the right person. Suck up to Ted, not me."

She flips her curls over her shoulder. "As if I need to find an *in*, Juniper." She cuts in front of me and sprints to catch up to Gabe.

A teeny, tiny part of me feels sorry for Gabe and almost wants to warn him about Chloe Horrible, but another, slightly larger part wants to let this play out on its own and see how Mr. Hot Young Celebrity handles it.

Chapter Eleven

GABE

I'M AS READY FOR MY FIRST DAY AT HARPER-RENTON HIGH SCHOOL as I'll ever be. Last night, Janie sent me a text to let me know that I was all set to start Tuesday morning, she'd meet me in the school office to help me register, and Juniper had offered to drive me every day. Sure she did.

Today, Juniper's hair is up in a high ponytail. She's wearing a brown cardigan covered with what appear to be tiny, embroidered orange and white foxes set at various angles, a khaki-colored corduroy skirt that lands mid-knee, brown leather boots that almost reach the hem. And glasses with bright orange frames, like the foxes. She'd fit right in back in LA. Maybe not at my celebrity-saturated pretentious prep school, but in general.

The ride to school is awkward as hell, and even though I have no idea where I'm going, when we get there I don't waste any time. I pull open the front door of the old, worn brick building. I'm not sure what I was expecting—something from a movie, maybe?—but there are no security guards, no metal detectors. Just miles of sea green lockers and handmade banners on the wall cheering on the football team and announcing a Homecoming Dance.

Oh God. I'm really in high school. There's no going back.

I will get through this day, and then the next one. What did Gran used to say? Worse things happen at sea?

"Hey," I say to a girl wearing jeans, a Rolling Stones T-shirt with a dozen different-colored tongues, and bright red rubber boots. "Can you tell me where the office is?"

She narrows her eyes. "Do I know you from somewhere?"

I'm surprised the news hasn't spread. I shrug. "Don't think so. I just moved to town."

"What's your name?"

"Gabriel." I'm not sure why I use my full name. Elise and her parents are the only people who ever call me that. "Big Rolling Stones fan?"

She screws up her mouth. "What?"

I wave a hand toward her. "Your T-shirt. You must like the Stones?"

"Oh, right, the band. I saw this at Target and just like it, you know? I swear I know you from someplace. Where'd you move from? Esko? Did you play soccer there?"

I shake my head. Who doesn't know the Rolling Stones? "Doesn't matter."

The girl frowns. "Well, Gabriel from doesn't matter, take a right up there underneath that football banner and you can't miss it."

I nod and turn in that direction as she walks away, but bony fingers on my arm stop me. I look first at the fingers—nails painted a shiny, glittery pink—and then up to a face with a pale, pointed chin, bright pink lipstick, and curly red hair.

"You're Gabe Hudson," she says as she sticks her chest out and nods to herself. "I'm Chloe. Chloe Harland. I overheard you ask Riley where the office is. If she had any manners at all, she'd have walked you there herself. I guess we can't all be generous and helpful, though. I'd be happy to show you."

She smiles but I frown, lifting her hand to remove it from my arm. Nobody touches this jacket. I think about my conversation about it with Juniper in the car. *That jacket should be in a museum.* I can't decide if it's cool that Juniper recognized it or if I'm annoyed by it, if it's weird that she thinks about the original owner of the coat or endearing.

Chloe stands before me and blinks her heavy eyelashes, waiting for me to say something.

"I'm good," I say. "I'm sure I can find it on my own."

"No, really! It's no trouble at all. Have you registered? I can tell you all the best classes to take. I hope we have some classes together. You're a senior, right? I'm a senior, too."

She takes my arm again and this time pulls me in the direction of the football banner and the hallway that leads to the office. "I was so excited when I heard you were staying! So excited. You're Ted's cousin, right? Ted and I are such good friends. I'm sure you'll go to all the football games, although you've already missed three."

I can tell this girl isn't going to back down. I follow her down the hall, the heels of her ankle boots clicking, until we reach a set of glass doors that lead to the office.

"Here we are!" Chloe trills. "Should I wait for you? Give you a tour?"

"Oh, no," I say. "This might take a while. You know."

"Are you sure? It's not a problem." Chloe looks up at me with wide eyes and a wide smile. I'll have to ask Ted about her, what she's like, if she's genuine. God, I'm losing it if I think that a small-town girl in northern Minnesota is after something.

"Well, you go on in, then. The office ladies will take care of you. Maybe I'll see you at lunch! Or we'll have some classes together! Bye, Gabe!"

Chloe leaves me at the door, her heels clacking and her hair bouncing against her back as she speed-walks down the hall.

✧ ✧ ✧

The office ladies, as Chloe called them, welcome me to HRH and gush over me and my curls (just like Chris's when he was my age, apparently). Janie handles everything, as she said she would. Barlow-Winston Academy for the Arts faxed over my transcript yesterday, and she and the principal here hashed out a plan so I can graduate in May. This trimester: World History, Creative Writing, Horticulture, Calculus, and Entrepreneurship & Business Management.

"Horticulture?" I ask after I scan the schedule. "No offense, but it's not really, you know, my wheelhouse."

Janie clucks. "Well, the fact of the matter is, we have an Earth Science requirement, and none of the classes you took at that fancy LA arts school qualify. Horticulture fits perfectly into your schedule this trimester. You're living on a farm now, a farm that will partially belong to you in a matter of weeks."

Ah yes, there's that. Not that I need reminding. It's all I can think about, especially after the meeting with Allan—the farm and the money. Always the money.

Ted's words from the park at the river come back to me: *Only an ass would sell.*

Suddenly, I'm hot and short of breath. I'm clutching the schedule, looking at it but barely registering the words. The school office is small, desks and copier and cubbies crammed into the small space. There's not enough air. I gotta get out of here.

"You can get through this, Gabe," Janie says gently. "I know you can."

I snap my head up. Those words—not the exact lyrics, but close enough. *Get through this, I know you will.* The lyrics to "Juniper Blue." I wonder if Janie even realizes it.

"Sure. Thanks," I mumble. Sweat drips down my back.

"Here's a map of the school. Do you want me to walk you to your first class? Or I could call Ted to come down and take you? Or Juniper?"

I shake my head. "I'm good. Thanks for everything, Janie."

I leave the office, lean against the brick wall, pull out my phone, and type in the search bar. Cell service and Wi-Fi in the building are crap, but after a few seconds of spinning, my search results pop up.

Commercial real estate Frederick Lake mn

I find the link for the company I saw on the yellow-and-black signs Sunday night and click *Call now.*

Chapter Twelve

JUNIPER

SOMEHOW, I MAKE IT THROUGH ALMOST AN ENTIRE DAY WITHOUT seeing Gabe, except for the few minutes when I ended up right behind him in the à la carte line at lunch. He didn't say a word and, after he paid, walked right past the table where Ted and Amelia were sitting. He pushed open the door to the courtyard and sat down at one of the picnic tables. Alone. As in, he was the only person out in the courtyard on a typically chilly, cloudy fall day in northern Minnesota. At least he's got Watson's Army jacket.

My luck runs out in fifth period, Entrepreneurship & Business Management, when Gabe, still wearing the jacket, strolls in and introduces himself to Mrs. Marxen, who raises her eyebrows at his disheveled, rock star appearance. I look down at my notebook, my blonde curls falling over my face, hoping that he won't notice me.

"I'm Gabriel Hudson," he says. I'm surprised to hear him use his full name.

"Yesss!" Chloe Horrible, who sits one row over and one seat up from me, isn't shy about expressing her excitement. She turns in her seat. "Oh my God, I hope I get paired up with him for the project. Wouldn't that be so amazing?"

"So amazing," I repeat.

"Ah yes," Marxen says. "Chris Hudson's boy. I heard you'd be gracing my class with your presence. Lucky me."

I almost snort.

Marxen has been around a while. She's not from Harper's Mill originally, but she's well versed on the Hudson family lore.

"Yes, ma'am," Gabe says. Someone laughs, and Marxen shoots a glare in that direction.

"Call me Mrs. Marxen," she says, "not ma'am. There's an empty desk behind Juniper Bell. I'm sure you're already well acquainted. Perhaps she can help you get up to speed."

Chloe turns around again, her mouth open and her eyes wide. "Oh my God," she says again. "He's so *hot.*"

I roll my eyes as Gabe walks down the row toward his seat. He doesn't say anything, not that I expect him to. He even goes so far as to scoot his desk back a little to put more distance between us.

"Your timing is perfect, Mr. Hudson," Marxen says after he's settled. Why does she call him that? She's never called me Ms. Bell or Chloe Ms. Horrible. "Today, you'll be assigned partners for your trimester project. Thanks to you, we now have an even number of students in the class."

She goes on to describe the assignment, most likely for his benefit because the rest of us already know: Create a comprehensive business plan for a small business that includes an executive summary, company mission statement, keys to success. . . . Marxen doesn't stop talking for a long time. I hope she never stops talking and the bell rings before she can get to partner assignments. I cross my fingers that Chloe gets her wish.

"And now," she says dramatically, "the moment you've all been waiting for." She marks up a piece of paper that must be the "partner" list. She reads off names, pair after pair. My dread increases with every name that isn't mine or Gabe's. Chloe is paired up with Olivia Parker, a quiet junior who also can't take her eyes off Gabe. Chloe sighs loudly. Of course, the last names on the list are mine and Gabe's.

"So unfair!" Chloe stage-whispers.

I don't hear any sound from the person in the seat behind me. Nothing. No reaction.

"With that," Marxen says, "scooch together and brainstorm a list of ten possible businesses. Share phone numbers or email addresses or Snaps or however you want to communicate with each other. Tomorrow, you'll need to have that list narrowed to three. There can be no duplicate businesses, so think outside the box, people. And please, no coffee shops or bakeries. I'm sick to death of coffee shops and bakeries."

The other fourteen students move next to their partners. Not me or Gabe. I turn around to find him staring at me.

"What?" I snap as I stand partway to flip my desk to face his.

He doesn't say anything but locks his eyes with mine, those beautiful, unforgettable green eyes. So this is how it's going to be. A stare-down. I don't think we can pass the class if all we do is stare at each other. I raise an eyebrow. I'm not going to be the first to say something. I'm not. I swear, I'm going to beat him at his own game.

"Do you have any ideas?" I blurt.

He shakes his head. "Not a one."

"Oh, come on," I say. "You can't be serious. I'm sure you're dying to suggest some sort of trendy vegan all-day-breakfast food truck or specialty shaving supplies store? Hipster beard oil? Something super LA?"

He shakes his head. "That's not the LA I know. I'll be honest here. This project, this class—they're not at the top of my list of priorities right now."

I bite my bottom lip. "Look, Gabe, I know you have a lot going on. But I need an A in this class." I don't tell him why, that I can't afford to lose my scholarship at Cloquet Valley State University in Fred Lake. I'm already planning to live at home and commute to save on housing costs, and I'll be able to keep my job at the park reserve, too. I've been setting aside most of what I've earned so far for books and tuition.

He's quiet for a minute, then, "Fine. Fifty-fifty. You come up with five ideas, I'll come up with five ideas."

I scowl. "Fine." I open my notebook and tear out a sheet of paper.

> *Trendy vegan all-day-breakfast food truck*
> *Specialty shaving supplies*
> *Recording studio for underprivileged youth*
> *Roadside farm stand*
> *Donut shop*

I slam my pen down and slide the paper onto his desk. He barely glances at it.

"Recording studio for underprivileged youth? What even is that?" he asks.

I widen my eyes. "What, not altruistic enough for you?"

He ignores me. "She said no bakeries."

"You *were* listening! Donuts only. Specialized. Your turn."

He picks up his pen and writes, carefully and slowly, pausing between each list item. He slides the paper back to me when he's done and smiles.

His smile about knocks me over. Perfect straight white teeth, lines like twin parentheses on either side of his broad mouth. I swallow hard, then glance down at our list, surprised by his neat, all-capitals penmanship.

DRIVE-IN RESTAURANT WITH CARHOPS
FASHION EYEWEAR/INSTAGRAM INFLUENCER
VINTAGE CLOTHING STYLIST
GROCERY DELIVERY SERVICE
CLASSIC CAR RESTORATION

"Carhops?" I ask. "Is that still a thing?"

"It could be."

"Isn't that a little sexist? Pretty girls in short skirts delivering burgers and cherry limeades on roller skates?"

"No one said anything about girls."

"Male carhops?"

He shrugs. "Any gender. And retro is big right now."

I read through the list one more time and sigh. I think the

grocery delivery service might have been intended as a jab, but overall, the ideas aren't horrible.

"Good enough?" he asks.

"Yeah, good enough."

The bell rings and Gabe practically launches himself out of the chair and out the door.

"Lucky you!" Olivia Parker squeals.

"Lucky me," I mumble.

✿ ✿ ✿

At dinner, Mom grills me about Gabe.

"How was his first day? Did you show him around?"

I take a spoonful of chicken and wild rice soup and fight the urge to roll my eyes. "No, I did not show him around. As far as I can tell, he survived. He didn't say one word on the drive home, not even *thank you* after I dropped him off."

Mom sets down her spoon and links her hands together, elbows on the table. "Do you have any classes together?"

"One. E-biz. And wouldn't you know, we got paired up for a project. I'd rather be paired up with Chloe Horrible." I fill her in on the assignment.

"So? Did you narrow your list down to three?"

I know that, as a woman who runs a business herself, she's genuinely interested in our brainstorm session. She was thrilled when I told her that I wanted to follow in her footsteps and study ag and horticulture, that I'd like to stay on at the farm and continue my work in Dad's greenhouse. I would stay here forever if I could.

I can't shake the worry, though, of what Gabe might do after he inherits. I dip my spoon into the bowl of soup, lift the spoon, let the soup drip back into the bowl.

"We didn't get that far. Hopefully we can figure it out on the way to school tomorrow. Thanks for the executive carpool order, by the way. Not awkward at all."

Mom sighs but otherwise doesn't acknowledge my comment. "He's only been here a couple of days, Juniper. Give him some time. Give him a chance."

Give him a chance to do what? I push my bowl away.

I look back up. Mom's eyes are soft, kind. Unlike my blue eyes, hers are a light brown. I may have gotten Dad's eyes, but I definitely take after Mom in the height department. What she lacks in stature, she makes up for in strength. Physical and mental. I've seen her lift a 120-pound ewe like it was nothing, and I haven't seen her cry since the day Leona died. She's compassionate and sensitive to the needs of everyone around her, but she rarely lets her own emotions get the better of her.

That's another way we differ. I can be a bit salty, as Ted likes to point out, and it doesn't take much to set off my waterworks. I've been known to cry when a bird flies into the picture window in the living room.

"We've weathered some storms over the years," Mom says, "some of them real storms, like the year a hailstorm completely obliterated the pumpkin crop. For a while, after your dad died, I thought I wouldn't be able to do this without him. I was this close to packing it in and moving to Wisconsin to be closer to my folks."

"You were? You never told me!"

She smiles. "There are some things you don't tell your young daughter who's just lost her father to cancer. Leona told me that she'd felt the same way after Hal died, that she couldn't stand to live here without him by her side. But she also said that one day, I wouldn't see only pain and heart-ache around me. And that I had to stay because it was the right thing to do for you, like it had been the right thing for her to stay for Chris and Janie, even though they were much older when Hal died. She was right. She was right about a lot of things."

"Why did Leona leave the farm to Gabe?" I don't want Mom to know that I'm worried, but I can't help asking the question. "And why only fifty-one percent and not the whole thing?"

"It's complicated," Mom says. "But she had her reasons. There were some rough years before Chris got clean. She didn't think Gabe should know when he was younger, because she didn't want that extra pressure on him. He's had enough to worry about, more than any kid should have to deal with."

I nod and she continues. "I assume you're up to speed on everything that's going on with him right now? What happened in LA?"

"Yes."

"You know, then, that he's going through some things right now. Imagine how lonely and out of place he must feel. He could use a little grace, Juniper."

I think about him in that video, crouched against that car, seized by panic. I think about the statement from the record label. I think about Leona's funeral and how he's all alone in the farmhouse. Maybe she's right.

"Talk to him, hon," Mom says softly. "Show him around the farm. And don't forget, you'll catch more flies with honey than you will with vinegar."

As I clear the table and rinse dishes before putting them in the dishwasher, her words echo in my mind: *Catch more flies with honey. Catch more flies with honey.*

That might be the answer I'm looking for.

Chapter Thirteen

GABE

TURNS OUT THAT PUBLIC SCHOOL ISN'T THAT MUCH DIFFERENT THAN Barlow-Winston except for the lack of uniforms and considerably less gossip, other than a few people I've noticed whispering about me as I pass by in the hall. And the fact that I have no music classes. I wonder if that was intentional on Janie's part or if they don't offer anything.

Laurel has invited me up to the little red house every night for dinner, but as much as I would love a home-cooked meal rather than another frozen pizza, I've declined. Being around Juniper in Entrepreneurship & Business Management—or e-biz, as she calls it—is stressful enough. I know three things: One, she treats me like I'm some Joe Schmo off the street, not the rich-kid son of two celebrities with his own chart-topping album (and one horseshit follow-up album); two, I'm not sure how I feel about the fact that she treats me like some Joe Schmo off the street; and three, I realize how fucked up it is that I'm not thrilled about it.

In e-biz on Wednesday, we choose our project topics. First we narrowed it down to three: roadside farm stand, donut shop, and the grocery delivery service, which was meant to be snarky. If she noticed, Juniper didn't mention it.

"Donut shop?" Marxen has been walking around the classroom peering over shoulders. "I said no bakeries."

I smile to myself while Juniper stumbles over an explanation. "It's a specialty pastry shop, not a bakery!"

"Don't argue semantics with me," Marxen says. "I've made your decision easier."

After Marxen moves on to the next students, I say, "You know, I really don't care. Pick whatever you want."

I know exactly which one she'll choose. She circles *roadside farm stand* on the paper.

"Excellent," I say, slouching down in my chair and stretching out my legs. "I was hoping you'd pick that. You already know everything there is to know about running a farm stand."

She opens her mouth to say something, closes it again, opens it. I can almost see her biting her tongue.

"Well," she says slowly, "we don't exactly have a farm stand at Stone & Wool. Mostly we take vegetables to the farmers' market, and occasionally a customer will stop by for larger quantities."

"Sounds similar, at least."

"Why don't I give you a tour of the farm after school today, and you can get a feel for it?" She sounds . . . less snide? "I mean, I assume you haven't had time with your important, busy schedule to have a look around."

Ah, there it is. I almost laugh. She can't help herself.

On the other hand, she's not wrong. I've got a guy from the commercial real estate company coming to "have a look around" right after school.

"Sure," I say. "I do have something on my important, busy schedule that will last about a half hour, but I could take a tour, sure."

"Fine. I'll meet you at the farmhouse."

That might be tricky if the real estate guy is still around. I think fast. The greenhouse is behind the little red house and not completely visible from the road, so maybe she won't see the agent. "How about I meet you at the greenhouse instead? You'll be working there anyway, right?"

She narrows her eyes at me in suspicion. "Yes," she says slowly. "I will be working in the greenhouse, as it happens."

"Perfect," I say.

"Perfect," she echoes. "And hopefully, once you've had the tour, you'll start to contribute more to this project."

"Maybe I will," I say as the bell rings.

Probably not, not when I've got other shit to worry about.

✧ ✧ ✧

There's a black luxury SUV in the driveway when Juniper drops me off. I guess the agent decided to show up early.

"Who's that?" Juniper asks.

"No idea. Maybe Chris is here finally and it's a rental?" The lie sounds flimsy even to me. But I'm out of the car and slamming the door before she can ask any more questions.

The SUV is unoccupied, and there's no sign of the agent. Luckily, Juniper's halfway up the road back to her house before the guy walks out from behind the garage.

"You must be Gabe," he says. "Eric Dunbar, Riverside Commercial Properties. I'm so glad you called the best agency in northeast Minnesota, and you will be, too. Here's my card."

Eric Dunbar, Riverside Commercial Properties, has got to be about six and a half feet tall, with a mass of brown hair and pale white skin covered in freckles. He's dressed in a poorly tailored charcoal gray suit with a bright red tie and brown loafers crusted with soil. His handshake is firm but sweaty.

"I hope you don't mind that I came a little early," he says before I can return his obnoxious greeting. "I kept myself fairly well out of sight, though. Don't want to give the caretaker anything to worry about now, do I?" He chuckles to himself. "I took a good look around, got a good idea of the lay of the land. You've got a tremendous property here, Gabe. Tremendous. The river on one side, park reserve on the other. Land like this is highly sought-after. I think this could be a very attractive property to the right buyer. Now, what kind of time frame are we looking at here?"

"I'm not sure, to be honest," I say. "This whole thing was sort of dropped on me, and I'm not quite up to speed yet. I only met with my attorney a couple of days ago."

"Good, good." Eric Dunbar nods.

"I'm only interested in valuation at this time," I continue.

"Sure, sure." He nods again. "Ideally, we'd get this on the market before the snow flies, of course, but you let me know once you've got all the details. Now, do you have any questions for me?"

"Yeah," I say. "Do you want to come in the house or—"

"No, no, I'm a little short on time this afternoon." His voice booms across the yard. "That's why I came early. I didn't go into any of the outbuildings, of course, but I doubt that will matter in the long run. I'm sure you're wondering dollar amount, correct? Who might be interested in this land, things like that? I'll need a day or two to put together the information you're looking for. Sound good?"

"Yeah," I say again. "Exactly what I'm looking for. I do have some questions, so—"

"Fantastic." He cuts me off again. "Great to meet you, Gabe. I'll be in touch. Give me a call if any other questions come up."

This guy's a jackass, but I have a feeling that he's a jackass who could potentially get me a ton of cash, and that's what matters most right now.

His phone starts to ring as he walks across the driveway to the SUV. "Eric Dunbar here," he says as he gets into the vehicle, on to the next thing before he even drives away.

Chapter Fourteen

JUNIPER

I'VE BARELY GOTTEN STARTED ON THE SOIL-TESTING PROJECT I'M working on for my independent study when Gabe shows up to the greenhouse, much sooner than I expected.

"That was quick," I say. "Is Chris back?"

"No," he says. He seems shaky, rattled.

"Who was at Leona's, then?"

"Oh, a friend of Chris's. Eric something. Do you know him? He came over to meet with Chris about something and didn't realize Chris wasn't here yet."

I look down at the vial in my hand and try to keep my tone light and, well, not suspicious. "I don't know anyone named Eric. Where was he from?"

"Are you almost ready?" he asks, not bothering to answer my question. "I've got a paper due tomorrow."

I want to ask him for which class or when he started caring about homework but bite back the snark, reminding myself about the honey.

"Sure. I can do this later," I say instead, tucking aside my project. "Well, this is the greenhouse. We typically grow our market produce in the fields—pumpkins, summer and winter squash, radishes, tomatoes. We use the greenhouse for herbs and salad greens mostly. Less likely to be damaged by hail or eaten by critters."

He walks up and down the rows, glancing at what's left of this summer's crop. I can't tell if he's genuinely interested or killing time. He doesn't ask questions or make any comments, so I keep talking.

"My dad was working on some renovations to make this a deep winter greenhouse so we could use it all year," I say. "He got sick before he could implement the changes, so I've got a shorter growing season. I've always wanted to pick up where he left off, though. We'll see."

Still nothing from Gabe.

"Should we move on?"

He nods and follows me outside. The weather has turned gray and a bit drizzly, not unusual for this time of year.

"Great," Gabe mumbles as we step out into the mist. "A tour in the rain."

"Rain is usually a good thing for farmers," I reply.

"Can we make it quick?"

A quick tour of a farm this size. I shake my head and head past our house, beyond the willow tree, and toward the pumpkin patch in the north field.

"Stone & Wool is known for two things, basically," I tell him. "Fleece, obviously, and pumpkins in the fall. We've talked about doing some sort of u-pick in the fall, but it's too much with only Mom and me. That's why we focus on the farmers' market."

"Do you make enough money that way?"

How interesting that his first question is about money. I don't want him to think the farm's not doing well. I don't want to give him any ammunition.

"Yes," I answer, not bothering to explain that on a farm, some years are better than others, that fifteen minutes of hail or high winds can change the course of a year.

We cross the road to the west field, and it's raining enough now that the water is starting to collect in ruts in the gravel.

"In this field, we grow zucchini, yellow squash . . ." I trail off as Gabe, instead of following me, heads down the road toward the barns. "OK, then."

We walk past the farmhouse into the big barn. I flick on the lights and shake the raindrops from my hair once we're inside. The big barn is mainly where we store equipment and vegetables we've harvested, and where we prep for the farmers' market each week. I give him a quick rundown. There's not a whole lot to see, but Gabe doesn't seem even remotely interested in any of it.

"So, for the farm stand project," I say, "we need to decide whether the retail space will be near the roadside of our hypothetical farm or farther into the property. Either way, we're going to have to think about storage space and if the storage will be in the same location as the retail portion."

"Whatever you think," Gabe says. "You're the expert. How much do we have left?"

I take a deep breath. He is trying my last shred of patience. "The round barn. The sheep."

"Do we need to know about the sheep for the project?"

"No. It's a farm stand, right? Vegetables."

"I think I've got the general idea, then."

"That's it? You don't want to see the rest of the farm?" I can't keep the irritation out of my voice.

"Yeah," he says absently. "Thanks for the tour, though."

Gabe leaves the barn door open and sprints across the yard to the farmhouse. I watch him run through the rain, stare after him long after he's gone up the porch steps and into the house. I stand in the doorframe until the rain's coming down so hard, the farmhouse and the trees blur in front of me.

Chapter Fifteen

GABE

I EXPECT JUNIPER TO BE PISSED AT ME AFTER I DITCHED THE TOUR of the farm, but Thursday morning when she picks me up, she hands me a travel mug.

"What's this?" I ask.

"Hot chocolate."

"Why?"

"Well, I would have brought you coffee, but I wasn't sure how you take it."

"Black."

"Like your soul?" she asks, then laughs. "Just kidding."

"I didn't realize you had a sense of humor," I say drily.

"There's a lot you don't realize about me," she says.

"Thank you," I say. "For the hot chocolate."

She lifts one shoulder as she drives out of the farm.

"Sorry I cut the tour short yesterday," I offer. "The rain and, you know, homework . . ."

"Really?" she asks. "It's supposed to be sunny and in the fifties today. You want to try again after school?"

"I'm not that sorry," I say. I take a drink of Juniper's hot chocolate, and she scowls.

Marxen gives us time to work on our executive summaries during class. Juniper's given this some thought.

"We need to make a list of vegetables and their growing seasons and determine what kind of volume we're looking at. Square footage of the stand itself and how many employees we'll need. Oh, and we need a name."

Juniper hands me the executive summary worksheet Marxen gave us earlier.

"What do you want me to do with this? You have all the answers."

"Your handwriting's better than mine," she says. "Fifty-fifty, remember?"

We work through the questions on the sheet. Every few minutes, Juniper will ask for my opinion and then huff with frustration if I don't sound interested enough. My phone vibrates with a text, and I pull it out of my pocket to check. Eric Dunbar, Commercial Real Estate Jackass. This has to be the fourth or fifth text today. I power the phone off.

"Don't let Marxen catch you with that," Juniper warns. "She's got a desk drawer full of confiscated cell phones."

"I'd like to see her try."

"I suppose you think that because you're *the* Gabe Hudson, she wouldn't dare."

I don't disagree with her.

The last question we answer is the name of the farm stand. When Juniper suggests Beet Street, I don't argue, mainly because I want to get this over with. I've never eaten a beet in my life.

"I can't believe you've never tried beets."

"Juniper. I can name probably five vegetables that I've eaten in my life."

Her mouth drops open. "Five? What five?"

I think about it. "Carrots. Peas, which I hate, by the way. Green beans—not a fan of those, either. Does lettuce count, like in a salad? Let's see, that's four. Oh, right. Gran used to make chocolate zucchini cake. Did you ever have it? You couldn't even tell."

"You're joking."

"About the cake? No."

"Gabe. You live in LA. You've traveled, like, all over the world. You have access to amazing restaurants. And you've eaten *five* vegetables?"

"I don't think geography has anything to do with it. I don't like vegetables." I shudder.

"How do you know if you've never tried? And what if, like, you're at a restaurant and the signature dish comes with asparagus or something?" She snaps her fingers. "You're at, I don't know, an awards dinner and the starter is prosciutto-wrapped asparagus. What do you do?"

"I don't eat it. You know, restaurants around the world will accommodate picky eaters."

"What about egg rolls? With the vegetables right inside?"

"Don't eat them." I grin. She's getting really worked up about my eating habits. This is kind of fun.

"OK, what about pizza?"

"What about it?"

"Can you honestly sit there and tell me that you've never eaten supreme pizza?"

I look at her, eyebrows raised. "Can you elaborate?"

"Supreme pizza. Pepperoni, sausage, onions, green peppers."

"OK, fine. Maybe I've had seven vegetables."

"Aha!" she cries and leans back in her chair, arms crossed.

"You're very . . . passionate about vegetables, Juniper," I say, smiling.

She shakes her head in disbelief.

The bell rings and Juniper turns in our executive summary prep work as we walk past Marxen's desk. I make a big show of pulling my phone out of my jacket pocket and checking it in front of the teacher, who rolls her eyes. She can see that it's not even on.

Juniper doesn't say much on the drive home. Maybe I've stunned her with my vegetable confession. When she pulls into the farmhouse driveway and puts the car into park, though, she says, "You know you're always welcome to join us for dinner. However, I think we're having shepherd's pie tonight, and sometimes Mom uses corn in the veggie mix. Technically, corn is a grain and not a vegetable, but I wanted to give you a heads-up, anyway."

"You're funny," I tell her.

I've eaten frozen pizzas—pepperoni only, not supreme— and sandwiches all week. A hot, home-cooked meal sounds like a dream come true right now.

"I'll think about it." I open the door to get out. I really

will think about it. Today has been a good day. "Thank you for the ride."

"You're welcome," she says. "Six o'clock, if you can make it."

I get out, then lean back in. "I like corn, especially the Mexican street corn from this taco stand near my school."

I close the door and watch her back out of the driveway, my stomach growling. Before her car disappears up the road, though, my phone buzzes with a text. I pull it out of my jacket pocket and swipe open the notification.

Rocky: Hey it's Rocky. How's it going in Minnie? Find the pot of gold at the end of the rainbow yet?

I guess I'm not as hungry as I thought.

Chapter Sixteen

JUNIPER

Friday night, Amelia and I and our friends Bunny and Youa pile into Bunny's old Saturn Vue and drive the twenty miles up to Eveleth, home of the World's Largest Hockey Stick, for the HRH game against the Golden Bears. The visitors' section is crammed with Screamin' Eagles fans dressed in green and gold—except for Gabe Hudson, rock star, who is dressed in head-to-toe black. He's even wearing a black wool beanie that he must have found in one of Leona's closets. He sits with Frank and Janie and some of the other football parents, and I can't decide if I should relish in that fact or feel sorry for him.

Today, right before the bell, Marxen returned the executive summary worksheets. She rejected the summary for Beet Street, saying that it was too elementary. *Not enough happening here,* she wrote across the top. *How will you make this business stand out from the rest?* Revisions are due Monday. There's no avoiding the fact that Gabe and I will have to work on this over the weekend.

Not long after the game starts, HRH takes the lead thanks to a rushing touchdown by Ted. Amelia whoops and we all stand and clap along as the pep band plays the rouser.

"Oh, wow," Youa says. "I will be so disappointed if this

game is a total blowout. Come on, Golden Bears! Make us work for it!"

"You're nuts," Bunny says.

"No," Youa says, not taking her eyes off the action on the field. "You wanna know who's nuts? My auntie Chia. So, you know, we were down in St. Paul over the weekend for my cousin Mailee's birthday—also, Amelia, you should be glad that this is the *other* side of my family."

"I've met them," Amelia says. She and Youa are cousins— their dads are brothers. Their moms, however, became best friends during the time that Amelia's parents were married, and that's one of the reasons why Amelia ended up moving to Harper's Mill after her parents' divorce. "Remember? Your sixteenth-birthday party or something?"

I grin. Youa's stories about her big family are often the highlight of these games. And as much as these people stress her out, she's lucky to have them. I've got Mom, and Ted and his family, too, but it won't always be like that.

"Oh God, that's right," she says, nodding her head. "Was that the time she tried to make tapioca? She is the worst cook. I don't know how she and Mommy are related. Anyway, so Mailee turned fifteen and she asks Chia if she can go to the Mall of America with friends, right, like, alone? Without Chia? And Chia says, of course, of course. And so Mailee invites a bunch of her friends and they all come over Saturday after lunch to take the light rail to the mall together. And all of a sudden, her brother Chewy comes downstairs and says he's ready to go to the mall."

"Oh no, she didn't," Amelia says.

"She totally did."

"Your cousin's name is Chewy?" Bunny asks.

"Chewy's his nickname, *Bunny*. He's a big *Star Wars* fan, right, and he's wearing this Han Solo jacket from, I don't know, *Empire Strikes Back*? Which, other than being short, Chewy looks *nothing* like Han Solo. He's got that mop-top hair and thick black Clark Kent glasses and he's *so* skinny."

"So Chewy was going to take Mailee and her friends to the mall dressed like Han Solo?" Amelia asks.

"Yes."

"But isn't he younger than Mailee?"

Youa nods. "A year younger, yes. So, Mailee, you can imagine, freaks out. She's crying hysterically because Chia doesn't trust them to go to the mall by themselves and Chewy is such a dork, plus, yeah, he's younger, she doesn't want to be seen with him. And all this is going down in front of her friends, right?"

"Which would totally be embarrassing," Amelia says, "except that her friends probably deal with the same stuff at home?"

"Totally," Youa agrees. "So meanwhile, *my* mom comes into the living room from the kitchen where she's been trying to reorganize Chia's nightmare of a pantry, and she pulls me aside and she says—"

"Oh no," Amelia says.

"Oh yes. She says, 'Chia, Mailee, calm down. I have the solution! Youa can take the girls to the mall.'"

"Oh no," Amelia says again.

"Wait a minute," Bunny says. "Didn't you have tickets to the St. Paul Chamber Orchestra Saturday night?"

"Yes!" she cries. "At the *Ordway*! And it was Schumann's *Piano Concerto*."

"Please tell me you made it back from the mall in time," Amelia says. Youa plays piano, cello, and clarinet and has started taking guitar lessons, too. Getting tickets to the St. Paul Chamber Orchestra was a huge deal.

She shakes her head. "Of course not! Mailee had to redo her hair and makeup after her little tantrum, and by the time we made it to the mall, it was after two o'clock, and on top of all the shopping, they had to go on every single ride at Nickelodeon Universe, even the Backyardigans swing. It was the worst."

"What about your tickets to the Ordway?" I ask.

She shakes her head. "Well." She sighs. "They didn't go to waste, exactly, although one might argue that they were wasted on Chia."

"She did not go!" Amelia cries.

"She did. She and Mommy took the tickets."

"Uffda," Bunny says.

"You can say that again," Youa says. Then she elbows me. "But enough about me and my loony family. What is going on at that farm of yours, Juniper, and do *not* play dumb. You know what I'm talking about, and I want some answers."

Amelia laughs. "Yeah, Juniper, why don't you give us some answers?"

I wish I had some.

"What do you want to know?" I know better than to try to fight Youa off. She's persistent.

"He sits, like, right next to me in World History and he barely says a word, even when I address him *directly*. I mean, obviously he's very, *very* good-looking, and I dig his music—well, his first album, anyway—but what's he *like*? Were you instantly best friends? You were, weren't you? Makes perfect sense. Your dad, his dad, best friends growing up and all. Now Gabe's inheriting the farm and it's, like, of *course* you'll follow in their footsteps."

"I have enough best friends, thank you," I say. "He's fine."

"Hold on," Bunny says, not taking her eyes off the field. Tonight she's got her long red hair in one thick braid and a Screamin' Eagles baseball cap pulled down low over her forehead. The quarterback is her younger brother Bucky, a junior, and I don't think she's ever missed one of his games. "Oh, sweet pass! Did you see that? Anyway. Chloe Horrible came into the store the other night and spent like thirty minutes at my register telling me how devastated she was that she didn't get Gabe for a partner on some project. She actually used the words 'one of LA's hottest celebrities.' You know I don't talk to Chloe Horrible if I can at all avoid it. And all you can say is, *he's fine*?"

"I wouldn't say he's one of LA's *hottest* celebrities," I argue.

"He's pretty hot, though," Amelia chimes in.

"She didn't mean that kind of hot," I say.

"He looks miserable sitting over there with his aunt and uncle," Youa says. She elbows me again. "I know a thing or two about that."

I bite my bottom lip and think about my plan. Maybe I should ask Gabe to join us. I should be making more of an effort with him. He didn't come to dinner for shepherd's pie, but he seemed close to giving in. I'm making progress, right?

I stand up. "Be right back," I tell my friends.

"Hi, Juniper!" Janie says after I make my way across the bleachers to the next section over. "Enjoying the game?"

"For sure," I tell her. "Ted's on fire tonight. Hey, Frank. Hey, Gabe."

"Hi, kiddo," Frank responds.

It's one thing for Gabe to speak to me in class or privately thank me for a ride home, but I'm not sure what to expect now, in public. He could ignore me or give me that trademarked rock star nod of acknowledgment. I'm surprised when he looks directly at me and says, "Hey. What's up?"

"I, uh, didn't know you were coming to the game tonight."

He jabs a thumb in his aunt's direction. "Janie can be very persuasive."

I snort. "True story."

"Well, I wasn't about to let him sit home alone on a Friday night in that big, empty house," Janie says.

"Chris still isn't back yet?" I ask.

"His return has been delayed," Gabe says indifferently. "He's not sure when he'll be back."

Yikes.

"I thought maybe you'd like to come hang out with me and my friends." I try to make my voice light and carefree and . . . genuine. "We're right over there. See, there's Amelia, who you met the other night, and Youa, who's in your World History class, and Bunny. You haven't met Bunny yet."

Janie chuckles. "That Youa's one of a kind."

Gabe opens his mouth to respond but doesn't get the chance.

"Gabe! I'm so glad you're here!" I hear the shrill voice before I see her. Chloe Horrible steps up and practically shoves me out of the way. She's wearing a white, cropped HRH T-shirt and black capri leggings. It's not even fifty degrees. "You said you weren't going to the game. You should come sit by us!"

Gabe looks at Chloe and then back to me, almost as if he's weighing his options and working out the lesser of two evils. He stands up.

"Oh, hey, Chloe," he says. "Thanks for the invite. I'm actually going to hang out with Juniper and . . . the others. Ready, Blue?"

My eyes widen at the nickname, and I step back as he moves closer to me, then takes my arm. He's *touching* me, and I'm more than a little shocked by the prickle of warmth from his grasp.

"Sorry," he says to Chloe, but he doesn't sound sorry at all. She pouts and her high ponytail flies up as she whips around and walks back to her friends in the next section.

"Thanks for the save," he says. "She's not horrible, necessarily, but she is annoying as fuck."

Oh, she's horrible. And annoying as fuck, both.

We make our way over to where the girls are waiting. "Hey," he says. "How's it going?"

"You know Amelia," I say as the pep band blasts "Proud Mary." "This is Amelia's cousin Youa, and this is Bunny. Not her real name."

"If you ever find out what her real name is," Amelia offers, "whatever you do, don't call her by it. And don't ask me what it is, because I will not tell you."

Bunny waves in our general direction, not taking her eyes off the action on the field.

"She's not even kidding," Youa says. "She looks nice and friendly, but she can be vicious if you cross her. Bit of free advice. Here, sit down before someone yells at you. You're, like, blocking the view." She yanks Gabe's arm, and he sits down hard on the metal bleacher in between Youa and Amelia. I sit on Youa's other side.

"How do you like HRH so far?" Youa asks.

"It's fine," Gabe says. "Different."

"Different how? I mean, besides the obvious weather and celebrity stuff?" Youa smiles.

"Well, I for sure wouldn't be taking a horticulture class at a music school."

"Wait, what?" Youa cries. "You went to a school for music?"

Ah, yes, these two are going to hit it off.

"An arts school, yeah," Gabe says.

"Oh my God, of course," she says. "Well, don't feel too bad about not taking any music classes here. Our band and choir programs are dismal. Embarrassing, really. I drive into Fred Lake for all my lessons, and even that's questionable."

She launches into an interrogation about his school,

his teachers, the classes he took. Even when musicians are on opposite ends of the style spectrum, the foundations are the same.

"Youa, cripes," Amelia says after a few minutes. "Give the poor guy a break."

Youa huffs and sticks her tongue out at her cousin. I'm hit with a feeling of gratitude for these friends and contentment for this crisp, fall night in northern Minnesota, for the air pungent with campfire and pine.

Bunny mumbles, "Come on, come on," and glances nervously at the scoreboard. How are we down by seven? I haven't been paying attention. We all look to the field as Bucky takes the snap and hands off the ball to Ted, who dodges a couple of tackles and runs it into the end zone.

Bunny and Amelia and Youa all jump up and cheer and hug one another, and I can't see what's happening on the field because they're blocking my view. I can barely hear the PA announcer signal the end of the half. Youa reaches down and pulls Gabe into their celebration. He looks down and smiles at me—a wide, real smile—and something deep inside me flutters. I look away.

"Get your lazy ass up here," Youa yells and pulls me up into their group hug, and we jump and cheer and act like idiots and I can easily forget about that beautiful smile.

"I have to pee something fierce," Youa says. "And we're getting pretzels. Juniper? You coming?"

I shake my head and sit back down.

"Gabe?" Youa asks.

"Nah, I'm good." He sits, too.

And then Amelia and Youa and Bunny are gone, and the crowd around us thins out, and it's me and Gabe. He slides closer to me but not close enough to touch.

"What are you doing?" I ask.

"I thought it would be weird with everyone else gone if there was this giant, gaping hole between us."

I laugh. "It was one tiny, Youa-sized hole."

"She's got a lot to say for a tiny person."

"Tiny person, big personality."

"I can see why you and she are friends."

"What's that supposed to mean?" My brow furrows.

"Tiny person, big personality," he echoes. "I like your friends, Blue."

There's that nickname again. Chris calls me Juniper Blue after the song, of course, but no one's ever shortened it to simply Blue before. I like it.

And, despite myself, I like that it's coming from Gabe.

"Well," I say, clearing my throat, "if you like them so much, you should definitely come out with us for pizza after the game. It's tradition. I'm sure Bunny won't mind giving you a ride home."

Gabe doesn't get a chance to respond, because Youa returns, dramatically dropping onto the bleachers next to me.

"Yes, for sure," she says. "God, the lines were *so* long. I've got an iron bladder. I'll pee at Pizza Snatch after the game."

Gabe's mouth drops open, and then he slams it shut again. "Uh? Pizza Snatch?" he says.

Youa nods. "Best part about driving all the way up here for a game. Mashed potatoes and fried chicken at Pizza Snatch. And pizza, of course, if you're into that kind of thing."

"Pizza *Ranch*," I clarify, which, come to think of it, doesn't sound much better. "Youa, come on. Don't be crass."

"Juniper, come *on*," Youa mocks. "Gabe, trust me. You haven't lived until you've feasted at the endless buffet at Pizza Snatch."

I cringe but Gabe grins and says, "Wouldn't miss it."

Chapter Seventeen

GABE

Pizza Snatch is like no other place I've ever seen, and that's saying something, considering I've been all over the world and have eaten in some very unusual restaurants.

First of all, they're playing Christian rock music, which is unexpected, but none of the girls seem to notice or mind. The walls are covered with Western-themed artwork: cowboys, wagon wheels, horseshoes, signs with quotes like "Never squat with your spurs on" and "Never give the devil a ride. He will always want the reins."

We pay for the "legendary" buffet at the register (it had better be legendary at that price point), the cashier hands us tall plastic cups, and we're let loose into a wide-open space with two buffets in the center and a drinks station on the perimeter.

"Grab a tray," Youa says. "I'll show you how it's done."

I follow her as she makes her way around the buffets, loading her plate with fried chicken, mashed potatoes, green beans, macaroni salad, and biscuits.

"What the hell are these pizzas?" I ask, squinting at the signs in front of the pies. "Stampede? Roundup? Where's the pepperoni?"

"Don't say hell, Gabe," Bunny advises from the other side of the buffet. "This is a very godly establishment."

"I can see that."

I choose a couple of slices of the Bronco, which appears to be all meat, and the Buffalo Chicken, as well as the mashed potatoes that Youa raved about and some hot wings. I fill up the plastic cup with ice and Coke and follow Amelia into the dining area to a large round table in a corner. Juniper follows after a minute or two, her plate loaded up with salad and a slice of pizza with too many vegetables on it.

"Is there any meat on that pizza?" I ask as she sits down.

"No, why?"

"It's not pizza if it doesn't have meat."

"False," she says. "I see you don't have any vegetables anywhere on your plate." She takes a giant bite, and a huge slice of tomato flaps against her chin. She laughs.

Youa sits down with a sigh, looking at her plate with longing. "Oh my God, it's been so long," she says. She digs her fork into the mountain of mashed potatoes and gravy and shovels it into her mouth with a moan. "There is nothing better than the Snatch! All you can eat, baby!"

I like this girl.

"Well, would you look at that," Bunny says, pointing her straw at Juniper before dunking it into her glass. "Juniper's eating the *exact same thing* as last time."

Youa squints and leans forward over the table for a better look. "And everything's on her plate in the *exact same order.*"

Juniper rolls her eyes. "Would you please let it go?"

"Let what go?" I ask. "I don't get it."

"I don't know if you know this about Juniper," Youa says, "but she's *very* set in her ways. She's been eating the same meal at Pizza Snatch for years. A big ol' salad and *one* slice of Tuscan Roma pizza. When she goes back for seconds, it's for two chicken drumsticks and waffle fries, dipped in barbecue sauce. Dessert? Cherry. Peach only if they're out of cherry."

"So what?" Juniper says. "I like what I like."

"But what about these mashed potatoes?" Youa cries. "Give them a chance, Juniper. You'll never know if you don't try."

Juniper shrugs. "I don't know. They're . . . lumpy. They don't look as good as the mashed potatoes from Happy's."

"What's Happy's?" I ask.

"This place in Harper's Mill with the best fried chicken," Juniper replies.

"Yes," Youa says. "Don't even bother suggesting fried chicken from anywhere else."

"It's delicious!" Juniper says and laughs. "With the perfect amount of crispiness."

"Poor Juniper, everyone picking on you," Amelia says. "Happy's does have the best fried chicken."

"But what if the apple dessert pizza is so amazing, it blows your mind?" Youa asks. "You'll miss out on that your entire life."

Juniper sighs. "I like what I like," she says again. "And I like my routine."

Youa is spot-on about these mashed potatoes. This is the best meal I've had all week, except for Janie's Sunday roast, of course. Maybe I should have taken Juniper up on her offer of shepherd's pie last night instead of eating cold leftover pizza.

We all go back for another round at the buffet, including dessert pizzas made with various pie fillings and soft-serve ice cream. Youa's right: Juniper comes back with two drumsticks, a few waffle fries, a tiny dish of barbecue sauce, and one slice of cherry dessert pizza. I stare pointedly at her plate.

"Don't even," she warns.

"So, Gabe," Youa says as she stacks her empty plate with others in the center of the table. "I have some questions for you."

Bunny groans. "Do you have to do this with every single person you meet?"

This will be interesting. Youa doesn't wait for me to respond before she launches questions at me like tennis balls from a Spinshot.

"Your house in LA. How close is it to the beach?"

"A few blocks. And we have a pool."

"You seem like you should have more of a tan. Not a big sun worshipper?"

"Both of my grandmothers had melanoma. One of them ultimately died from it. So I wear sunscreen."

"Valid point," she says. "How old were you when you learned to play guitar?"

"Seven. Chris bought me this amazing Martin acoustic guitar, a special edition for the company's hundred and seventy-fifth anniversary. They only made a hundred and seventy-five of them. It's still my favorite guitar."

"Seven? I had read somewhere that it was ten. You've been all over the world. What's your favorite place?"

"That's easy. Liverpool."

"Beatles fan, are you? What's your favorite Beatles song?"

I shake my head. "How can you even have only one favorite?"

She makes a sound like a buzzer. "False! The correct answer is 'Let It Be.'"

I laugh.

"What's it like dating a superstar like Marley Green?"

This one I'm not expecting. My stomach twists and I regret that last slice of Buffalo Chicken pizza. I can't set down the weight of Marley and the money, not even for one night.

"Ah. Well. Interesting. Never a dull moment."

"DC or Marvel?"

"DC."

"Really? Why?"

"Wonder Woman. How is this even a question?"

"See, Youa?" Amelia says. "I am not the only one!"

"What do you think of the Snatch?"

I think I would come back to the Snatch and feast on the legendary buffet every week if it meant I could hang out with these people. The only person missing is Ted. I reach over to Juniper's plate and take one of her waffle fries. She swats at my hand, but the corner of her mouth twitches.

Is this what real friendship looks like?

✿ ✿ ✿

Youa and Juniper and I cram into the back seat of Bunny's SUV after we've rolled out of Pizza Snatch. Amelia groans from the front seat that she's too full, and Bunny says she wishes she hadn't gone back for a fourth slice of Cactus Bread.

I lean my head against the window and listen to the girls talk about the game and their plans for the weekend. Youa's making two hundred egg rolls with her mom for an event at their church on Sunday. Bunny's training for a seventy-mile hike on the Willard Munger State Trail, and then she has an afternoon shift at the drugstore. Juniper works at eight in the morning at the park reserve. I didn't even know she had a job.

When Bunny drops me off and I walk into that big, empty house, I can't help but feel a little lonely. This has been a long week, and I haven't slept well. I've been sleeping upstairs in what was Chris's childhood bedroom, but I can hear every sound: the house creaking, the furnace sputtering.

It's late. I should go to bed. Instead, I flip open the cover of the piano in the living room. I've had a melody at the back of my mind all day, so I play around with it. It's slow and a little haunting, and I try to find a way to emulate the lonely howl of the coyotes. I find some notebook paper in the old rolltop desk in the study and scribble down the notes. It's not quite right, but I don't want to lose what progress I've made. After a while, I give up and play songs I've had memorized for years: "Levon" by Elton John, "A Whiter Shade of Pale" by Procol Harum, "Let It Be" and "Fool on the Hill," and always, Pink Floyd's "High Hopes."

I sit at the piano for nearly an hour, then move onto the couch with the Martin and play until my fingers ache. I miss my classes at Barlow. I miss playing out. I miss being in the studio. I miss the excitement of creating something new, something good.

I'm tired by the time I go back upstairs to Chris's old bedroom. I crack open the windows, and the crisp, chilly air cools down the room quickly. I get back into bed and focus on the night sounds: tree branches rustling, an occasional coyote wail, crickets. I'm relaxed and exhausted and comfortable. I think about the game and pizza with Juniper and her friends. Tonight was . . . fun, I guess. I haven't had fun like this in a long time. And Juniper seemed different tonight. Softer, somehow. Like maybe we could be friends after all.

Maybe that wouldn't be so horrible.

Chapter Eighteen

JUNIPER

SATURDAY MORNING, I WORK AT THE PARK RESERVE WITH A YOUTH group from a church in Fred Lake. I've been employed with the park district as a trail guide and a steward for the park's Adopt-a-Trail program for two years. I take out groups like this two or three times a month in the summer and fall. In addition to basic cleanup and trail grooming, we remove invasive species and sometimes collect seeds for the park system's nursery. Israel, the forest and conservation specialist, and I have worked with this group before, so we don't have to spend much time explaining or demonstrating the day's tasks. Mostly, we supervise the kids, help them identify the various plant life, and answer any questions.

Today's the last Adopt-a-Trail Saturday for the year, which usually corresponds with the first frost. After this week, I'll transition to my off-season position at the nature center on the north side of the park reserve. Part of my role is to explain the importance of the program and environmental stewardship in general, so at the end of the two hours, I congratulate the group for all they've accomplished. I talk about how much others will enjoy the trails because of their efforts and ways they can continue to conserve and protect our natural resources during the fall and winter months.

"Thanks for your hard work, everyone," Israel says when I've finished my wrap-up, "and let's all give Juniper a hand for her awesome stewardship and assistance this summer."

The kids and group leaders pack up their things and start down the main trail to the parking lot. We follow at a slightly slower pace. I think we're both a little sad that the season's over. "Have they told you what you'll be doing at the center?" Israel asks.

"I'd be surprised if they don't put me in the gift shop or snack bar." I sigh. "I really hope I'll be able to teach a few classes, though."

"I heard that they're thinking about giving you birthday parties," Israel says.

"Please, no." I groan. "I like plants, not people."

Israel elbows me. "That's my line, young lady. And even if you claim that you don't like people, which I don't believe for one minute, you can't deny that people like you."

Israel has worked for the park since I was a kid. He's tall with deep brown skin and scruffy gray hair. He's about Mom's age, maybe a little older. His wife died a couple of years ago, and their only son is grown with a son of his own. Israel sold his house in town and moved to a one-bedroom cabin farther out in the country. He jokes that he's married to Mother Nature now.

"What's going on these days in that greenhouse of yours?" Israel asks.

I fill him in before saying goodbye and continuing down the trail toward home. Today's an unseasonably warm fall day. The warmth of the sun feels like a luxury on my skin as I walk across the yard to the greenhouse. As I open the door, I shoot a text to Gabe and try to block out my worry about our e-biz project.

This is the space where I feel most like myself, where I can experiment with different growing techniques and flavors. I started making tea about two years ago and even planted a *Camellia sinensis* shrub, a tea plant that takes three to five years to mature. For now, I make mostly herbal tea blends or buy base teas from a co-op in Duluth. A few months ago, I started experimenting with the idea of making my own essential oils, and it's been a lot of trial and error since then.

Today, I'm full of new ideas, not surprising considering I spent the morning on the trail at the park. I've always turned to nature to tune into my creative self, another habit I picked up from Dad.

We didn't go on many vacations or weekend trips as a family, but twice Dad and I were able to plan special hikes out of town, both in early spring before the work on the farm got too busy. Once, we drove up past Duluth and hiked along Lake Superior. Another time, we camped at Banning State Park, about an hour south of us, and hiked a four-mile loop. I was nine and complained nearly the whole way that my feet hurt. I'd give anything to have that time with him back.

I move through my daily tasks quickly and then sit down at the desk. I pull down a book on herbal teas and a notebook to jot down an idea for a cranberry-cinnamon tea for Thanksgiving. I've got to make this quick because there's a pile of homework waiting for me, including the revision of the Beet Street executive summary. Neither one of us brought it up at the game last night, and Gabe hasn't responded to the text I sent about it after work.

As much as I've tried not to worry about the project and the farm, as much as I tried to let it all go on the trail this morning, I can't help what I'm feeling. This is our life, our home.

I need a cup of my comfort blend tea ASAP, and I need to up my friendship game with Gabe Hudson. Last night was a start. He seemed to have fun hanging out with us. Youa can be a lot to take in, but he was a good sport. And that smile he gave me after HRH tied the game right at the half—when I closed my eyes last night and tried to sleep, it's all I could see.

I stand up, tuck the book on herbal teas back on the shelf, and turn toward the door. I'm surprised to see Gabe standing only a few feet from me. He smiles—not like the *one*, but close enough.

"Oh, shoot," I say, pressing a hand to my chest against the pounding of my heart. "You startled me."

"Clearly," Gabe says. "You were pretty deep in thought."

"Oh, right," I stammer, not wanting to give away that I've been deep in thought about him and that smile and how I can't seem to figure him out. "What are you doing here?"

"I went up to the house, and Laurel said you were here."

"Why did you go up to the house?"

"To talk to you."

I wave my phone. "You could have sent a text."

Gabe shrugs. "Battery's dead."

"So charge it?"

He shrugs again. "Every now and then, I like to discon-nect. Seemed like a good time to do that. Dead battery and all."

"Are you . . . charging it, then?"

"Why are you so worried about my phone battery?"

"Well," I say with emphasis, drawing out the word, "what if someone needs to get ahold of you? For example, me. I sent you a text. We need to work on the executive sum-mary revision."

"Well," he mimics, "here I am. That's why I went up to the house looking for you. Let's talk about our executive summary."

I put my hands on my hips, then drop them again quickly. This is so frustrating. If he'd charged his phone battery like a responsible human, I wouldn't have spent the last hour and a half wondering why he wasn't responding to my text, wor-rying about getting the executive summary revision done on time. Which spiraled into a sick feeling in the pit of my stom-ach at the thought of not acing this class, what a poor grade would do for my GPA and my scholarship.

"Can we talk about it at the house?" I ask. "I haven't had lunch."

He nods, drops his sunglasses down over his eyes, and fol-lows me out of the greenhouse and across the lawn.

Mom's at the stove stirring an enormous stockpot of chili.

"Perfect timing," she says. "Slow-simmered two hours. I've set out all the toppings. Scrub up and help yourselves."

I half expect Gabe to decline, but he surprises me and Mom, I think, by rolling up his sleeves and stepping over to the sink to wash his hands.

"Smells amazing," he says.

I watch, stunned, as he picks up a bowl and holds it out for Mom to ladle up the chili, then moves around the island, choosing cheddar cheese, jalapeños, sour cream, avocado, and Fritos.

Mom beams. "You must be hungry."

"I think it's this crisp northern Minnesota air. I opened the windows last night and slept better than I have in weeks."

"You know there are tomatoes in chili, right?" I ask.

He grins. "Aren't tomatoes fruit?"

"Well, yes," I sputter, "but what about the onions? And the jalapeños? Peppers. Vegetables."

"Maybe I've decided to expand my vegetable repertoire." He laughs.

"How was the game last night, Gabe?" Mom asks.

"Better than I expected, considering it was my very first high school football game."

"No way!" I say. "You've never been to a high school football game before?"

He shakes his head as he sits down at the table with its mismatched antique chairs and French stripe place mats. "That wasn't really . . . my scene back in LA."

Mom hands me a bowl of chili. I add toppings and sit down next to Gabe, who is already chowing down.

"I took a walk around the farm this morning, too," Gabe says in between spoonfuls. "It looks different in the sunshine."

"So," Mom says as she sits down across from us. "What do you think?"

"Delicious," he says. I narrow my eyes. He knows she's not asking about the chili.

"I meant about the farm," Mom prods gently.

He crunches a corn chip, then says, "I think it's got a lot going for it." *A lot going for it*? What does that even mean? I open my mouth to ask the question, but he continues before I get the chance. "Tell me about the round barn."

She smiles. "That's our favorite place on the farm, isn't it, Juniper? It's one of only a handful of round barns in the Midwest made with fieldstone. It was originally used as a dairy barn. When your great-grandfather bought the farm, it was called the milk house, but he sold off the cows and raised sheep instead. That's how he came up with the farm's name, too."

"Has it ever been renovated?"

"Not a complete overhaul. The exterior has held up well. The walls are twenty-four inches thick, so it would take a lot to damage them."

"The interior looks a bit run-down," he says.

I lift a spoonful of chili to my lips and blow on it to cool it. He suddenly seems very interested in the farm, considering he couldn't get away fast enough the day I gave him a tour. And why is he asking so many questions about the round barn? Who cares when it was built or that it's a little run-down? I agree, the inside could use some sprucing up, but the sheep don't seem to mind. It's an iconic fixture on the farm, visible from the overlook at the park reserve and by anyone canoeing on the river.

"I've asked Chris about renovating," Mom says, "but it's in good-enough shape right now that I've been able to focus on other repairs or equipment needs. Eventually, I'd like to expand the flock, which will require moving the sheep to the larger barn, and then we can renovate the interior."

"Why are you so interested in the round barn?" I ask, trying to keep my tone innocent and even.

"I'm interested in all the buildings," he says, "but wouldn't you say the round barn is something of a focal point? Iconic, even? As you say, there aren't too many of them around."

"Oh, I agree," I say pleasantly. "Mom, we should contact the county historical society about the barn again. Maybe they can help us get it listed on the National Register of Historic Places."

"Interesting," Gabe says. "This chili is delicious. What's your secret ingredient?"

He changes the subject so smoothly that I don't think Mom notices. She beams again. She loves when people ask her for the secret ingredient.

"*Two* secret ingredients. Cinnamon and *honey*." She gives me a pointed look, a reminder. Honey and vinegar.

"Honey," Gabe echoes. "I wouldn't have guessed. How many sheep do you have?"

Once Gabe has had his fill of chili (two heaping bowls)

and insider information, Mom clears the table and offers to clean up the kitchen so we can work on our project together.

"So," he says, once I've gotten my laptop and pulled up the shared doc Marxen sent with a blank executive summary worksheet. "How do you want to do this?"

I'm crabby. I don't like how he's been digging for information. "What do you mean? Marxen told us we need more, that our business needs to be more than a place that sells vegetables. We need to add two or three additional components to show that we can manage multiple objectives."

"You're the subject matter expert here. What the hell do I know about farming? Not a damn thing except there's something near the big barn that makes me sneeze. So, I defer to you."

I pause. Even after last night, I don't trust him. A large part of me wants to tell him this, but a larger part thinks it's probably not wise to poke the bear. Remember the honey. Bears like honey. "You defer to me," I repeat.

"Yes."

"May I remind you that I technically have no experience besides running a stand at a farmers' market, and even that's cursory."

"Which is way more experience than I have with any of this. You run a *successful* stand at a farmers' market. I fucked up the one thing I know how to do."

Well. I finally listened to the second album this morning while I was getting ready for work, and I can't disagree with him.

"Tell me your ideas," he says.

I sigh. Yes, I'm worried about Stone & Wool. Yes, I'm wary of his motives and his sudden interest in the round barn. But I remind myself that this is a school project, completely separate from reality. I've been practically begging him to take this project seriously, and now he is. I take a deep breath.

"OK. Let's say the farm stand is the focal point. Maybe we make it more than a stand. An entire barn filled with produce and other items, and we call it a farm store." At his nod, I keep going. "Pony rides, a hay wagon. Corn maze. Strawberry picking and a u-pick pumpkin patch. School field trips. Freshly baked apple fritters and donuts and apple cider. Any of those sound good?"

"All of them sound good," Gabe says. "I would murder an apple fritter right now."

"You just ate two bowls of chili."

"If you put an apple fritter in front of me, I'm going to eat it. Gran used to make the best apple fritters. Oh, and cinnamon rolls."

I smile at the memory of Leona baking in her kitchen. "Yes, with that maple icing. And her sour cream coffee cake? So good."

"Funny, Allan said the same thing. You don't happen to have the recipe, do you?" he asks.

I nod. "I'm sure if we don't have it, we could find it at the farmhouse."

"Put that in the bakery, too. What about sheep?"

"What about them?"

"Should we have them on the farm? If we're having ponies, we should have sheep, right? Don't kids like sheep?"

"I guess."

"Could we do sheep shearing or something?"

"I don't know much about sheep shearing. I've never done it myself."

"But you can tell people how it's done, right?" Gabe asks. "In theory, you could stand in front of a group of people and describe what the person is doing? And, you know, it's not like you *really* have to do this. Beet Street is completely fabricated."

"You know we only shear sheep once a year, right? People can come see the sheep any time of the year, but we'd need to call it something else."

Gabe nods and thinks for a minute. "Right. How about something like a living farm tour? Annual sheep shearing can be a special event."

"Sure, that sounds good. And visiting the lambs in the spring." My fingers fly across the keyboard as I list our ideas.

"This might be a dumb question, but what do you do with the wool once it's been sheared?" Gabe asks. "I mean here, in real life."

"We take it to a fiber-processing farm in northern Wisconsin."

"All the way to Wisconsin? Why not do it yourselves?"

"We don't have the time or the equipment to skirt or scour the wool pieces. Mom buys some of it back to card and spin herself."

Gabe shakes his head. "I have no idea what any of that

means, but whatever it is, I think we can put it into the proposal. Eventually it becomes yarn, right? We could sell the yarn at the market?"

"Sure, we could sell yarn. We could sell the wool at different stages for people who like to process it themselves. Maybe even some of the equipment, like hand carders. Finished products, too, like what Mom makes now."

"What types of things does she make?"

"She uses felted wool to make bowls, purses, slippers, coasters, that kind of thing. She also makes mosaic wall-hangings."

"Mosaics? Out of wool?"

"Felted wool."

"What's the difference?"

I stand up. "Follow me." I lead him into the office off the living room where two of Mom's designs hang: a seascape and a mountain sunset.

"Hmm," he says as he tilts his head to inspect the mountain sunset. "Interesting."

"Interesting?"

"Well, they're amazing. She's really talented."

I nod. "She is."

"So, all of this," Gabe says. "We need to add all of this. We can sell yarn and felted wool stuff and whatever else. I think this all works well together. Now we need a new name. Beet Street doesn't really work if it's more than a vegetable stand."

A name comes to me out of nowhere. "How about Field & Flock?" I ask. "We've got the growing side of the business and the sheep side."

"Field & Flock. Like Stone & Wool. Hmm." He doesn't say anything more, and I expect him to tell me that it's too similar. Then, "I like that. A lot. Field & Flock it is."

This is going well. Almost too well.

"You should come to the farmers' market tomorrow," I say as we walk back into the kitchen, surprising myself.

"Yeah, that would be cool," he says, and he gives me another one of those devastating smiles that sends little flutters from my stomach to my throat.

I shake my head to clear it. I think I'm starting to like those smiles—and the flutters—a little too much.

Chapter Nineteen

GABE

"Field & Flock?" Ted laughs. We're in his truck on our way to the farmers' market in town. "What the flock, Gabe? Careful what font you use."

"The name works," I say. "It evokes a simpler time, an invitation to slow down and enjoy what nature provides." I didn't come up with this—it's what Juniper told Laurel when she asked about it yesterday.

"Oh, like you're doing now, according to all the gossip sites?"

"Exactly like that," I agree.

"What does Juniper think about the idea?"

"She loves it. All of it."

Ted laughs again. "Does she now? She hasn't argued with you?"

"She does like to argue, that's for sure. We seem to have come to an agreement over Field & Flock, however."

Ted turns off the main road toward the community center. The vendors are set up in the parking lot in front of the building, so we drive around back and park on the street.

"What does the farmers' market have to do with Field &

Flock?" Ted asks as we get out of the truck and walk around to the front of the building.

"One of Field & Flock's main attractions is the farm store. I'm here to steal ideas."

"At least you're honest," Ted says. "I've got some advice, for what it's worth. Don't let on that you're stealing ideas, even for a school project. You're an outsider, even if you are a Hudson. And whatever you do, don't let anyone know that you don't like Juniper. Everyone loves Juniper. Everyone is very protective of Juniper and her family. You don't want any of these farmers coming after you with a pitchfork."

I stumble in the gravel at that. "What do you mean, don't let anyone know that I don't like Juniper? Who said I don't like Juniper? And are you serious about the pitchforks?"

"Do you like Juniper?"

"Well . . . well—" I stammer.

"You see? Do you want to know what I think?"

I laugh, partly to cover up the fact that he caught me off guard. "I'm sure you'll tell me whether I want to know or not."

"Exactly. I think you need to lighten up and allow the magic of Juniper into your life."

I burst out laughing at this. We round the corner and I see her standing at a long table covered with a red-and-white checked tablecloth. Sunlight streams across her face, making her hair—in two long pigtails today—pure white and glowing. She does look a little magical in this light. She lifts a hand to shade her eyes against the glare of the sunlight, and then she smiles—big and genuine—when she sees us, and I can't help but smile back.

"Hey!" she calls over the head of a customer who has three very oddly shaped vegetables in front of her on the table. "You made it!"

"I take my chauffeur duties very seriously," Ted says. "I smell apple fritters. I'll be right back. Don't kill each other while I'm gone."

"Goddamn," I say. "I've been craving an apple fritter. Get me two, would you? And one for Blue."

"Blue, huh?" Ted says, raising his eyebrows. He takes a bow. "I am at your service."

Today, Juniper is the epitome of farm girl fashion: jeans, boots, a black-and-red plaid shirt, and a black puffy vest. No glasses, though. All she needs is a piece of hay to chew on and a cute little lamb to carry around, and she could star in her own sixties sitcom.

I watch as she spends the next few minutes chatting with a customer and the customer's young daughter.

"Mirabella, can you name all the types of squash today?"

The little girl points at each one and mumbles something I can't hear. But Juniper beams as she repeats the names.

"Yes! Butternut, acorn, carnival. Carnival has always been my favorite. I love the stripes and the dots and all the different colors. Every single one is unique!"

"Thanks, Juniper. Say hi to your mom for us," the woman says as she holds open a canvas tote and Juniper carefully sets each squash inside. Canvas totes. Perfect for the Field &

Flock farm store. We could offer three different sizes. People would eat that up. And we'll need a logo, but I don't know anything about graphic design. I wonder if Juniper does, or Ted, or if they know someone who could design a Field & Flock logo.

I shake my head a little to clear it. Sometimes, when I think about Field & Flock, I think that it's actually happening, that all these plans we're making could work at Stone & Wool. Which is ridiculous.

Juniper hands a small mesh bag to the woman. "Here's a sample of my latest tea, Fall Fireside. And Mirabella, isn't tomorrow your birthday? Here's a fairy to add to your collection! This one is called Tulip."

The woman puts her hand on her heart as the girl reaches out for the fairy Juniper's offering—a diaphanous, delicate doll no more than two inches high with bright pink wings. "You remembered! Thank you! We love your mom's fairies, don't we, Mirabella?"

Juniper reaches across the table and tugs on one of the little girl's braids. "Bye, Mirabella. Come by the nature center soon!"

I can see why people love Juniper. She's friendly. She remembers their birthdays. She gives away small, handmade fairies. Why is she *giving away* her mom's fairies and not charging for them?

"Where did that woman get her canvas tote?" I ask as I step up to Juniper's picked-over display of squash, pumpkins, and other vegetables that I don't recognize. "Tell me about these tea samples. Do you have any larger packages available for sale? Or are they a teaser? And why did you give away that fairy? How much is it worth?"

"The fairies sell for six dollars each," Juniper says. She frowns. "Hello to you, too."

Ah, right. I launched into my questions without even saying hello. "Hey, Blue," I say quietly with a small grin.

That seems to do the trick. The muscles in her face relax, and she blows out a breath. "Hi, Gabe. She's one of our best customers."

My grin widens. "I'm sure she is if you give them things for free."

"But it's Mirabella's birthday!" She turns on the charm again as another customer steps up to her table. "Israel! I'm so happy to see you. And twice in one weekend!"

The man rubs his frizzy white hair, a stark contrast to his deep brown skin. "The boy and his family showed up last night and surprised me! I'm here for some of your mama's finest beets."

"You're in luck," she says. "I happen to have two of our best bunches left. On the house." She gives me a pointed look and smiles at Israel.

They chat for another minute or two, laughing about something that happened at the park reserve yesterday, and then Juniper says, "Here's the Fall Fireside I was telling you about. Tell Rafe I say hello and squeeze that baby's cheeks for me!"

Israel waves as he walks away with two bunches of beets.

"Now, what were you saying about a tote?" Juniper lifts her hand to shield her eyes again.

"Don't you have sunglasses?" I ask. I slip mine off and hand them to her. "You need them more than I do."

She looks down at the sunglasses in her hands, then looks back up at me, eyes wide. "Thanks?" she says, like she's not entirely sure. Like what I've done is completely out of character. Which, I guess, it might be.

"The totes. The woman who was here a few minutes ago put her squash in a tote. Did she get that somewhere at the market?"

Juniper shrugs. "It's a canvas tote, Gabe. You can get them anywhere. The market encourages reusable bags. Most people bring their own, but we keep a small supply of paper bags on hand in case."

"Right. I see. I was thinking Field & Flock should sell some. Do you think you could design a logo?"

She shakes her head. "No, but Amelia could throw something together for us."

"Great. Can you ask her? I'm going to walk around and get a feel for the market. Do you need anything?"

She shakes her head again and finally slips the sunglasses on. They're black, like her vest. "Thanks," she says again, this time like she means it.

She looks good in my overly expensive sunglasses. I wish I had that money back, and the money I've spent on all kinds of shit over the years: shoes and watches and even guitars. Not that I'd be able to bring myself to sell my guitars.

But I don't want to think about that mess right now.

"See you around," I call as I walk away to catch up with Ted.

The truth is, I'd rather hang out here and watch Juniper with her customers than find Ted and eat apple fritters.

The truth is, Juniper Blue is growing on me.

○ ○ ○

Later that afternoon, I'm restless. I make myself a sandwich and nose around the kitchen. The cabinets are bursting with old Pyrex glassware, teal and white with a snowflake pattern, green and white with daisies. Heavy ceramic mixing bowls. Lightweight plastic mixing bowls. I pull open the drawers, crammed with utensils. Eggbeaters, whisks, a large device with a canister covered in small holes and two red metal handles with the paint chipping off. A quick Internet search tells me that this is a potato ricer, commonly used for preparing potatoes for lefse or mashing. (Youa would love this thing.)

I move from the kitchen to the study off the living room and snoop through the drawers in Gran's rolltop desk. Receipts from the country store from ten years ago. Old electric bills. Black-and-white photographs with yellowed edges. Prayer cards from funerals. Shit. She really didn't throw anything away, did she?

I move upstairs to Chris's bedroom with its big walk-in cedar closets, racks and shelves filled with clothing and shoes, men's and women's. The pungent odor of cedar feels like a comfortable blanket, and I lift one of Gran's sweaters to my nose, hoping that it still holds her sweet, cakey smell, like buttercream frosting. It doesn't. I open a shoebox that's filled with dried roses and baby's breath. The petals crumble beneath my fingers.

It's getting late and I might as well go to bed, so I move down the hall, cool wood floors creaking, to Chris's childhood bedroom, my room now. I pull open a deep drawer of a desk that looks to be handmade. Lined notebook papers filled with meticulous, fading handwriting. Old comic books and magazines, including an old *Spin* from August of 1991—right before Chris left Minnesota for Seattle—with Paul Westerberg of the Replacements on the cover. The headlines read: *Paul Westerberg: Rock's Last Bastard and the Cult of the Replacements* and *In Search of the Soul of Rock 'n' Roll: Is Rock Dead? SPIN's Writers Cross America to Find Out*. Chris is still a huge 'Mats fan. I pull this one out to read later.

There's a folded sheet of graph paper stuck to the back of the magazine. I gently peel it off and unfold it. The handwriting on it is misshapen and of various sizes—if I had to guess, that of a ten-year-old who maybe didn't like school all that much (or so I hear). Chris drew a map of the farm, sketched and labeled all of the buildings. The round barn's in the center. From there, he must have used a compass to fill in a series of concentric circles out from the round barn. *Silo, farmhouse, big barn, climbing tree, garage, machine shed, river, east field, west field, the Beehive.*

The Beehive—Juniper's house.

The circles continue.
Town
School
Fred Lake
Big Louie
River (again)
Airport
California
The Sunshine, The Sea, The Wild Air
The World

I sit down on the bed, the map clutched in my hand, amazed at how Chris knew from such a young age where he wanted to go. For him, everything began at the round barn and moved outward, and he knew that one day, he would see the world. He mapped it out. He's moved away from the round barn his whole life.

I'm moving inward.

Chapter Twenty

JUNIPER

WE FALL INTO SOMETHING OF A ROUTINE. GABE COMES UP TO THE house a couple of times a week for dinner and to work on our project. Amelia designed a simple logo with a sheep's head surrounded by a wreath of wheat, although wheat is not a crop on our fake farm. She was proud of her work, Gabe said it was good enough for a fake farm, and that was good enough for me.

We still argue a fair amount, but that seems to be the nature of our friendship. Friendship—not a word I ever thought I'd use to describe our relationship. One day, we spent fifteen minutes of class time debating whether we should have dressing rooms in the farm market so that people could try on the wool sweaters in privacy. I insisted on customer privacy, but Gabe figured a mirror near the sweater display would be sufficient *and* deter shoplifters from taking things into the dressing room and stuffing them into their canvas totes.

"Are you kidding me?" I asked. "Who is going to *shoplift* from a market on a *farm?*" I blurted out, loudly enough that Marxen glared at me from her desk at the front of the room. "This isn't LA, Gabe. Honestly!"

"You don't know that! I've seen some dodgy people at the SuperValu hanging around the candy aisle. The same people who are tempted to stash a Snickers bar down their pants might have the same urge to pinch a . . . I don't know . . . one of your mom's six-dollar fairies!"

"Oh my God, you're never going to let that go, are you?" I laughed.

"Never." He grinned and brushed one of his deep black curls out of his eyes.

"Bell! Hudson! Keep your voices down or you're outta here," Marxen warned.

In the end, I gave in with a shake of my head and another laugh. No dressing rooms.

Some nights, we study World History together even though I'm in a different class. He regales me with facts he's learning in Horticulture, and he even helps me with some of my end-of-season tasks in the greenhouse.

"What is this?" he asks the afternoon we harvest the last of the mint. He's standing in front of my tea plant, which has grown to about two feet tall.

"*Camellia sinensis*. A tea plant."

"A *tea* plant? How do you *grow* tea?"

I laugh. "Where do you think tea comes from? I planted this two years ago. In the summer, it lives here in the greenhouse, and then I bring it into the house for the winter. There's a small chance I might be able to harvest some of the leaves for next summer, but more likely it'll still need another couple of years."

"Hold. On," he says. "Are you telling me that you're growing a plant that takes three to five *years* to produce anything?"

"That's right."

"You're willing to wait three to five *years.*"

"Totally worth it. Right now, I have to buy the tea to add to my blends. This way, I'll be able to experiment with drying times to develop different flavors."

"That's amazing, Blue. Sounds like writing music. Fuck, I couldn't even wait three months to have Chris help me with my album. Maybe I should grow a tea plant and learn some patience." He laughs but it sounds hollow.

"That's why you didn't wait for Chris? Because you weren't *patient*?"

He shakes his head. "No. I mean, that was part of it. But a bigger part was that I thought I was invincible, right? 'Burden' was a huge hit, the album was making me a ton of money, and, I don't know, I figured I was talented enough to bang out a new album without really doing the hard work to get there."

"I'm sorry." I don't know what else to say, but I'm glad that he feels comfortable enough to open up to me.

"Nothing to be sorry about," he says.

"Have you ever wanted to do anything besides music?"

He shakes his head and moves over to the sink to wash the dirt from his hands. "For about half a year, I went to this rad school for kindergarten where they didn't teach the alphabet or anything like that, but we learned by 'experiencing life.'" He makes air quotes with his fingers. "We went on field trips to the fire station and museums, and we got to throw paint at big canvases on the walls and call it art. So back then, I thought it would be cool to be a firefighter or an artist like every other kid in my class. But other than that, no. Music has always been my thing. I miss my guitars. I brought one of my acoustics with me, but I'm thinking about having the rest shipped here. Or I won't have the patience and I'll go buy some new ones." He laughs again.

"Patience is definitely one thing you learn when you grow up on a farm," I say as I pluck stems from the mint leaves and place the leaves on a cookie sheet. I'll warm them in the oven to dry them when I go back up to the house. "We used to have this small garden behind the house where Mom would grow vegetables for our family. It was so hard for me to wait for the vegetables to mature. I'd pull carrots up too early and wipe the dirt off on my shirt and take a big bite of this bitter, earthy thing. When the peas were finally ready, I'd sit down between the rows and pop the pods open right there."

I look over at Gabe to see him smiling at me. He doesn't say anything.

"What?" I ask.

"I can picture you with dirt all over your face and your clothes. It's pretty easy, considering half the time you still have dirt all over your face and clothes." He smirks.

"Ba-dum-bum. He's here all week, folks."

"Didn't the carrots, you know? Taste like dirt?"

"That's part of the charm," I say.

"That's part of the reason why I don't like vegetables," he says.

"I'll make it my life's mission to change your mind."

"You're on." He smiles.

✿ ✿ ✿

Mom invites Gabe and the girls over for dinner Friday night before the home football game. Gabe declines because Chris is finally coming back from LA, and Bunny has to work a short shift at the drugstore, so only Amelia and Youa ride home with us after school. We drop Gabe off, and I bring iced tea out to the front porch. It's sunny today, and even though the air is a bit crisp, we want to take advantage of one of the last days of nice weather.

Amelia sits down and puts her feet up on the railing, tilting her face toward the sky and closing her eyes. "The sun feels so good."

"God, I know," Youa agrees. "The weather's got to hold. We've got that big festival at church on Sunday. I will die if it rains like it did last year."

"What are you doing this year?" Amelia asks.

"We're running the ring toss," she says. "Boring. You're coming, right?"

Amelia rolls her eyes. "Oh, I'll be there. Your mom roped me and Kat into working the popcorn stand."

"Ha!" Youa says. "Welcome to my world. Juniper, you should stop by."

"Thanks for the invite." Mom and I don't go to church, but I've gone to the carnival a handful of times. "I'll try."

"You should bring Gabe," Amelia says. "The two of you seem pretty chummy these days."

"Mm-hmm," Youa agrees. "He was talking about you and your e-biz project the other day in World History, and it was like you walked on water. *And* he called you Blue. What's that about?"

I can feel my cheeks warming, so I take a long sip of iced tea to try to cool down. "Oh, you know, 'Juniper Blue.' It's his nickname for me. Chris calls me that, too."

"No," Amelia disagrees, "Chris calls you Juniper Blue, the whole thing. Not Blue."

"Po-tay-to, po-tah-to," I say.

Youa snorts. "Hardly. The two of you sure spend a lot of time together. You've got a firm grip on that tea, Juniper. Now spill it."

I consider telling them everything. How I couldn't stand to be in the same room when he first arrived, how I came up with the fake friendship plan as a way of possibly saving the farm, how he makes me laugh, how the friendship feels less and less fake every day. How his smile gives me the flutters. How his nickname for me sends a rush of warmth through me every time I hear it. I almost wish he'd kept it a secret between the two of us.

I don't tell them any of this, though. It's too new, too fragile, and it's not part of the plan.

"I guess . . . the more time I spend with him, the more I see he's a regular person, you know? Overall, he's . . . OK."

"Hmm," Amelia says. "Interesting. And what about the farm?"

"What about the farm?"

"Him. Selling the farm next month."

My stomach drops. "Wait. What do you mean, he's selling the farm next month?"

"No, sorry, I meant what happens *if* he decides to sell the farm next month?"

I close my eyes. "God, you scared me."

"Are you still worried about it?" Youa asks. "I mean, you must be. Didn't he screw the pooch on that last album? This place is probably worth a lot, don't you think? Right on the river?"

"I'm worried," I admit. "Of course I'm worried. I mean, I'd live and work here forever if I could. If they decide to sell, then what? I don't want my mom to lose her entire livelihood because Gabe didn't manage his money properly."

"They both need to agree to it, right?" Amelia asks. "It's all or nothing?"

I nod.

"Not to make you even more worried, but I could see Chris agreeing to it," she says. "He's hardly ever around as it is."

That doesn't help.

"What are you going to do?" Youa asks at the same time Amelia says, "Keep your friends close but your frenemies closer."

"What movie is that from?" I ask.

"*The Godfather: Part II.* They didn't say frenemies, obviously. But you get the idea. Sleep with one eye open."

"You're so dramatic, Amelia," Youa says. She rolls her eyes. "You've seen too many movies."

Amelia shrugs. "Life imitates art and all that. Doesn't Gabe have a song called 'Life Imitates Art' on his first album?"

"No," I say. "It's called 'Imitation of Life.'"

"Oh, is it now?" Youa snickers. "How familiar *are* you with his fine back catalog?"

"Wow, Youa," I say.

"All I'm saying, girl, is keep that frenemy as close as you can."

"You're ridiculous," I say.

"On the other hand, he seems pretty trustworthy to me," Youa continues. "Trust that boy to give you the shivers when he sings." She thinks for a minute. "Or whispers sweet nothings in your ear. Or—"

I cut her off. "Stop!"

"That's not what you'll be saying when he—"

"Oh my God, Youa, stop already!"

She laughs.

"This conversation is over," I say. I stand up. "I'm going to help Mom with dinner. I'll call you when it's ready. Do *not* set foot in this house until then. And whatever you do, do *not* talk about Gabe's back catalog in front of my mother!"

They laugh as I walk into the house.

Amelia's got a point about keeping your frenemies close. It's a different version of the honey/vinegar thing.

I have to remind myself and my fluttery heart that Gabe is the enemy.

Chapter Twenty-One

GABE

I'VE BEEN SLEEPING BETTER.

The sleeping issues, the restlessness, all started long before I came to Minnesota, even before I got back together with Marley the second time. If I had to pinpoint a date, I'd say it was the day I told the label I'd work with their second-rate producer for *Embrace the Suck*, even though I knew Chris would be pissed when he found out. But I'd waited long enough for him to keep his promise. Too long.

Chris flies in from LA. I'm pissed myself, considering he didn't make the trip—or me—a priority. But he brings some guitars and gear with him. He had to rent a small moving truck to bring it up from the airport. Unloading and unpacking the crates is like Christmas and my birthday and divorce guilt gifts all in one. This lessens my irritation with him *slightly*.

For now, we store everything in the living room and the study. "You planning on staying long?" I ask.

He nods. "Why not? You're going to be here, so I might as well hang out, too. Let's order pizza and build a fire. There's nothing like sitting at a fire down by the river and playing your blues away."

"Who said anything about the blues?" I ask, grinning as I

strum my Gibson Hummingbird. I think I'm actually feeling something close to happiness for the first time in weeks. "God, this feels good. There's nothing better."

He snorts. "You've obviously never been in love before if you think the best thing that you'll ever hold in your arms is that guitar."

He's got a point, but guitars don't lie.

"You ever build a fire?" he asks as we walk down the path from the big house to the river.

"No."

"You never go camping?"

"In LA?"

"You can get out of LA, you know. Plenty of places to camp and explore in California."

"Why haven't you ever taken me camping, then?" I ask.

Chris laughs. "Got me there. You're more of an indoor pet, anyway."

"Indoor pet?"

He nods. "Never bring an outdoor pet into the house, Pa told us, and don't let your indoor pets run wild in the woods."

"Good advice," I say. "Makes me question how I ended up here."

"Funny."

Chris talks about his childhood pets—a cat named Dusty Springfield and a dog, Sparky—while he clears the firepit and pulls a few pieces of wood from a pile stacked between two trees.

"Watch and learn," he says and stacks the firewood like a

log cabin. There's a small shed near the firepit. He unlocks the padlock and brings out a cardboard box full of newspapers and small branches. "Kindling and tinder," he explains. Soon enough, he's got the fire going, and then he brings out two camp chairs from the shed.

We sit at the fire as the sun sets and the sky darkens. We play and sing for what feels like hours. Pink Floyd, "Wish You Were Here." Alice in Chains, "Down in a Hole." The Rolling Stones, "You Can't Always Get What You Want." Every now and then, Chris pokes at the fire with a stick or adds another log.

"This is good, yeah?" he asks.

"Yeah. It's good."

It's all good—the fire, the calm river, the unbelievable night sky filled with bright stars and a full moon, the guitars, the harmonies. I could get used to this.

"I'm thinking about sticking around for a while. Christmas, New Year's. Maybe longer. And maybe it's time to set up a studio somewhere." He plays a melody I don't recognize.

I'm relaxed and loose and I can't help but think that if Chris stays in Minnesota a while, if we spend more time together, maybe I can convince him that now's the time to sell.

"What are you thinking?" I ask. "Clear out one of the spare bedrooms?"

The farmhouse is big, but not big enough for a music studio. Except for Gran's bedroom, where Chris sleeps now, all of the rooms upstairs are small and crowded with antique furniture and knickknacks. The basement's unfinished and smells dank and moldy.

"Nah. The garage is heated. Maybe I'll set up there."

"Acoustics would suck," I say.

"Yeah, I might need to have somebody come in and fix that."

"I had somebody out to look at the property." The words stream from me without a second thought.

He lifts an eyebrow. "Hmm," he says.

That's it. I don't know what I expected him to say. "Only to get an idea of a possible selling price."

"I don't know that you needed to have someone out to the farm to tell you that. Allan told you what the farm's worth."

"Sure, he told me what it's *worth*, not how much I could get for it. I mean, that round barn alone . . ." I realize as soon as the words are out of my mouth that I sound like a spoiled rich kid from LA who only cares about himself.

"I see," Chris says. "Did he tell you what you wanted to hear?"

"I guess." Eric Dunbar, Riverside Commercial Properties, sent me an email with a number and calls me every few days "to check in."

"Well, now you'll never hear the end of it. They'll be on you like flies on shit. Land this close to the river and the park reserve? It's a gold mine."

"That's why I wanted somebody out sooner than later. I wanted to have all the facts in front of me so I can take the time to think things through."

"Yeah? And what do you think?"

What do I think? I think the number Eric Dunbar gave

---

me was good. I think that Chris is right. This land is a gold mine.

"I think I've still got a lot to think about," I say. The familiar sense of dread shifts in my gut, reminding me.

"I think you should be careful who you trust around here," Chris says. He's not kidding. "Talk to me before you do anything stupid."

Too late.

My bank account is dwindling, my credit cards are maxed out, and Rocky's words are in a constant loop in my brain: *I'm counting on you, Gabe.*

Chris pokes at the fire. A log falls and sparks fly up into the dark sky. "I'm sorry I was away so long and left you on your own here. It was a shit move."

I'm surprised as hell by this apology. "It *was* a shit move," I agree.

For long minutes, neither of us says a word. I wonder if I should come clean, tell him the truth about the money from his account and get it over with.

I think about the time that I fucked up his '79 Fender Telecaster, the used guitar he bought when he was fifteen, blonde with a black pick guard. His first guitar, his baby. I hadn't been playing long myself, a couple of years, and I don't know what got into me that day, but I wanted to play that Telecaster. I *needed* to play that Telecaster. So I did. I taught myself Soul Asylum's "Somebody to Shove" and Led Zeppelin's "Communication Breakdown." I felt like a fucking rock god. I felt like a fucking king. And then I dropped the fucking guitar and snapped the headstock and Chris lost his shit. He didn't even try to stay calm. His face turned purple and he cussed me out using words I'd never heard before and he sent me to stay with Elise.

"I can't even look at you right now," he said. A driver took me to the airport, and I didn't see or talk to Chris for the two weeks it took for him to get the guitar fixed and simmer down.

No, I can't tell him. Not now. Not when things are calm and quiet and we're not being assholes to each other.

I play a riff quietly. The strings of this guitar feel like old friends. Maybe, after everything settles down and I figure out a way to fix this mess, we don't have to be assholes anymore.

"That sounds good. Is it new?" he asks.

I nod. "Still working out the kinks."

"Janie says she's been checking up on you, and Laurel told me you've finally started eating dinner there once in a while."

"That's true."

"I'm glad you're here, Gabe. I should have brought you home a lot more when you were younger, before Ma died. This farm's a part of us. Yeah, I wanted to get out of town and make something of myself as soon as I could, but this land, our family, our roots, they're always here. I've fucked up a lot in my life, people come and go, but one thing I can always count on? This family. This farm."

"Is this your way of telling me to call off Eric Dunbar?" I ask.

"Oh, hell no. Tell me you didn't call that tool."

"You hit the nail on the head, no pun intended," I admit. "I called that tool."

He shakes his head. "Good luck with that. No, I'm not telling you what to do. I'm giving you some more things to think about."

"Noted," I say.

"You've got a good thing going here, Gabe."

"Yeah," I agree.

"Have you had any panic attacks? How's the anxiety? That's what's going on again, right?"

Again, he surprises me with the observation, and I wonder how much he remembers from the times—when I was ten, eleven—my anxiety ran high. When the panic attacks came on suddenly and frequently, over little things: worry that my Frisbee would be swept away in the ocean or Persephone would forget to pick up the cupcakes for my birthday. Or, you know, that my parents would OD and die like Jensen Philips, Elise's costar in *Friends, Unlimited*. For a while, when I was recording music and touring the first album, the anxiety all but disappeared.

"Not lately," I say. "Things are OK."

"Only OK?"

Being on the farm and away from the bright lights of Hollywood has solved some of my problems, sure. I don't have to worry about the paps following me around, for one. A guy from one of the gossip sites made the trip to take a photo of me on the steps of the high school, but the story fizzled when there was no actual story.

"I've got some shit to work through, you know?" I say. Like figuring out a way to get that money back in his account.

Chris chuckles. "Understatement of the year. You want to see somebody about that?"

"About what?"

"Keep up, Gabe. A therapist."

"A therapist? Here?"

"Uh, yeah. You know, therapy's not only an LA thing. I've got a good one in Fred Lake."

"I didn't know you had a therapist in Fred Lake."

"There's plenty of shit you don't know about me, mostly because you like to keep to yourself. And keep things *to* yourself." He pauses and clears his throat before he continues. "I know I haven't been the best dad, and I haven't always been there when you needed me. But I'm here now, and I want to be here in the future. And you can talk to me. About anything. I hope you know that. I'm an all right guy once you get to know me."

It's a nice idea but I don't know if I can believe him. I strum a few chords on the Gibson. The fire crackles and snaps.

"Seeing somebody would help with the panic attacks, too," he says quietly.

I don't respond.

"It's OK, you know. It's OK to ask for help."

"No, thanks," I say quietly. "I don't want to see your guy in Fred Lake, OK? Or LA, when I go back."

"My guy in Fred Lake is a chick, actually. I don't think you can see the same guy as me, but I can call up there tomorrow and make an appointment with one of the other therapists."

"I said no, Chris."

"Fine. That's cool. I get it if it doesn't feel right for you yet. Someday, it might. And I can help when that day comes."

"Sure."

"You know," he says, "I can only speak from experience. But whatever's going on with you is probably going to get worse before it gets better."

Maybe that's true. But tonight, I've got my Gibson, and that's like a year's worth of therapy right there.

Chris starts playing the opening riff of "Every Other Day Hero," a song about the weight of fame, about losing yourself and the people you love. The song that inspired me to write my own dark anthem, "Burden." I join in. Neither of us sings the lyrics, too raw, too close. I know it's an apology.

He sets his guitar aside and stands up to add a log to the fire, moving the burning wood and hot embers around with campfire tongs. A spark pops onto his hand and he swears. He looks out over the river, lost in thought. This place means more to him than I ever thought. His ties to this place, his roots, are strong.

Roots. That's one thing I've never had.

"God, it's good to be back home," he says. He sits down again, pulls the guitar to his lap, starts playing the opening riff of "In My Life" by the Beatles.

In this moment, in those few words, those notes, I know

for certain that Chris won't ever sell Stone & Wool. In the back of my mind, I've always known it, like I've known that Marley won't repay me in time. I'm on my own with this mess. I try to swallow down the panic—*it will get worse before it gets better*—and play along.

Chapter Twenty-Two

JUNIPER

"Goats."

Gabe slaps his hand down on the table in front of me, and I jump. I'm studying for an ag production quiz, and I didn't hear him come in through the back door. He and Chris were planning to come for dinner, but he's early.

"Goats?"

"Yes. Goats."

"What about them?"

"Goats are the answer." He grins.

"What's the question?" I ask.

"The question is, how are we going to save this project?" He sits down across from me and picks up a napkin, twisting the ring around and around the fabric. I'm mesmerized by his hands and his long fingers, imagining them at the piano or playing guitar. Or reaching out to brush a strand of my hair off my cheek.

"Hello? Earth to Juniper?"

I blink a few times. He's waiting for me to say something. I track backward in the conversation. "Hold on. Since when does our project need saving?"

"OK, fine. Maybe it doesn't need saving. But it needs

something more exciting than baby lambs and pony rides. The answer is goats."

"Baby lambs are the cutest," I protest. "But do tell, how do goats fit into the equation?"

"Products made from goat milk. Goat milk soap. Goat milk lotions. Goat milk lip balm!" The more he talks, the more his face lights up. "Essential oils are all the rage right now, right? Flavor up the goat milk soap with some of that shit, and the stuff will be flying off the shelves!"

"I don't know. We've already got so much. I wouldn't want Marxen to tell us that now we've bitten off more than we can chew."

"No, listen. Here's the best part. I did a quick Google search. There's this restaurant in a place called Door County. It's in Wisconsin. They have *goats on the roof*. That's it! We throw some sod on the roof of the farm market and the goats hang out up there, and everyone will flock to Field & Flock to see the flocking goats!"

I can't help but laugh at his unbridled enthusiasm. "Goats on the roof. I like it. I like it a lot. And it's weird enough that Marxen will like it, too. You've given this a lot of thought, I take it?"

"I do my best thinking when I'm playing guitar. Hey, can you show me the round barn now?"

I glance out the window. "It's raining."

"No, it stopped."

"Fine. Let's go." I close my textbook. "We've got thirty minutes until dinner."

At the back door, I slip on my rain boots and my mom's raincoat. The weather's been rainy and drizzly all week. We've got the last outdoor farmers' market of the season coming up on Sunday morning, and we don't need rain to keep the customers away. I say as much to Gabe as we walk toward the round barn.

"If you're worried about selling your pumpkins, why not have a stand down at the end of the road? Other people do that, right? I mean, I've seen all these wagons with pumpkins and cardboard signs with the different prices on them, but never any people. What is it, run on the honor system? You put cash in a box or something?"

"A lot of people do that. But we like to talk to our customers, you know? These days, people want to know about how things are grown or who's growing them."

"Even if it's only a pumpkin for carving jack-o'-lanterns?"

"You'd be surprised. Plus, most of what we're selling is squash or pie pumpkins."

"Pie pumpkins?"

I glance at him. "You know, pumpkins for making pie? Pumpkin pie?"

"Oh."

"What did you think? That pumpkin pie filling only comes in a can?"

He shrugs. "The only thing I think about pumpkin pie is that it'd better have whipped topping."

"I'm working on a pumpkin tea. It's tricky."

"When can you start selling your teas at the farmers' market?" he asks. "I have a feeling you'd sell out every week."

"How do you know they're any good? Have you tried any of them?"

"Well, no. But Janie raves about them, and I rarely see your mom without a cup. And your samples go fast, right?"

I shrug. "Because they're *free*. It's one thing to sell someone squash and carrots. It's another to sell them specialty tea blends."

"I don't see the difference," he says. "I should try some of your tea, though."

I tilt my head, considering him. Is it possible that he's trying the honey approach, too?

I stamp my feet once we make it to the entrance to the stone barn just past the big house. We're not inside the small, attached entryway for more than a minute before the skies open in a downpour, pounding on the roof.

"Good timing," Gabe says, shaking his head so that droplets fly from his black curls, spraying me.

"Hey," I say, "knock it off."

"Why? You're already wet." He grins.

I push open the door to the main barn, fifty-two feet in diameter, pens curving along most of the wall, a set of stairs that leads to a partial second level and the ladder to the cupola. Because the barn was built into a hill, there's a ramp that leads to a set of double doors at the back of the barn that open to the pasture. The familiar smell of earth and wool settles over me, calms me.

"Hello, babies," I call to the sheep, then turn to Gabe. "Well, this is it. Not much to see, really."

"Tell me why you love it so much," Gabe prompts.

"Well, for one, the sheep." I step toward the pen, and one of the ewes butts her head up against my hand. "Then there's the unusual architecture and the stone exterior. And of course, the rules."

"Rules?"

"Come on," I say, and before I know what I'm doing, I tug on his hand to lead him along. He falters a little at first, but then grips my hand solidly as we walk up the ramp toward the double doors, sending a wave of warmth through my every cell.

On the right-hand door, a fading inscription reads:

THE RULES OF STONE & WOOL FARM

1. ALWAYS TELL THE TRUTH.

2. ACT AS A STEWARD FOR THE ANIMALS, THE EARTH, AND OUR LIVELIHOOD.

3. PLANT WITH HOPE, GROW WITH HEART, HARVEST WITH GRATITUDE.

4. GIVE, AND IT SHALL BE GIVEN UNTO YOU. —LUKE 6:38

5. LIVE IN THE SUNSHINE, SWIM THE SEA, DRINK THE WILD AIR.

—RALPH WALDO EMERSON

Gabe's quiet for a moment as he reads. Then he squeezes my hand before he drops it.

"Who wrote those rules?" he asks, his voice quiet and thin.

"Your great-grandfather," I reply. "I knew the rules of the farm before I could read. For generations, the Hudsons have worked hard to make a living from the land, and to make a life as well. I find a lot of inspiration in that."

He doesn't speak for a long minute. Finally, he says, "I've had a lot of time on my hands lately, so I've been snooping around the house. Closets, dressers, desks. I found this handwritten note in Chris's bedroom from when he was a kid," Gabe says. "It's a map of the farm. The round barn's right in the center of it all. From there, he drew all these perfect, concentric circles out from the round barn. Like everything begins here, at the center of the farm, and moves outward from there. He labeled all the buildings, some trees, even the river. Your house, too."

"I'd love to see that."

"What I found the most telling about the drawing," he continues without acknowledging me, "are the circles beyond the farm. Town, school, Big Louie, the airport, California. The last circle was the world, but right before that was one I didn't understand. The sunshine, the sea, the wild air. I get it now."

"Oh," I say as I let out a long breath. "God."

"Yeah," he agrees. "He's always been moving outward, to something bigger, you know? But at the same time, he's moving inward, coming back. Does that make any sense?"

I nod. I've lived my whole life trying to live in the sunshine and breathe the wild air right here on the farm. Chris took those words literally and went out in search of the things beyond the confines of the farm, but he values its legacy. Gabe's had sunshine, sea, and wild air his whole life. He must feel so constricted here.

I swallow down the knot in my throat. "What about you?"
I ask. "Are you moving in or out?"

"Isn't that what we're all trying to figure out?" He smiles.
"This is an amazing building. I can see why this place means
so much to you."

As we walk back to the house, I feel something I haven't
in a long time: hope.

Chapter Twenty-Three

GABE

ERIC DUNBAR, RIVERSIDE COMMERCIAL PROPERTIES, CALLS ME the next day on our way to school. I'm sitting in the front seat of Juniper's Impala, so I answer the call and tell him that now's not a good time, but I'll call him back after school. Chris is right. This guy has been on me like flies on shit since that first phone call.

"Who was that?" Juniper asks.

"Guy from the label," I lie smoothly and immediately feel horrible for doing it, thinking about the first rule: *Always tell the truth.*

"Isn't it five thirty in the morning there?"

Shit. I forgot about the time difference.

"Those guys never sleep. Should we plan to work on Field & Flock tonight?"

She shakes her head. "Can't. I've got a staff meeting at the nature center tonight. It's my first weekend on birthday parties."

"Sounds horrible," I say.

"Well, I don't *love* the birthday parties," she admits, "but I do like spending time with kids who are interested in nature."

"I'm interested in nature," I say, and she bursts out laughing.

"Sure you are. Want to go for a hike this weekend?"

"Absolutely. Where should we go?"

"Well, rookie, we should start with something easy, like the park reserve."

"I look forward to it." I grin at her. "See you later."

✧ ✧ ✧

Eric Dunbar calls back twice more before noon. This guy's getting on my nerves. At lunch, I sneak out a back door near the band room where the vapers hang out, walk around to the other side of the marching band trailer for a little privacy, and call him back.

"Gabe," he says as soon as he picks up. "Good to hear from you. Thanks for calling back."

"Sure," I say. "What can I do for you?"

"Look," he says, "I know you said your timing was still pretty far out, but I wanted to run something past you. Listen, I wanted to have someone out to give you an estimate."

"An estimate for what? You gave me the info I needed. I'm not sure what else I'd need at this point."

"Right, right."

I roll my eyes. This guy gets more annoying every time he opens his mouth.

"Look, Gabe, based on the layout of the property, we'd have to make a few adjustments. Of course, you knew that going in. I'm not telling you anything you didn't already know."

"Adjustments for what?"

"If you decide to sell to a developer, for instance. A few of the buildings would have to come down, of course."

"I never said I wanted to sell to a developer."

"Who else would you sell it to?" he asks.

My stomach drops. Who else would buy it? He's right. And "developing" the land probably means razing it. He takes my silence as his cue to continue.

"Now, I'm not saying anything has to be done right away, but I'd like to have my guy come out and take a look, give you an idea of timing and cost. How does next Wednesday afternoon sound for you? I know you're in school, but no worries, you don't need to be there for this."

"I don't think that's actually—"

"Good, good," he says. "I didn't think it would be a problem. I'll let him know. I've sent him the pictures I took when I was out on the property. He needs ten, fifteen minutes tops. I'll make sure he doesn't bother anyone. And I'll let you know if I need more photos."

"Eric, listen—"

"Now, I know you said you weren't ready to move on this yet, but I've got someone who might be very interested in this property. I'm talking a significant dollar amount, Gabe, and, with my experience in the industry, this would be a smooth transaction. Quick. If we move forward on this right away, we could wrap things up by the new year, and you'd be set for a long, long time."

I swallow hard. "I don't think so, Eric."

"Well, think about it. Gabe, good to talk to you. I'll be in touch soon."

He hangs up before I can get another word in. Shit.

Think about it. On paper, this would be an easy decision. I fucked up and need to come up with a lot of money fast. This guy wants to make that happen for me. In reality, it's not going to happen.

I kick the tire of the trailer. "You dumbass," I mutter to myself. "You've got to think of some way out of this mess."

Back in the cafeteria, I pick at my lunch and make a half-assed attempt at joining the conversation.

"Hey," Juniper says after the first bell and we all stand up to leave. "You OK?"

I give her a half-assed smile because that seems to be all I can do right now. "Fine." Something inside of me twists when I think of how Juniper would hate me if we sold the farm. "Got a lot on my mind today."

In e-biz later, as I walk down the row to my seat, Chloe leans in and reaches out to grab the hem of my shirt, stopping me. "I couldn't believe the news when I heard!" she says.

I turn to her, sighing. I don't know that I have the patience for this today. "Heard what, Chloe?"

She shoves her phone at me. There's a photo of Marley from the *Real Hollywood* website.

"What's this?"

"So you don't know? The news that leaked today?"

"Is she OK?" I ask. That's all that really matters. Anything else coming from Hollywood could be complete bullshit.

"She's still in rehab, if that's what you're wondering. But a source close to Marley says that she is hundreds of *thousands* of dollars in debt. Is it true?"

My stomach twists. Hundreds of thousands of dollars in debt. I'll never see the money she owes me.

"We dated, Chloe," I say, trying to cover my dismay. "I wasn't her financial advisor."

"Well," she huffs, "you must know *something*. Didn't you talk to each other about this kind of thing?"

Oh, we did, unfortunately. I can't get the image of her, sobbing and begging me for help, out of my head. "Not really," I say, swallowing hard.

"You know, Gabe, I don't believe for a minute that she didn't really love you. There's no way your relationship was *fake*. She was having a hard time, that's all."

"Thanks for your input," I mutter and walk past her to my desk. I glance at Juniper, who's watching this exchange with wide eyes.

"I'll send you the link to the article," Chloe says. "Can I have your number?"

I shake my head. I'm not giving this girl my number. "You have Juniper's number, right? Text it to her and she can send it to me."

Chloe scowls and Juniper's lips twitch.

Well, so much for lying low. That *Real Hollywood* article will have at least ten links to shit about me and Marley, our relationship, that night at the wedding, the album. Even Chris and Elise and their shitshow of a marriage. *Real Hollywood* is known for dredging up every last scrap of sediment from the water under the bridge.

Marley's broke. I feel shaken, desperate. What am I going to have to do to get that money back in Chris's account? Put Gran's antiques on eBay? Beg Elise for a loan even though she's told me time and again that as a Scorpio, I must embrace my complicated relationship with money, learn how to discipline myself and accept my difficult financial lessons? Sell my guitars, the one thing I don't think I could actually do?

As I sit behind Juniper and half-listen to Marxen's lecture, that familiar brick of dread settles in. I do not need this right now. I try to slow my breathing. I focus on the little orange price sticker on the notebook I picked up at the drugstore in town, the print fading: *Ehlers Drug, $1.25.* I rub my finger across the corner of the sticker where it's pulling away.

Fuck. This room's too small, too many people. Not enough air. I can't catch my breath. I stand up and my desk shoots back toward the wall.

"Mr. Hudson?" Marxen says, startled.

"Gabe?" Juniper says. I look down at her, see the worry in those clear blue eyes.

I can't answer but I can walk, at least for now. The dread brick spreads from my chest down to my belly, up to my throat. Why here?

I'm out the door, down the hall. There's a door here, and it's only seconds before I'm outside and sucking in the cool air. I slide down against the wall and place one hand on the cool grass, dig my fingers into the earth. That's real. I can feel it under my nails. The oxygen in the air is real. My heart rate is slowing down. My breath evens out.

"Gabe." Juniper's here and she's crouched down in front of me. She's holding her hands out, like she's not sure if she should touch me. I want her to touch me. God, it's been so long since anyone has touched me, has wrapped their arms around me and meant it. "Gabe, can you hear me?"

I burst out a laugh. "Yeah, Blue, I can hear you."

I drop my head onto my knees—and then she does touch me. She's got her fingers in my hair, and she's rubbing the back of my neck. We sit like that for what feels like hours but not long enough, when it's probably only thirty seconds or so.

"Tell me what I can do to help you," she says. "Are you—is this a panic attack?"

I lift my head and her hand falls away. I wish she would touch me again. Her eyes are wide and a little wet. She's so different from Marley, who wouldn't have touched me. Marley would have sighed in exasperation and told me to get over it. "Looks that way," I say quietly.

"It's OK," Juniper says. "You're OK."

"Yeah."

"Was it—was it the article?"

I shrug. "The article. A lot of things."

"Is it true, about you and Marley? Was your relation-ship . . . fabricated?"

"No," I breathe out. "A least, not for me. For her, well . . ."

"I'm sorry."

"Don't be sorry."

"What can I do?" she asks again.

I move to a standing position and lean against the wall. She joins me. "Keep doing what you're doing."

"But I'm not doing anything."

"You're here. That's what I need right now."

Even I'm surprised by those words.

Chapter Twenty-Four

JUNIPER

GABE'S PANIC ATTACK SCARES ME.

It's one thing to see a video on a celebrity news website. It's quite another to watch it happen before your very eyes. We stand outside against that wall, not saying much, until the bell rings.

"Thanks," he says when I drop him off after a mostly quiet drive home. "For everything."

"We don't have to talk about it," I say, "if you don't want to. But I want you to know that I'm here for you if you *do* want to talk about it." I mean every word.

He nods and smiles. "Thanks," he says again. "I know."

A couple of days later, Gabe and I arrange to work on our project after dinner. When I walk back down to the farmhouse, Gabe's on the porch, a guitar across his lap, working through a melody. He doesn't notice me at first, so I'm able to watch him closely. He looks good, not pale or shaky like the day of the panic attack.

I clear my throat.

"Jesus, Blue," he says. "I didn't see you there."

"Obviously."

He looks at his watch. He's one of the few people I know who still wears an actual timepiece, not a fitness tracker or an Apple Watch, analog with a black leather strap and roman numerals that's probably worth more than my car.

"I've been playing for over an hour. My fingers are cashed," he says.

"Do you still want to work on our project?"

Gabe stands up. "Actually, no, I don't."

I take a step backward. "Oh, OK, that's fine. I'll head home."

"No, no," he says quickly, reaching out and touching my arm, sending that stream of now-familiar warmth through me. "Let me put my guitar away. I want to show you something. You dressed in layers? You warm enough? Good."

I wrinkle up my nose. "This is weird. Why are you acting so weird?"

"Me? I'm not acting weird. You are. Look, it's a warm night. Well, warm is relative. I'm from LA. But I'm not freezing my ass off, so I want to take advantage of it while I can. Don't move. I'll be right back."

Gabe's practically giddy when he returns wearing a flannel barn coat and a black stocking cap, thick socks peeking from the tops of his hiking boots. He pulls a chunky, multicolored stocking cap down over my curls, too.

"Follow me," he says.

"Where did you get that coat?" I ask as we walk down to the river. "Another one of your grandfather's?"

He nods. "You can tell?"

"Well, yeah, I've got a good eye for vintage stuff."

"I've noticed."

He's noticed? My cheeks warm a little, and I'm embarrassed that I'm embarrassed by it. Today, I'm wearing an oversized shaker sweater from the mid-eighties, bright turquoise, with thick black leggings, three pairs of layered, colorful socks, and red Converse high-tops. I used Mom's old hot roller set and kept my curls big and loose like a blonde Julia Roberts, which are now flattened under this giant handmade stocking cap.

"It would be hard not to notice, Blue," he continues, then must realize how insulting that sounds. "No, I mean, that's a good thing. I'm seriously interested. Where did you get that sweater?"

"Nice save. It was Mom's."

"She saved all her clothes from the eighties?"

"We're farmers, Gabe. Nothing goes to waste, not even horribly bright, oversized sweaters. Why are we going down to the river?"

"I thought you were a patient person," he says. "You'll see."

When we reach the riverbank a couple of minutes later, he sweeps his hands out widely in front of him. "Ta-da!"

I'm thoroughly confused. The riverbank looks the same as it always does. Firepit, shed, woodpile.

"OK?"

"I'm going to build you a fire, Blue."

"Oh!" I can't hide my surprise. "Do you—do you know how to build a fire?"

"I should be offended by that question, but I'm not," he says cheerfully. "Until last week, I had no idea how to build a fire. Chris taught me."

"He did?"

Gabe nods. "He did. I even came down on Saturday afternoon to practice."

"To practice . . . building a campfire."

"Yes, because I really want to impress you right now. We're friends, remember? I want you to see that there's more to this LA boy than a pretty face."

I laugh. "OK, LA boy, show me what you got."

He unlocks the shed, and while he collects wood from the pile, I pull out two chairs and set them up next to the firepit. I sit, shivering a little, and watch as he carefully builds his log cabin and fills it in with tinder and kindling. When he's finished, he stands back proudly to admire his work.

"Well, what do you think?" he asks.

"Looks structurally sound. The real test, though, is how it burns. Got a lighter?"

"Oh, shit," he says. "I didn't think of that."

I snort. "Don't worry. I think there's a box of matches in here somewhere." I stand up and walk back to the shed to look.

"Want to do the honors?" he asks.

I hold out the matchbox. "Absolutely not. See it through, Hudson."

He does. He strikes the match against the side of the box, and my nose tingles with the sharp, potent smell. When he sits down next to me, he's smiling.

"Nice work," I say.

"Chilly?" he asks. "Do you need my coat?"

"No, thanks. I'll warm up in a minute. It's not a bad fire, city boy."

He laughs. His nose and cheeks are red from the cold. "I'll take that as a compliment."

"You should."

We're quiet for a few minutes as we watch the flames take hold. It's not awkward or uncomfortable. It's . . . nice.

"So," he says finally, "we're friends. You and me."

"That's the rumor," I say quietly.

"All right then. Let's do this properly. Let's sit at this well-built fire and get to know each other."

"Proud of yourself?"

"I am. After the dumpster fire I left behind in LA, this exemplary campfire is reassuring."

"Do you miss LA?" I ask. Might as well get right to it.

"Parts of it, yes. I miss the warm sun and the ocean, that's for sure. I don't miss the traffic or the assholes. There aren't as many assholes here."

"Oh, I don't know. Per capita? We might give LA a run for the money."

He laughs. "Doubt it."

"What do you like about Harper's Mill?"

"That's easy. The quiet. At first, I thought I would lose my mind. I couldn't sleep at night because it was *too* quiet. Or else I heard the coyotes, and that kept me awake." He pauses. "My turn. You've been to LA. What did you like about it?"

I'm a little surprised that he's bringing up my trip to California for the Grammys. He was living with his mom in New York City while she filmed a movie there and Dig Me Under was on tour for the album. The band was up for several awards, including Song of the Year and Rock Album of the Year.

"This is your song," Chris said when he called to invite me. "We wouldn't be here without you, so no ifs, ands, or buts. You're coming with me."

Leona took in one of Mom's old prom dresses and let me borrow a pair of fancy bareback, open-toed heels from the fifties, black with a rhinestone buckle. Mom flew out with me and styled my hair. She let me wear mascara and lipstick. I walked the red carpet and stuttered awkward answers to the few questions that reporters directed at me rather than Chris.

"We were only there for three days. I didn't see much, but Chris took us to Disneyland and to the Last Bookstore. Have you ever been?"

"Yeah, of course."

"I've never seen so many books in my life."

"What did you buy?"

"Chris told me to choose something special. I found a copy of *The Secret Garden* from the sixties. He wanted to buy me a first edition, but I put my foot down."

"Only you would turn down a first edition of *The Secret Garden*, Blue." He laughs.

"It was, like, five hundred dollars!"

"So you got, what, a musty old paperback instead?"

"That's exactly what I chose," I say. "I adore that book. I always thought that Mary Lennox was such a classic name, sounded so important."

"Mary Lennox is a fantastic character."

"You've read *The Secret Garden*?"

"Of course. Also, and I'm not sure that I should admit this . . . that remake that came out a couple of years back? Elise's debut as a producer."

My eyebrows shoot up. That was one of the worst adaptations I've ever seen. "Seriously?"

He shrugs. "Don't judge me based on my mother's catalog of films."

"Gabe. She set it in *New England.*"

He throws his hands up in surrender. "Preaching to the choir, missy. Moving on. Quick, tell me something you love about Harper's Mill."

"Where do I begin? Everything. Living out in the country, close to the river, close to the park reserve. Hearing the coyotes at night and waking up to birds right outside my window every morning."

"Oh, yeah, those fuckers," Gabe says. "Wake me up every goddamn morning at, like, four o'clock."

"How do you like being around your family?" I ask.

He considers this for a moment. "You know, I like it a lot. Vacations at the lake were always fun. I mean, who wouldn't have fun spending all day out on a boat or the water trampoline or playing cribbage?"

"You play cribbage?"

"Four-time Hudson Family Summer Vacation Champion. What about you? Tell me about your family."

"Not much to tell, really. What you see is what you get. Even after Dad died, though, Mom and I have never really been on our own. Your family has been so good to us."

"I remember when your dad flew out to Seattle to bring Chris here for treatment. I was so fucking scared that Chris was going to die. But Doug—he was good under pressure, wasn't he? He looked me in the eye and told me that he was going to take care of everything."

"He was my hero," I say, choking up a little.

"I know why my parents didn't have any other kids. What about you?"

I lean forward in my chair to take advantage of the heat from the fire. "Mom and Dad tried to start a family for a long time. Mom miscarried twice. They saw specialists and tried different treatments. Nothing worked. Finally, they stopped all treatment. Mom got pregnant three months later."

"Wow," Gabe says. "That's amazing. That's a wanted baby."

I look over in surprise. His tone seems almost bitter. "What about you?" I ask.

"What about me?"

"How did you come to be?"

He snorts. "Do you really need a lesson in the birds and the bees?"

I flush. "That's not what I mean, and you know it. Ass."

"Well, our stories couldn't be more different." He pokes at the fire with a stick. "Chris met Elise on the set of *Altered*.

Have you seen it? Chris had a small part playing the drummer in a bar band. They fell hard for each other, the story goes. Elise got pregnant, and they eloped to Hawaii when she was five months pregnant. I'm the bump in all the wedding photos."

I nod. I knew this. I've seen the photos of the wedding on the beach, both of them barefoot, Elise in a diaphanous empire waist dress with a single white rose tucked into her hair. Chris stands with his hand on her belly, looking at her with such love and reverence, my throat tightens when I see it.

"I've seen the photos," I say quietly.

"Everyone has seen the photos." He sounds resigned.

"Do you think they'll get back together?" I ask—and wish I could take it back as soon as the words are out of my mouth. "Never mind. Don't answer that."

"They're Hollywood's most on-again, off-again couple. It's a valid question. But this time, I don't think so. Did you know that she's engaged?"

This surprises me. Not that I spend a lot of time watching *Celebrity Tonight*, but I hear things. Hard not to in this town.

"I take it by the look on your face that you didn't," Gabe says. "So that's good. At least her plan is working."

"What plan?"

"She doesn't want the news to leak until after she's done filming. Apparently, this new movie has Oscar nod written all over it. And she doesn't want the news to be a distraction during the season, so they're planning to wait until spring to announce it."

I'm confused. "What season?"

"Oh, right. The NFL season. She's marrying Ty Callahan."

"Ty Callahan. Doesn't ring a bell."

He bursts out laughing. "Why doesn't this surprise me? He's a running back for the Seattle Seahawks. Guess she's got a thing for Seattle boys."

"Do you like him?"

Now Gabe turns to look at me, and I'm stunned to see so much emotion in his eyes. "Do you know that you're the first person to ask me that question?"

"Really?"

"Really." The word is soft. "You know what? I do like him. He treats her well."

We're quiet for a few minutes, watching the fire. I think about how different our lives have been, our childhoods. I can't imagine living in the spotlight like he has, his every move documented and criticized.

"Tell me about your plans for next year," he says.

"There's a state university with a good horticulture and agribusiness program right in Fred Lake. I won't have to go so far, and I can still live here." I pause. "And still work on the farm."

"Agribusiness? The business of agriculture?"

"You're catching on," I say and smile.

"That's good that you know what you want to do. And you'll stay in the area after you graduate from college?"

"If I can. What about you? You've lived all over, right? LA, Seattle, New York, even New Orleans for a couple of years.

But where's home? Where do you feel most at home?" When he doesn't answer right away, I quickly add, "If that's not too personal. You don't have to answer if you don't want to."

He tilts his head and regards me and my question. "Seattle, I guess," he says slowly. "Things were good in Seattle. Chris and Elise were together. The band was on a break, so Elise took one, too. We were just a normal family, you know? We lived on a houseboat, because Elise had wanted one ever since she'd seen *Sleepless in Seattle*. The houseboat from the movie wasn't available, so Chris bought one a few docks down."

"You lived on a houseboat? Really?"

"Yes, for almost two years. I went to a private music academy there. Tell me about your dad. I wish I could have known him better."

I'm not expecting that. I swallow down a lump in my throat. "Ah."

"Shit. I'm sorry. That was insensitive. Ignore me."

"It's OK. You caught me off guard, that's all. I usually only talk about him to my therapist, since Leona died, anyway. Mom doesn't talk about Dad much, but Leona had some stories."

"You must miss him so much," Gabe says quietly. "So, you . . . see a therapist?"

I nod. "Not as often as I used to. Leona was the one who convinced Mom I should see someone. God, I'm glad she did. I've worked through a lot of stuff these last few years."

"Hmm." He stares at the fire.

I want to know what he remembers about the day of Leona's funeral. I ask the question before I can chicken out. "Do you remember me? From when we were younger?"

He looks at me with such intensity, it's hard not to look away. The reflections of the flames dance in his eyes. "I remember that you wore a blue, long-sleeved dress to my grandmother's funeral that matched your beautiful eyes."

My heart leaps into my throat, and tears sting the corners of my eyes. I swipe at them. I don't know how much I should tell him. "I hurt so badly for you that day, Gabe. I knew how it felt to lose someone close. I mean, it hadn't been that long since my dad—" I choke back a sob and take in a long breath, breathe it out again. "I wanted to give you something, a piece of my heart, that you could take with you and think about when you were sad and missing her." I let out a small laugh. "You weren't receptive."

"Ah," he says. "I was an ass to you, wasn't I?"

I nod.

"Tell me," he says softly. "What did you want to give me that day?"

I remind him of the words that I shared that day, the words that had soothed me so many times. For long minutes, he stares at the fire, not saying anything.

Finally, he says, "I've been kind of an ass most of my life. I'm sorry, Blue." He reaches over and takes my hand. The warmth from his skin radiates through me, lights me up. "I wish we had been friends then. Because knowing you now the way I do, I can honestly say that I would never, ever want to hurt you."

I bite my bottom lip to steady it, guilt coursing through me. I'm no better than the boy he was, faking a friendship for my own selfish reasons.

"To be honest, I was a little jealous of you and your relationship with Chris. Leona's funeral was, what? A few months after the Grammys?"

I nod.

"I'm not making excuses," he continues, then gives a hollow laugh. "It's hard for me to make friends. I learned early on that people will use you for your connections or your money or both. Even Marley, and we've known each other our entire lives. So, yeah, it's hard for me to trust people. Still, I'm sorry for that day. I'm not that spoiled little brat anymore. Forgive me."

We fall silent and watch the fire burn down as we hold hands across the space between our chairs. After a while, I say, "It's late, Gabe," and he nods. He spreads out the embers with a stick while I take a bucket to the river for water to pour over the coals. Once the fire's out, we walk back up to the big house, not speaking. Leaves and twigs crunch beneath my feet. An owl calls out in the distance. I shiver, and as we walk, Gabe puts one arm around my shoulder and tucks me in close.

I fit perfectly, my head at his shoulder.

He walks with me all the way to the front door. I don't know what I'm expecting, I don't know what this night has meant for him, but I can't help wondering if he's going to kiss me. Do I want Gabe Hudson to kiss me? God, I think I do.

I want to kiss Gabe Hudson.

I shake my head to clear the thought. This is *not* what Mom meant when she told me you can catch more flies with honey than with vinegar.

Right?

"Thanks for walking me home. I would have been fine on my own, but thank you."

He pulls me into a hug. "Oh, I know you would have been fine. I wanted to anyway. Thanks for listening tonight and for opening up about . . . things. I'm glad we're friends, Juniper."

Right. Friends. That's what we are.

Chapter Twenty-Five

GABE

ONE THOUGHT FOLLOWS ME HOME AFTER I LEAVE JUNIPER ON HER front porch. I've got to get that real estate agent off my back and tell him that there's no way his demo guy can set foot on this property.

Chris is home from an NA meeting in Cloquet, drinking a glass of chocolate milk at the kitchen table.

"Where've you been?" he asks. "Do I smell smoke?"

I grin. "I built a campfire for Juniper tonight."

"Is that right, you sly dog. You sure know the way to that girl's heart."

"It's not like that, Chris," I say as I sit down across from him. "How's your day been? How was the meeting?"

"Good," he says and takes another large gulp of chocolate milk. "Also saw my therapist. Two-for-one deal today."

"Everything OK?" Before coming to Minnesota and the farm, asking would have felt awkward and uncomfortable, and I would have ignored his comment.

"Yeah, everything's good. Wanna stay on top of it, you know?"

"Yeah."

"You give it any thought?" he asks.

"Seeing a therapist?" I shake my head. "I'm good."

"Keep an eye on it. Panic and anxiety are sneaky little fuckers."

"That's the truth," I mutter. I don't tell him what happened at school. "I will."

"Good. Remember what your gran always used to say: *Worse things happen at sea.*"

"Truer words," I say. "You were right about that real estate agent, by the way."

"Which part?" he asks.

"Flies on shit. He's calling me two or three times a day when I'm in school."

"What does he want?"

I sigh. This one's gonna sting. "He thinks we should have someone come out and give us a quote on a demo. For some of the outbuildings."

Chris leans back in his chair. "First of all, there's no *we* or *us* in this equation, pal. We may own this farm together, but this business with Dunbar is all you." I'm surprised at his calm tone. "Secondly, if you have any doubts about what should or shouldn't happen here, you go out to that round barn and read the rules. You've read the rules of the farm, right?"

I nod. "Juniper showed me."

"Well, live by the fucking rules, Gabe. Act as a steward. Tell the fucking truth."

A sickening rush of guilt washes through me. "OK, I get it. I'm sorry. I'll call Dunbar and tell him I don't need his services. Again."

"Excellent. I'm headed up. Close up shop before you go to bed, OK?"

I make sure the doors are locked and leave the light above the stove on. I go upstairs and take out the Martin. I play until exhaustion takes over, and then, finally, I let myself sleep.

✧ ✧ ✧

The next morning, before Juniper comes to pick me up for school, I call Eric Dunbar. It's early and he doesn't answer. Leaving a message without him interrupting me every two seconds makes it much easier to be a LAsshole.

"Eric, Gabe Hudson. Wanted to let you know that I'm no longer interested in working with you regarding the Stone & Wool property, so you can go ahead and remove my information from your files. My attorney and I have begun the process to list the round barn on the National Register of Historic Places. Thanks. Take care."

I hang up and dial Allan's office number and leave him a message as well. "Allan, I've got a project for you," I begin and then lay out my plan.

Too bad I still don't have a plan for putting that money back in Chris's account before I run out of time.

Chapter Twenty-Six

JUNIPER

When I power my phone back on Saturday afternoon after a short birthday party shift at the nature center, my notifications blow up with texts from Gabe.

Gabe: Hey whatcha doin today? Wondering if you wanted to study for world history test

Gabe: Chris went to mpls for a buddy's gig at First Ave. but the asshole wouldn't take me. What the hell? I'm Gabe Fucking Hudson.

Gabe: That's a joke, you know.

Gabe: Blue? Are you ignoring me or are you actually doing something important with your life?

Gabe: Seriously, though, I could use your help studying for that test. I'm shit at dates. I can play any song on the piano by ear, but I can't remember dates.

Gabe: BLUE I'm lonely can you help a guy out?

Gabe: K fine, I get it. Obviously you ARE busy doing something important with your life.

Gabe: Text me when you have a minute.

I smile. I can't help it. He texted *me*. He wanted my

company, not Ted's or anyone else's. Although I don't think
he was serious about studying.

Me: Was working. 15 ten-year-olds who only wanted to feed slugs
to Smaug.
Gabe: Smaug the dragon?
Me: Redbelly snake.
Gabe: This is disturbing on so many levels.
Me: You're telling me. You hungry? I could grab a ten buck cluck from
Happy's on my way back.
Gabe: First, do you really think I'm hungry after you told me about a
snake that eats slugs? Gross. But yes, I'm hungry. Second, ten buck
cluck sounds . . . dirty.
Me: You're terrible. It's a bucket of chicken.
Gabe: Finally! Chicken from the famous Happy's! Can you get a side
of mashed potatoes?
Me: And coleslaw?
Gabe: That feels too much like a vegetable. Just the mashed.
Me: See you in twenty.

I grin all the way into town. I grin while I wait at the hostess stand for my to-go order. I grin on the drive home.

As I walk up to the farmhouse, it occurs to me that I'm not
trying very hard to be nice to Gabe because being nice to him
is easy. I don't have to try. And I like it.

He practically rips the door off the hinges in his enthusiasm. "Holy shit, that cluck smells amazing. Get in here

with that bucket. I set the table. What do you want to drink? Water? Lemonade? Chocolate milk?"

I raise my eyebrows. "Chocolate milk?"

He shrugs. I follow him into the dining room and laugh. Gabe has indeed set the table, complete with woven place mats, Leona's wedding china, and heavy silverware.

Gabe asks me about my day, about the birthday party, about Smaug and the other reptiles that live at the nature center.

"Do you have to, I don't know, touch them? The snakes and other things?" he asks after we're completely stuffed.

I push away my empty plate. "I admit, snakes aren't my favorite. I absolutely hate feeding them. It's my least favorite birthday party theme, that's for sure. I'd much rather work the family farm display."

"You are a true farm girl at heart, aren't you, Blue?" Gabe smiles at me across the table. "Thanks for bringing dinner. That was an *unforgettable* cluck." Now I think he's smiling at himself and his cleverness.

"You know, I think you're the first person to ever make that joke, Gabe."

"Wow, the sarcasm. I didn't realize it ran so deep."

I stand and begin to collect the dirty dishes from the table.

"Oh no," he says. "You cooked. I'll clean up."

"Did you not just say I was a true farm girl? Farm girls don't stand around and let other people do the work while they sit with their feet up. Farm girls help. You wash, I'll dry."

"How do you know that I'm not planning to load everything in the dishwasher?"

"Gabe." I pause for emphasis. "If you put your grandmother's mid-century platinum-rimmed Bavarian dinnerware in the dishwasher, I will never speak to you again."

He throws back his head and laughs. "How do you know so much about my grandmother's fancy dishes?"

"I broke a plate when I was nine. I cried for hours, I felt so bad, but Leona told me not to worry. She called this china replacement company in North Carolina and boom, she had a new plate within the week."

"I promise not to break anything," he says. He gently slides the plates, white with delicate blue flowers, into the sudsy water and tells me about his day. "Everyone deserted me. Ted's in Duluth for some eligibility meeting. Chris left before breakfast. You were ignoring me."

"I was *working*."

"So you say. I was all alone."

"Listen to you. I thought you weren't here to make friends." I'm serious but make sure my tone is light and joking.

"Har har," he says. "I only need a few. I spent my entire day alone, going through a storage closet in the basement."

"Find anything interesting?"

"A few boxes of toys I remember from when I was really little. This old wooden clock that played 'Grandfather's Clock' when you wound it up."

"Oh, I remember that. I always thought the lyrics were so sad. *It stopped short, never to go again, when the old man died.*"

"Me, too, mainly because my grandfather died when I was a baby."

I dry the forks carefully and set them on the counter. "What else?" I ask. "Did you find the fairy-tale blocks, too?" Leona had kept the set of wooden blocks, each one with illustrations that told the stories of various fairy tales, on the bookshelf in the living room so I could play with them on rainy days.

"No, but I'm sure they're around here somewhere."

Gabe rinses the last plate and I dry it. He pulls the stopper, and the water swirls down the drain. I hang my dish towel on the stove handle.

"Now what?" I ask. "Ready to study for World History?"

"God, no. I can't read one more thing about—you know, I can't even remember what we've been studying."

"French Revolution ring a bell?" I ask.

"Ah yes, how boring. I've seen *Bill & Ted's Excellent Adventure*. That's all I need to know."

"Are you trying to fail out of school?" I ask. "Fine. We don't have to study."

"What do people do around here on Saturday nights?" he asks. He leans against the counter and crosses his arms.

I shrug. "I'm sure there's a party somewhere, if you're into that scene."

"You're not?" he asks.

"Farm girl, remember? Gotta be up before dawn to milk the cows."

"You don't have any cows, Blue."

"It's a figure of speech."

"Well, parties aren't really my scene, either."

I raise my eyebrows at him again. "That's not what I read on *Celebrity Insider.*"

"You shouldn't read that trash, Blue. Also: You read about me on the Internet, huh?"

My cheeks warm, and I turn to walk into the living room to hide my embarrassment. "Maybe." I sit down on the couch and Gabe follows, sitting in Leona's favorite recliner.

"I only went to those parties for publicity. Kinda goes with the territory, you know? I'm not fun at a party, I've been told."

"Why's that?"

"No booze. No drugs."

I can't help it. My mouth drops open before I even have a chance to think about it. He laughs.

"Your face! What, you don't believe me?"

"Well—I mean, what Marley said."

"Oh, thanks a lot. You're going to believe a troubled, addicted teen actress who you don't know over me? I see how it is."

Now I really blush. "God, I'm sorry. I shouldn't assume."

"Chris always tells me that if you don't tell your own story, someone else is going to tell it for you. And it might not be the truth. He learned that the hard way, and I have, too."

"I'm sorry," I say again.

He shrugs. "Not your fault. But it's the truth. I've never even tasted alcohol."

"Was it hard, you know, spending time with Marley when she was using?"

"She was good at hiding it. We'd go out to dinner and

she'd snort something in the bathroom, and I wouldn't even know. But yeah, it got a lot harder toward the end. She was getting more and more out of control, not hiding it as well. I was really worried about her. I hope she's getting better." He smiles, small and sad. "Amazing, isn't it? She used me, she humiliated me, and still, I want the best for her, you know?"

"You're a good person, Gabe," I say quietly.

He shakes his head. "I don't know about that."

I'm glad that he's opening up to me about Marley and life in LA, but I miss the lightheartedness of earlier. "Will you play something on the guitar?" I ask.

Gabe holds up his hands. "Shit, I should have had *you* wash. I can't play when my skin's so soft from the water. But I can play piano."

He stands and walks over to the piano, flipping the lid open as he sits on the bench. "Did you know, this piano was built in 1908? Gran reminded me every single time I sat down to play when I was a kid. That woman had a lot of stuff, but she treated everything with respect."

"She was amazing."

He plunks out a simple version of "Grandfather's Clock."

"You weren't kidding. You can play by ear?"

"And memory, I guess. I haven't heard that song in years, not until this afternoon when I played it on the little toy clock."

He plays parts of classical pieces that I recognize— Chopin, Satie, Vivaldi—and some that I don't. He plays "Let It Be" and sings with conviction. He plays snippets of "November Rain" by Guns N' Roses and Stevie Wonder, "Superstition."

"Wow, that's a wide range," I say when he pauses.

"My music instructor was hands down the best thing about the school in LA. We studied every style of music, every era. And I've taken classical piano and guitar lessons since I was about ten."

"Impressive."

"I want to learn everything about every kind of music. It makes me a better musician." He pauses. "Well, maybe not country."

"Oh, you are for sure not from around here. We've all got a little bit of country kicking around in our blood up here."

"Is that right?" he asks. "Even Chris?"

"Have you never heard the story about how Chris and my dad drove down to the Twin Cities in the dead of winter to see Johnny Cash? And on the way back, Chris hit an icy patch and ended up in the ditch. They were, like, seventeen or something, no cell phones, so they had to wait for the state patrol to come drive them to a gas station so they could call home."

"OK, Johnny Cash makes the cut."

"I like a little *Lo*retta Lynn myself," I say, emphasizing the first syllable with a thick twang.

"I'd play you some, but I don't know any." He turns back to the piano, and his hands hover over the keys for a minute before he begins to play.

Melancholy, slow, with long spaces between notes. One hand playing notes like a bell, the other playing the haunting melody. I don't recognize the song. His voice is clear and strong and sends goose bumps through me.

When he finishes, neither one of us says a word for a moment. "What song is that?" I ask quietly.

"Pink Floyd. 'High Hopes.'" He pauses, then says, "I chose that song for a school talent show once. I hadn't been playing long, and I probably had no business choosing *that*. I mean, I've been working on that song for years, and I still screw it up every time. But I wanted to impress my dad, you know? Pink Floyd's his favorite band. Apparently, when I was a toddler, I couldn't go to sleep without that CD playing on my boom box. So, I practiced my little heart out. If I wasn't at school, I was at home playing 'High Hopes' for my tutor." He laughs. "God, she was sick of that song by the time the talent show rolled around. I played until my joints ached, but I was ready. I was going to play 'High Hopes' and prove to my parents that I was worth their time."

Gabe's voice cracks a little when he says that, and my heart aches for him.

"What happened?" I ask.

"The day of the talent show rolled around, and our little school auditorium filled up with parents. The rich, the famous, the not-so-famous. My Benson-Beckett grandparents even made the drive from Beverly Hills to see and be seen."

"But?"

"But Chris and Elise didn't show. Elise was having an elemental balancing massage, whatever the hell that is, and Chris had flown up to Seattle but hadn't bothered to let anyone know. After the talent show, I tried calling but couldn't get through to either one of them. For all I knew, they were both dead." His laugh is quiet, tinged with a hint of bitterness. "When Chris got back from Seattle, you know what he said when I asked him about it? He said, 'Oh, was that this week? There'll be other talent shows, Gabe.'"

"Was he using then?" I ask. "Not that it makes a difference."

"Oh yeah, no question about it."

"I'm sorry," I say. "I don't know that Chris. Everyone tried to shield me from that side of him."

"Nothing to be sorry for." He plunks a few notes on the piano. "I'm glad you didn't have to see Chris like that."

I try to hide a yawn behind my fist. "Gabe, I'm sorry, but I should go. I've had a long day with the snakes and the birthday hooligans. Farmers' market tomorrow, remember? I've got to get up really early."

"Right, the farmers' market. Can I come with you? Or will Laurel be there and I'll only be in the way?"

"It's the first indoor market of the year," I say. "Maybe you want to wait until we work the kinks out."

"I get that," he says. "No problem. Can I walk you home?"

"I drove, remember?"

"Right, of course." He shakes his head. "Sorry I'm acting so weird tonight."

He is, in a way, but I think I get it. He's alone, and he's lonely, away from his friends and his music.

"It's OK," I tell him as I walk to the front door and lift my coat off the hook.

"Do you know," he says, "that I've never seen you in such . . . *regular* clothes before?"

I look down at my outfit. I'm wearing a green park polo shirt, khaki pants, and hiking boots. My work uniform. Even my hair's in a boring single braid down my back. Still, he reaches out and flips the tail of it between his fingers. He lets it drop and runs a finger along my jaw from my ear to the center of my chin. I practically hum with the sensation of his touch. I want to lean into it.

"Sweet dreams, Blue," he says. "Text me when you get home safely."

I nod and repeat his words back to him. "Sweet dreams," I whisper.

Chapter Twenty-Seven

GABE

I'M RESTLESS.

I've been restless since Saturday, when Chris took off early to get down to the Twin Cities for the gig. Yesterday, Juniper worked early at the farmers' market, then had a long shift at the nature center. By the time she got home, it was past dinner and she was tired, she said. So except for Saturday night, when she brought the bucket of chicken, I've been alone. Not long ago, I would have relished that time alone. Now, it makes me antsy and nervous.

I'm glad to be back at school and around people again, even if one of those people is the inimitable Chloe Annoying AF.

"Gabe!" she calls to me, waving, as I walk down the hall toward World History. Her ponytail swings wildly. "I'm having a few people over Saturday night for a small party. A bonfire. You *have* to come."

This isn't exactly what I had in mind. "I don't know, Chloe. I'm not really in the party mood."

"Did I say party? More like a gathering." Her eyes grow wide. "Oh my God, that's right! You're in treatment, right? And you don't want to be around alcohol?" She slaps her hand over her mouth.

"Actually, I'm *not* in treatment. I'm not an addict, no matter what the tabloids like to say. I meant that I'm not really in the mood to be around a bunch of people I don't know."

She drops her hand and starts running off her mouth again. "Oh! Is that all? Well, *get* to know us. Seriously! You'll be so glad you did."

This girl is insufferable. I have to think of a way to shut her up and shut her down.

"Well . . ." I draw out the word like I'm thinking about her offer. "I can bring Juniper, right?"

Her eyes grow wide again. She glances around the hallway like she's looking for the right answer. For sure, she's going to say no, and then I can get out of it, too. "Of course! Bring her along! The more the merrier, right? What's your number? I'll text you the address."

Well, that backfired. "Text Juniper," I say. This girl has got to stop trying to get my number.

Juniper storms up to me at lunch, holding out her phone.

"What is going on? Did you tell Chloe Horrible that we'd come to a *party* at her *house* Saturday night?"

"Chloe Horrible? Come on, she's not that bad. And it's more of a bonfire."

"It's more of a bonfire," she mutters. "What is *wrong* with you? Why would you subject us to such an experience?"

I grin. She's mad at me, yes, in her typical Juniper fashion, but she said *us* and I kinda like it. "What, you don't like to go to Chloe's parties?"

"You are the worst."

"You love it! Who would you argue with if I weren't around?"

"Me," Ted pipes in.

"Me," Amelia follows.

"Oh God, so much me," Youa adds. "But you should know, Gabe, that Chloe's parties *are* the worst. Everyone gets hammered and stupid and *someone* whose name starts with T and rhymes with Fred ends up buck naked on a picnic table singing 'Rednecker' by Hardy. I'm so glad I'll be at my church retreat this weekend so I won't have to see *that* again."

"That was one time!" Ted roars. 'God, I wish you people would stop bringing it up, OK? And I don't drink anymore! I mean, my family is riddled with addicts." He looks over at me. "No offense."

"None taken," I say. "Although *one* addict doesn't equal riddled. But I don't drink for the very same reason. Well, that, and I don't want to end up drunk and naked on a picnic table singing some horrible country song."

"Same," Amelia chimes in, looking pointedly at Ted. "Which is why none of us go to those parties. None of us drink. And watching drunk people act stupid and take selfies to post on Instagram isn't that much fun."

If she thinks HRH parties are bad, she should go to an LA club once.

"Listen," Juniper says. "I will go to this 'bonfire' with you, but you have to promise we'll only stay for one hour. *One.*"

"Done."

"Even an hour sounds miserable," Amelia says.

Juniper turns to her, eyes narrowed. "Well, guess what? Misery loves company. You're going, too."

✧ ✧ ✧

Chloe's "small gathering" spills out from her backyard to an empty field where a giant bonfire's flames lick the dark night sky. I'd say the guest count is well past fifty by the time the four of us arrive.

"Yesssss," Ted says. "Look at that awesome fire."

"I can't believe you're making us do this," Amelia says.

"Chin up," I say. "It's one hour of your life. Think about how many awful Hollywood parties I've had to attend."

"Oh, poor you," Juniper says. "It must be so terrible to have to mingle with Tom Holland and . . . Selena Gomez."

"Selena Gomez? That's the best you can do? I've never met either Selena or Tom. I have met Demi Lovato, though. Come on, let's get this over with."

"This is your fault, you know," she says.

I sling my arm around Juniper's shoulders. "Hang in there, Blue. We can get through this together."

Juniper bites her bottom lip but doesn't say a word. We walk toward Chloe, who's surrounded by a few people I recognize and many that I don't. Chloe pulls away from the group and practically charges for me, grabbing my arm.

"Gabe!" she shrieks. "You made it!"

"Yeah, hey, Chloe. We can't stay long."

"Oh, you will," she says. "Come say hi to everyone!"

She tugs me away from Juniper, Ted, and Amelia, none of whom make a move to prevent this. Juniper crosses her arms and lifts one eyebrow. I'm beginning to recognize this as her "I told you so" look.

"Have fun!" Amelia says, lifting one hand and wiggling her fingers at me mockingly.

"Look, everyone!" Chloe announces loudly as we walk over to the bonfire. "Look who's here! Gabe Hudson."

"Hey," I say. "How's it going?"

"Dude!" a guy I recognize from my horticulture class calls. "Did you bring your guitar? Can you sing 'Burden' for us?"

"Nah, man, I didn't bring my guitar."

"Next time, man, next time."

"Yeah, for sure." I nod.

Chloe grabs my arm again and tugs me away. "Come on! We've got more people to meet!"

One hour. I glance down at my watch. I can do this for one hour.

Chapter Twenty-Eight

JUNIPER

Chloe Horrible walks around like a Queen Bee from a KidCo Original Teen Movie, showing off Gabe to all her friends, her arm linked through his. She pets him, smiles up at him adoringly.

I think I'm going to throw up.

Amelia sighs and leans against the side of the pole barn. "I'm bored," she says.

"Want me to see if they have any Coke?" Ted asks.

"Nah. I'm so bored," she says again.

Jasper, one of Ted's football buddies, comes over and offers him a beer. "Hey, Ted, get your ass over here. We want to talk to you about Wednesday night's game."

Ted doesn't take the beer, but he follows Jasper over to a group of guys at a picnic table, all with blue plastic cups.

"I don't understand how I got here," Amelia says. "Things are weird since Gabe came to town."

"You can say that again." I can't seem to stop watching Chloe and Gabe. Slowly, Chloe has been inching them away from the bonfire and the crowd. Now, they're mostly separated from the group, in the shadows. I can't hear what they're saying.

Amelia glances at her phone. "Only forty-five more minutes."

"Is that all?"

I stare at them for another minute or so. Chloe touches him, she laughs, he smiles, even though it's not his full, brilliant smile. Still. Is he having a good time? He's not supposed to be having a good time with Chloe Horrible.

"Let's go inside," Amelia says. "At least we won't have to stare at them."

She's got a point. I follow her into the pole barn, where a couple of small tables are set up in the one corner that's not filled with lawn mowers and utility vehicles and other small equipment. There's another, longer table tucked against a wall with small bags of chips, water bottles, and a deck of cards. We've got the place to ourselves.

"This must be where the losers hang out," Amelia says.

"I can't believe no one has found the stash of Cheetos yet."

"Want to play cards?"

"Sure."

We sit down and Amelia shuffles the deck. "I could be at home watching *The Great British Baking Show* right now."

She deals out a hand of Trash, a game we've been playing almost daily since the weekend in eighth grade we spent at her haunted church camp on Snowdrift Lake, and continues. "I could be, I don't know, washing my hair. Oh! I know! Cleaning the hair out of the shower drain with that plastic snake thing."

"I get your point, Amelia."

"No, no, wait. I could be organizing Mom's spices alphabetically."

"Wait a minute. Your spices aren't already alphabetical?"

She rolls her eyes. "Draw a card."

We play the first round of Trash in silence. Amelia wins by one. I gather up the cards, shuffle, and deal.

"So," she says as she draws her first card. "You like Gabe."

"Why do you say that?" I ask, staring intently at the ten face-down cards in front of me while Amelia plays her turn.

"Well," she says softly, "maybe because as soon as Chloe dragged Gabe away, you stared at them like you hoped a hole would open up in the ground and swallow Chloe whole."

"No. I didn't." I draw a card from the pile in the middle. A queen. No good. Amelia takes her turn and flips up three of her cards in quick succession.

"And I've seen how your face gets when you talk about him. Or when someone else is talking about him," she says. "It's like all your muscles relax or something. Your eyes get gooey, and one corner of your mouth turns up like you're trying not to smile but you definitely want to."

My eyes get *gooey*?

"I don't know what you're talking about," I say.

"Sure you don't." She draws a card and then slaps it into the discard pile, a five. I glance at my cards. The only one I've flipped so far, of course, is the five, so I can't use it. I draw a king and my turn ends. She finishes out the round in a flourish.

"Your deal," I say as I gather the cards into a neat pile and slide it to her.

She shuffles and deals, then flips an ace and a two before drawing another ace. I pick it up.

"Well, well . . ." I sputter. "What about you? Why are you in here playing cards with me instead of out there with Ted?"

"That's different," she says.

"How is it different?" I draw a card, a jack, a freebie. I flip and face three more cards before my turn ends. "How will you know if you don't ask him? Today is someday."

"Nice run," she says. "It just is. And we're not talking about Ted here. We're talking about Gabe."

She draws and then discards the two of hearts. She doesn't need it, but I still do. I take it from the discard pile.

"Oh, look," she says. "The two of hearts."

I glance up to see Ted and Gabe walking into the barn. "Oh, look," I say. "Maybe now's your chance."

"Maybe now's *your* chance," she echoes.

"Chance for what?" Ted asks as they walk up to the table. "What are you doing in here? The party's out *there*."

"This party's lame," Amelia says. "Can we go? Is our hour up?"

"That's the best idea I've heard all night," Gabe says.

"May I remind you," I say as I stack the cards, "this was your idea."

"I learned my lesson."

Ted laughs. "I'll say."

"Oh no," Amelia says. "What did Chloe do?"

Gabe visibly shudders. "I can't talk about it. Too soon."

I frown. What *did* Chloe do? My brain immediately pictures Chloe reaching up on her tiptoes and trying to kiss him. Did she kiss him?

"Come on," Ted says, "if we sneak out the other door, no one will see us leaving."

We follow Ted through a maze of various lawn equipment and out the service door in the opposite corner of the pole barn. When we step out into the cool, dark night, I feel like I can freely breathe again for the first time in—I check my phone—forty-two minutes.

"Well, kids," Ted says as he puts the truck in reverse and backs down Chloe's long driveway. "Where to?"

"I could go for some Spuds," Gabe says from the front seat.

"Yes," Ted shouts. "Got it in one. Uncle Bud's it is."

"Only if we get to eat inside. It's too cold to take our food to the park," Amelia says.

"It's Saturday night. Do you honestly think we're going to get seats inside?"

"You're related to the owner!" she cries. "Call ahead! Tell them to reserve us a table!"

"I'm not going to abuse my power like that, Lee," Ted says sincerely.

"OK. Gabe'll do it. Right, Gabe?"

Gabe snorts.

When we get to Uncle Bud's, Gabe walks up to Violet at the hostess stand and asks for a table for four. She's sorting through a stack of menus and doesn't look up.

"It's about a ten-minute wait," she says. "That OK?"

Violet's mid-thirties, with buttery blonde hair in a massive beehive, bright red lips, and rhinestone cat-eye glasses. She's wearing a pink Uncle Bud's bowling shirt tied at the waist, her name embroidered above the pocket, jeans rolled to mid-calf, and saddle shoes. I wonder if they sell those bowling shirts. I would rock that outfit.

"Ten minutes is fine," Gabe replies.

"Name?"

"Abe Froman, Sausage King of Chicago," he deadpans.

Ted bursts out laughing, and Violet looks up, finally, from Gabe to Ted and back to Gabe. "Oh, is it Gabe? Little Gabey?" She comes around the side of the hostess stand and pulls Gabe into a hug. "Oh my gosh, honey, I haven't seen you since Leona's funeral, God bless her. It's Violet! And aren't you the spitting image of cousin Chris!"

"Hi, Violet," Gabe says.

"Now, let me see if I can get you a table right away."

"No need," Gabe says. "We can wait. We'll take a look around the gift shop."

"You do that, honey, and I'll call you back as soon as I can."

"Nice Ferris Bueller reference, Gabe," Amelia says as we step into the side porch that serves as a gift shop. I browse through a rack of T-shirts and sweatshirts but don't find a bowling shirt.

"What are you looking for?" Gabe asks as he comes up behind me.

"I want an Uncle Bud's bowling shirt," I say. "I don't see them here, though."

"How about a giant mug shaped like a stack of pancakes?" he asks, picking up a large ceramic mug from the shelf next to us.

"Those aren't merely pancakes, Gabe," I say, "those are Uncle Bud's World Famous Blueberry Pancakes."

"So," he says, setting the mug down, "do you want to talk about the party?"

"What about the party?" I ask.

"You didn't seem too thrilled that I spent time with Chloe, which, I guess, was the point of us being there."

"What gives you that idea?" I ask, my cheeks warming.

"You know, your cheeks always turn this cute shade of pink when you're embarrassed. Like cotton candy."

Now I'm sure my cheeks are deep red, not cotton candy pink.

"I saw you watching us," he says. "Why?"

"Well," I say slowly, trying to buy some time, "weren't you, I don't know, miserable talking to her? I would have been."

"You know," he says, "she's not that horrible. Annoying—"

"Yes, yes," I cut him off. "I know. Annoying as fuck."

"Blue, I don't think I've heard you swear before!" He grins.

"Why are you so nice to her, anyway? You don't even like her." I pause. I sound like a toddler. "Do you?"

"I'm not going to go out of my way to be friends with her, if that's what you're asking. My whole life, I've had to put up with people who are much worse. Shallow, materialistic, manipulative dicks who only want to be friends with me because I can introduce them to Chris or Elise or—shit, one time a guy asked me if I could introduce him to David Bowie, and I was like, you realize he's dead, right? David fucking Bowie." He shakes his head.

"I still have to be nice to them," he continues. "One of the best parts about being here in Minnesota is that I don't have to constantly worry about the paparazzi or wonder if someone is taking a video of me, I don't know, having a panic attack in public." He runs a hand through his messy curls.

"I'm sorry," I say as I pick at a loose thread at my wrist. "Sometimes I forget that you're—you know. Famous."

He leans forward, smiling again. "I wonder, though, if maybe, just maybe, you were a little bit jealous?"

My cheeks go cotton candy pink *again*. Was I jealous? The truth is, I do want him to have a good time with *me*, be with *me*, not Chloe Horrible. Not anyone else.

He's right. I'm jealous.

I try to cover up my embarrassment. "I wonder," I mimic, "if maybe, just maybe, someone's a little conceited?"

He laughs. "You know what, Blue? Don't take this the wrong way, but I'm thankful every day that I got paired up with you for this project. I don't know that I could have tolerated anyone else."

"What do you mean, don't take this the wrong way? Are you being sarcastic?"

"Nope," he says. "I'm serious. I can't imagine arguing with anyone but you. And in case you were wondering, I didn't kiss her."

"What? I—I never said—" I sputter.

"She *tried* to kiss *me*, but she was pretty sloshed, and I was able to dodge it. In case you were wondering," he repeats.

From the other room, Violet saves me from further embarrassment when she calls for Abe Froman, Sausage King of Chicago. Gabe looks down at his watch. "Three minutes," he says. "Not bad."

"It's not what you know," Ted says. "It's who you're related to."

I follow Ted, Amelia, and Gabe through the crowded diner to a corner booth in the back. Not a minute later, Uncle Bud himself comes over with a tray of root beer floats.

"On the house," he says as he sets a foamy drink in front of each of us. "Busy night or I'd stay to chat."

"This beats Trash in Chloe Horrible's pole barn," Amelia says as she reaches for a glass.

Gabe holds his float out to the center of the table. "To Chloe Horrible," he says, "without whom—and without whose boring, annoying as fuck, horrible party—we would not be here today, enjoying complimentary root beer floats and soon, Bud's Spuds."

"Here, here," Ted says, and we all *clink* our glasses.

"Cheers," Gabe says. "There's no place I'd rather be at this moment."

I couldn't agree more.

Chapter Twenty-Nine

GABE

Football season ends in a brutal loss in sectionals, and Ted's out of sorts. Janie pulls me aside in school one day and implores me to get him out of the house. "He's miserable," she says. "See if you can get some of your friends together and get him to the movies Friday night. Otherwise, he'll sit on Twitter all night to see the prep football scores and complain about missing his chance."

"I'm on it," I tell her. More and more, I'm finding that I like doing regular, American teenager things—parties, movies, even homework. It doesn't erase the worry about the money or Marley, because that worry has settled in like a squatter, low in the pit of my stomach, and finds its way into my thoughts constantly. But it helps me feel like someone who *doesn't* have to worry about a famous, addicted ex and financial fraud.

Ted skips lunch to shoot hoops in the gym, so I loop Amelia and Juniper in.

"Yeah, totally," Amelia says. I'm no idiot. I know that Amelia has a thing for Ted, and since that first dinner at Ted's house, I'm pretty sure the feeling is mutual. "I'm in. So, you, me, Ted, Juniper. Anyone else? Your new friend Chloe Horrible?"

Juniper snorts. Today, she's wearing a big, bright, billowy

skirt, sky blue and covered with embroidered rainbows, and a sunshine yellow cardigan. She's also wearing flip-flops (even though it's fucking cold outside), and her toenails are painted a glittery purple. Her bare legs are muscular and tanned. She's small, but she's strong.

I like this girl.

I clear my throat. "So? Blue? You up for the movies?"

"For sure."

Ted's a little harder to convince.

"Nope. Not going. I'm depressed," he says when I catch him in the hall after school before he heads to the weight room with his depressed teammates. "Plus, I gotta watch the games."

"All the more reason to go," I say. "It'll take your mind off things."

"No," he says again.

"Come on, man. The girls are looking forward to it."

"What girls?" Now he seems interested. Girls > football.

"Juniper and Amelia, who else?" I watch carefully as his eyes flash. Part of me wonders if I've got it all wrong and he's got a thing for Juniper, not Amelia, but I shake the thought away.

"Fine." He sighs like it's such a hardship to go to the movies with friends. "Fine, I'll go. I don't want to let the girls down."

"Great. You're driving."

"As if I'd let anyone else drive," he says as he walks backward toward the weight room. He throws up his hand in a wave, then turns and jogs down the hall.

Friday night, Ted picks Amelia up first and then drives out to Gran's, where Juniper and I have been working on the Field & Flock project while we wait. I can't help but laugh at myself and how I've so easily fallen into this lifestyle. Half the time, I didn't bother to go to classes on Fridays when I was in LA. Now I'm studying on a Friday night.

Before Juniper and I are even buckled in the back seat of Ted's enormous pickup, Ted and Amelia are bickering about which movie to see. Juniper and I haven't argued about anything in days, I realize. I sort of miss it.

"We watched a slasher flick last time," Amelia says. "I'm tired of blood and gore and jump scares. I want to see *Greenwich Calling*."

"No. No way. No more romantic comedies," Ted says gruffly.

"What else is playing?" I ask.

Juniper shoots me a look that screams *Warning*! "It's better if you don't share your opinion and let them hash it out," she says quietly.

"But Mindy McAdams is in *Greenwich Calling*, and you love her," Amelia says. "Oh! And Tess Daniels, too."

"You make a good case, but no fucking way. I can't stand Jake Washington. I can't sit through two hours of Jake Washington."

Amelia scrolls on her phone. "Fine. No *Greenwich Calling*. But we are definitely not seeing another stupid slasher movie. Especially one that is actually called *Another Stupid Slasher Movie*. I'll see what else is playing."

"I'm going to veto anything animated, FYI."

Amelia grumbles. "What about *First Harvest*? That's gotten really good reviews."

"Absolutely not," I say.

Now Juniper whacks me on the arm. "I thought I told you to stay out of this."

"Yeah, Gabe," Amelia agrees.

"I don't care," I say. "We can't see that movie."

"Why not?" Juniper asks.

I turn to look at her. "Because that's Elise's latest movie. According to *Hollywood Today*, she had an affair with her costar, Early Bingham. Not that I believe everything the tabloids say, of course, because she's usually rumored to have affairs with all of her costars. But this time I really hope it's not true, because she was already engaged to Ty Callahan when she filmed it."

Everyone falls silent.

"Wait a damn minute," Ted says. "Your mom is engaged to Ty fucking Callahan and you're just telling me this now? What the fuck is wrong with you, man? Can I meet him? When can I meet him?"

"Oh my God," I say dramatically. "Are you serious, Ted? You're using me to meet someone famous? And all this time, I thought we were really friends."

"Har de fucking har," he mutters.

"Who's Ty Callahan?" Amelia asks.

"Who's Ty Callahan? How are we even friends?" Ted roars. "He only averaged ninety-two rushing yards a game

BEND IN THE ROAD

last year. He's already had three games with over a hundred this season."

"You know that means nothing to me, Teddy," Amelia says.

It doesn't mean anything to me, either, but I like Ty, and he's good for Elise. "Ted, you can't tell anybody. Seriously. She's trying to keep this under wraps until she gets back from Australia. So zip it, OK?"

"OK, OK," Ted says. "So we are definitely not seeing *First Harvest*."

"*Another Stupid Slasher Movie* it is," Amelia mumbles.

☼ ☼ ☼

Not five minutes into the movie, Amelia squeals and covers her eyes and, at one point, turns toward Ted and buries her face in his chest. He puts his arm around her and tucks her in close.

"You big baby," he says.

I'm so right about this. I wish the two of them would admit their feelings for each other and get on with their lives already. I lean over and whisper in Juniper's ear, "Is it me, or are those two perfect for each other?"

Juniper nods.

"Will you hold me if I get scared?"

She smacks my arm. "Shh," she says. "I'm trying to watch the movie."

"Big fan of slasher movies, then?"

She shakes her head. "Quiet, Gabe."

I lean in close again. "I've got a surprise for you. I'm on the soundtrack. End credits."

"Shut up!" she says loudly, then slaps her hand over her mouth.

"You shut up!" someone calls from the back of the theater.

"Shh," I mimic her. "It's true. Song's called 'All Right Guy.'"

"Shut up!" she says again, this time in a loud whisper.

The movie is truly awful, made even more unbearable by the fact that more than anything, I want to hold Juniper's hand like I did at the campfire or put my arm around her shoulder and tuck her in close. We share a bucket of popcorn, and every now and then our hands brush together when we reach in at the same time. It's torture.

Juniper's jaw drops when the credits roll and my signature sound—grungy guitars and scrappy lyrics—fills the theater. Well, signature sound until I fucked it up with *Embrace the Suck*.

"What the hell, Gabe?" Ted says as we're walking through the parking lot. "You've got a fucking song on a movie soundtrack, and you don't think to tell us? When we're literally going to see that movie? You are full of secrets tonight, aren't you?"

I shrug. "Didn't seem like a big deal."

"Oh, listen to Mr. Big Shot. Didn't seem like a big deal, my ass."

"Well, I only hope 'All Right Guy' has got some legs, because after *Embrace the Suck*, my career could use a boost."

And I could use a big fat check. Too bad I'm so deep in the hole, even a nice royalty check won't help me.

"It's so good," Juniper says. "It reminds me of your, uh, earlier stuff. 'Burden.' 'Imitation of Life.'"

I look at her and smile. "You know my first album?"

She blushes—hard to see under the bright lights of the parking lot, but it's there. "Everyone in town bought your album, Gabe."

"Did they now?" I ask. "Amelia, did you buy my album?"

"Nope," she says.

"Me neither," Ted offers.

"Asshole. You got one for free."

"I'm hungry," he says. "Hell, I wish Uncle Bud's was still open."

We go to a late-night walk-up taco place instead and take the greasy bags over to Riverview Park to dine with Big Louie.

"Why are we eating outside?" I complain. "I'm freezing my ass off here."

"Could be worse," Juniper says. "We haven't even had a hard frost yet."

"I have no idea what you mean," I admit, "but it sounds horrible. Is that going to happen? A hard frost?"

Amelia snorts. "Wow, are you in for a rude awakening. Have you never seen snow before, Gabe?"

"Very funny."

"Tell us how you got a fucking song on a movie soundtrack," Ted says, then shoves half a stuffed taco into his mouth.

"I guess you could say I'm friends with Miro Abernathy."

"Who's Miro Abernathy?" Juniper asks.

"He's the head of Capstone Pictures," Amelia chimes in.

"Of course you would know that," Juniper says.

Amelia nods. "Yeah, he's one of the youngest studio execs in Hollywood. He made some big play at Sundance a couple years back, and now he's a superhot ticket."

I'm impressed. "Yeah, that about sums it up."

"So how do you know him?" Ted asks.

I shrug. "How do I know anyone in Hollywood? Pretty sure I met Miro through Elise, though it could have been Chris. Might have been at Edie Garcia's Christmas party, maybe?"

None of them say a word. I look over at Juniper, whose mouth has dropped open a little. I guess they all know who Edie Garcia is, but then again, every nine seconds someone in this country watches an Edie Garcia movie.

"I'm not trying to name-drop and sound cool, really," I say quickly. "I mean, I barely know the guy. Miro, that is. But we got to talking—wherever it was, but I think, yeah, I think it was at Edie's—and he asked me to write a song for the film."

Ted snorts. "Fucking hell. That's awesome. You wrote a kick-ass song and it's on a fucking soundtrack to a kick-ass movie."

"Teddy," Amelia says, "no. That has got to be the stupidest movie I've ever seen, no offense, Gabe. I mean, a mannequin serial killer? A *mannequin*."

"You loved it," Ted says. "Admit it. So much better than *Greenwich Calling*."

"I wouldn't know," Amelia bites back, "since I haven't seen *Greenwich Calling*, no thanks to you."

I look over at Juniper, who's scrunching her taco wrappings into a small ball. "How do you stand all their bickering?" I ask.

She shrugs. "You'll get used to it."

For the first time in a long time, maybe my whole life, I feel like I've got friends who understand me. People who want to be friends with me for me and not my name or my famous parents or grandparents or the fact that I go to parties at Edie Garcia's beach house. Genuine friends who don't ask for cash to cover their drug habits.

Juniper's right. I could get used to this.

Chapter Thirty

JUNIPER

I DON'T MEAN TO FALL ASLEEP ON THE WAY HOME FROM THE MOVIE theater in Frederick Lake, leaning on Gabe in the back seat of Ted's truck, but I do.

I wake to Gabe's whispers. "Blue, wake up. We're home."

Home.

My first thought is that yes, it seems like Gabe is more at home here now. And *then* it occurs to me that I'm sort of snuggling with him. I don't think this is what Mom meant about the honey. I sit up abruptly and scoot as far over to the door as I can. "Oh, shoot, I'm sorry," I say. "I didn't mean— God, I didn't drool on you, did I?"

Gabe laughs. "No, you didn't drool on me."

A coyote howls in the distance, and Gabe's face freezes. "I'm going to walk you to your door," he says.

I raise my eyebrows. "It's a coyote, Gabe, and based on that howl, it didn't sound close. I don't need a bodyguard."

He shakes his head. "Nope, not happening. Don't even think about arguing with me. I'm walking you to your door and that's it."

"*You're* the one who's freaked out about the coyotes and you're trying to protect *me*?"

"Stop arguing about it and get the fuck out of the truck," Ted chimes in. "I've got to get Sleeping Beauty here back to her comfy bed."

"You. Stay. Here," I say, punctuating each word with a finger to Gabe's chest. He sighs. "Hey. Amelia," I say, sticking my head in between the two front seats. "Today is someday."

And then I'm out the door and up the sidewalk in a flash, and Ted's peeling out of the driveway and barreling down the road toward the farmhouse.

I push the front door open. Mom's still up, waiting for me like she always does, the TV playing softly across the room.

"Hey," I say as I toe off my shoes.

"Hi, sweetie," she says. She picks up the remote and clicks the TV off. "How was the movie?"

"The movie was horrible. But *surprise*! Gabe recorded a song for the soundtrack."

"No kidding?"

"Yeah, he dropped that bomb after we were already in the theater."

"Good for him. Do you work tomorrow?"

"No, I've got the weekend off. Thank goodness. I'm sick of birthday parties. And I could use a good, solitary hike."

"We've got the farmers' market Sunday."

I plop down on the couch next to her. "I'll be ready." I rest my head on her shoulder. "Mom, can I ask you something?"

"Anything," she says and puts her arm around me.

"How do you handle being such close friends with Chris?"

She laughs. "How do you mean?"

"Like, he's one of the biggest rock stars in history. And he's your *friend*."

"Well, he's your friend, too. How do you handle it?"

"That's different. He's always been a rock star to me. You knew him before."

"Right. I knew him before. And I think that's what makes it easy, like you think it's easy because you've always known him as a rock star. I've known Chris and his family most of my life. You know that Chris and your dad were best friends. Thick as thieves, that's what Leona used to say. And I was lucky enough to have both of them in my life." She pauses, and then, "But you know all this. What's this really about, Juniper?"

I shrug against her shoulder. "Do you think Gabe will sell the farm?"

"I see. You're still worried about Gabe."

I sit up. "Of course I'm still worried about Gabe. Even if his latest album hadn't been such a huge loss for him, I'd be worried about Gabe and what he plans to do with the farm."

"Is there more to it than that?"

I sink back into the couch, nestle against her again, and blow out a long breath. "Yeah, I think so," I say, but I don't continue. I'm not sure how to put my feelings into words.

She kisses the top of my head. "I think that you made up your mind about Gabe a long time ago. You decided that he wasn't someone who was worth your friendship because of how he acted or who you thought he was or what you saw about him on the Internet. But now, now that you're getting to know him as a person and not as a celebrity, you're finding out that he's not a bad guy. He's someone that you might actually be friends with, and—if I can take a guess here? Maybe more than friends?"

Well, that about sums it up. Couldn't have said it better myself.

"Gabe's a household name," I say. "He's never known a life outside of the spotlight. I'm a girl who lives on a farm. Let's say—hypothetically—that I have . . . well, feelings for him. Beyond friendship. How could I possibly expect him to feel the same? Look at Chris. He married a *film star* who makes, like, twelve million dollars a movie."

"How do you know how much money Elise makes? You know, she wasn't a film star when they met and fell in love. They both worked hard to get where they are today and had to overcome some serious obstacles besides their addictions. It's a tough business."

"But why would someone like Gabe be interested in me? Hypothetically. And let's say—hypothetically—that we have a relationship. What happens when he gets bored and packs up for LA and he and Chris decide to sell? How would I deal with a broken heart when his face is *everywhere*?"

"Whoa, whoa, whoa," she says. "Let's back up a little. First of all, here's why *anyone*, famous or not, would be interested in you. Because you're smart and determined and you stand up for what you believe in. You're as beautiful on the inside as you are on the outside."

I laugh. "Are you required to say that because you're my mother?"

"I'm saying it because it's true."

"Well, thank you."

"Please don't ever assume you're going to get your heart broken. That shouldn't be your default setting. Life is short, Juniper. Every day with the people we love is a gift. Your dad and I met in junior high. We started dating when I was a junior and he was a senior. I'm grateful for every single day I had with him."

I snuggle in closer, tightening my arms around her waist in a hug. "I love you, Mom."

"I love you, too, sweetie. Why don't you get some sleep?" she says. "Maybe things will seem clearer in the morning."

Maybe. After I go to bed, though, I lie awake and think about Gabe. I analyze every interaction we've had since he came to Minnesota, looking for evidence that he could truly have feelings for me beyond friendship.

As I'm finally about to drift off to sleep, my phone buzzes. I lift it from the bedside table to read the display.

Gabe: You promised me a hike. How about tomorrow morning?

I grin.

Me: You're on. Meet me at the greenhouse at 9.

Chapter Thirty-One

GABE

Saturday morning, I'm up early, almost as early as those obnoxious birds squawking outside my window. I make breakfast for myself and Chris, wash dishes, and throw in a load of laundry. All this before eight.

"What's gotten into you?" Chris asks. He's sitting at the kitchen table with his second cup of coffee and the old *Spin* magazine I found in his desk drawer, reliving the glory days of the Replacements.

"I'm taking Juniper on an adventure today."

He snorts. "I don't think I've ever heard the words *Juniper* and *adventure* in the same sentence. Good luck with that."

Juniper's already in the greenhouse when I arrive at 8:57, sweeping up a pile of dirt and leaves near the door.

"Hi, Blue," I say, grinning.

"Hey," she says. "I'll be ready in a minute. It's a beautiful day. The overlook should be so pretty today."

"We're not going to the overlook today."

She looks at me like I've sprouted horns. "Aren't we hiking?"

"We are. But not to the overlook. Not in the park reserve."

"But it's Saturday morning. And if I don't have to work, I hike to the overlook." She's starting to sound a little panicky, so I put my hands on her shoulders.

"Today, we're doing something different. Can I drive your car?"

"Can you *drive my car*?" she repeats. "Wh-why?"

"Because we're going to hike a different trail today, and it's out of town. So let's hit the road."

She shakes her head. "Gabe, I don't think I . . ."

"You don't think you what? Can try something new?" I keep my tone gentle, but she still gets her back up, her face pinched, eyes narrowed as she works up her response.

"I was going to say that I don't think I have time for a hike out of town today." She puts her hands on her hips. "So quick to jump to conclusions."

"I thought you were off this weekend."

"I am, but that doesn't mean I'm not busy. I have to get ready for the farmers' market tomorrow."

"I see," I say, but I don't think she's telling me the truth.

"You think I'm making excuses?" she asks. She pulls open the greenhouse door with a huff.

I follow her out. "I'm only saying that it seems like you're hesitant to try new things, to step out of your comfort zone. Would that be accurate?"

"You sound like my mother. I happen to like hiking to the overlook, OK?"

"OK, OK." I throw up my hands in defeat. "Show me the overlook."

The hike—across the Hudson property, into the park, and up a gradual incline—takes less than fifteen minutes. Juniper's no casual hiker. She means business. By the time we make it to the crest of the trail, a bit muddy and covered in wet leaves, I'm breathing heavily, and Juniper seems to have mellowed out.

"Welcome to the overlook," she says, and twirls with her arms outstretched. "I can't believe it's taken me this long to get you here."

It's pretty, I'll give her that. Most of the leaves have fallen, so the trees are dingy and bare. The view across the river is cool. I can see the round barn and the farmhouse. But there's nothing especially spectacular about the view.

"This is my favorite place," she says, sitting down on a small bench that faces the river below.

"Why?" I ask as I follow and sit down next to her. When she doesn't answer right away, I nudge her. "Blue?"

"I used to come here with my dad," she says quietly.

Ah, there it is. I get it now.

"He was so busy on the farm, you know? So coming to the park was convenient. He could give me an hour of his time, once a week, to come up here."

"Saturday mornings," I guess.

"Saturday mornings."

"I'm sorry you lost your dad."

She shrugs and puts her head on my shoulder, and we sit in silence for a long time.

I'm glad we came to the overlook today, glad that she shared her special place with me.

Being here with her feels right.

Being anywhere with her feels right.

Chapter Thirty-Two

JUNIPER

SUNDAY MORNING, MOM AND I DRIVE INTO TOWN FOR THE INDOOR farmers' market. Today, we've got extra pumpkins, many of them large and misshapen, perfect for jack-o'-lanterns. Halloween's less than a week away, so this is usually a busy market for us. We've also got pie pumpkins, a variety of winter squash, rutabaga and turnips, and beets.

Our booth sits in between a local honey producer (what are the odds) and Mom's hippie friend Guinevere, who owns a natural health store in Fred Lake called Sun & Moon. You never know what products Guinevere will bring with her on market day or what weird, wonderful advice she'll dispense.

After we set up, we've got a few minutes before doors open, so I sample some lavender honey, which would be amazing with my Restful Garden blend, and then inspect Guinevere's goods: handmade bath bombs and shower tablets, essential oils, bundles of lavender and sage, bars of goat milk soap (Gabe would be all over those), and leaf-shaped maple syrup candies.

"Good morning, sweet girl," Guinevere says as I browse. "Do you have a sample for me today?" She asks this every time I see her.

"Not yet, but I'm close with the cherry-vanilla roller."

"Lovely. I look forward to trying it. See anything you like?"

I smile. "Tell me about these goat milk soaps. Are they local?"

"Minnesota made," she says. "They're from a place called Rapha Farms. This summer, when I was down in the Cities visiting Lydia and my sweet grandbabies, I went to her farmers' market and discovered these soaps. They're made by a woman and her daughter who live on a goat farm. I've started carrying them in the store. You must stop by sometime and see the selection. And they're absolutely delightful humans."

Everyone Guinevere meets is absolutely delightful. She sees the best in everyone and wants to bring out the best in everyone. I wish I could be more like her.

"They smell amazing," I say, holding one of the smaller bars up to my nose. Hazelnut Coffee Scrub. "I'd eat this."

"Please don't." I hear a voice behind me, a voice that sends shivers down my back. I whirl around to find Gabe standing close, holding a to-go tea from Avant Garden, the coffee shop down the block. "Drink this instead. I know it's not one of your special blends, but I hope it will do."

"Hi!" I'm surprised to see him. I realize that I've *missed* him since our hike to the overlook yesterday. Lately, I've had the flutters even when he's not smiling at me, so when he does, it's a murmuration of flutters, whirling and diving like thousands of starlings in flight. The sight of him in worn denim, ripped at both knees, a long-sleeved gray thermal, and a *Dark*

Side of the Moon T-shirt—holding tea that he bought for *me*—nearly knocks me over. "You're here!"

"Laurel invited me to help out today so I can get a good feel for the market. I'm caffeinated and ready to go." He holds up his own coffee cup and taps it against mine. "Cheers."

"Juniper, aren't you going to introduce me to your friend?" Guinevere asks. I swear there's an extra gleam in her eye.

Gabe steps closer to Guinevere's table and offers her his hand. "Gabe Hudson."

"Guinevere Daily. Pleasure to meet you. And you look so much like a young Christopher!"

"Oh, you know Chris, then?" Gabe asks innocently. It's all I can do to hold back a snort.

"Of course, dear. Quite the troublemaker, that one. And my Lydia had such a crush on him for many years. I wasn't worried, though. He's quite a few years older than Lydia, and, of course, the universe has a way of bringing people into our lives who belong there. I knew, deep down, that Chris wasn't the right person for Lydia, or Lydia for him. Everything works out the way it's meant to. When's your birthday, dear?"

"Tomorrow, actually," Gabe responds pleasantly, not at all affected by Guinevere's strange ramblings or the abrupt change of subject.

His birthday. Tomorrow. A day I've been dreading since I found out about his inheritance, a day that now feels more like a gift.

"Oh my gosh," Mom says. "Tomorrow already?"

He nods. "And we're taking *you* out to dinner to celebrate, Laur," he says.

"Oh no, of course not!" she says. "I'll make you something special for dinner. And a cake."

"You're always cooking. Let us take you out instead." He turns back to Guinevere. "Tell me about these goat milk soaps. I have a special interest in products made from goat milk. And goats, for that matter."

"Do you now?" she says.

After a few minutes of chatting with Guinevere, he joins me behind the table, walking from one end to the other, examining the selection. "No fairies today?"

"We're out," Mom says. "I've been so busy that I haven't had time to make another batch."

"You're out!" Gabe says. "Must be a big seller. Or maybe Juniper gave them all away."

I jab him with my elbow. "Knock it off, or I'm going to give you all the worst jobs."

He laughs. "I have a feeling you'll do that anyway. Drink your tea before it gets cold, and try not to be crabby."

◇ ◇ ◇

Our booth is busier than it's been in weeks, which creates a positive ripple effect for Guinevere, the honey guy, and the microgreens vendor across from us. Gabe smiles and laughs as he chats with customers, occasionally admitting that he knows absolutely nothing about root vegetables and he'll let the experts handle the questions. He has a long conversation with one of our regulars about Pink Floyd and the state of rock and roll today. Midmorning, Janie and Izzy stop by and drop off a basket of radishes.

"This is the last of them," Janie says. "I can't believe we haven't had our first hard freeze yet."

"I hear that term tossed around a lot," Gabe says. "What does it mean, because I'm freezing and I don't believe you."

Mom laughs. "A hard freeze is when overnight temps drop to twenty-eight or lower. Crops should be harvested before the first one each year. We've been lucky with a warm fall, even with all the rain we've had lately."

"You must have brought the warm weather with you," Guinevere says as she hands one of her customers a receipt. She nods at the woman. "Thank you from the bottom of my heart. May your day be filled with love and abundance."

I'm taking a quick break around noon, sitting in the back corner of our booth eating a turkey sandwich and some of Janie's radishes. I check my phone and see a text from Amelia.

Amelia: Today is someday

I gasp.

Me: What does that mean??!!!!!!
Amelia: Ted brought pizza over last night and he asked me if I wanted

to go to the haunted ship in Duluth and I asked him if this was a date and he got super embarrassed and flustered and said yeah if I was cool with that and I'm so cool with it I can't even think straight!

I laugh. Finally!

Me: Finally!!!!!!

"What's got you so happy?" Gabe leans against the wall behind me.

"Ted's taking Amelia on a haunted ship tour today."

"Oh, really? Like a date?"

"Like a date." I nod.

"It's about time!"

"And you say you don't like rom-coms. They are a living, breathing rom-com."

He shrugs. "I never said I didn't like rom-coms." He pushes himself off the wall. "I'm going to the concession stand. Want anything?"

I hold up my radish. "I'm good."

Later, after we've sold out of everything but two especially deformed pumpkins, and Gabe is helping Mom carry empty crates back to the truck while I gather up our supplies, Guinevere steps over and puts her hand on my wrist.

"Pause with me for a moment," she says, shutting her eyes almost reverently. "I believe with my entire being that people come into our lives when we need them most. And in some cases, the purpose for their arrival does not become clear for quite some time. We must open our hearts and our souls to the possibilities, Juniper, because we cannot predict the impact of one person, weaving in and out of our lives or choosing to stay there forever."

She makes a sort of humming sound before she continues. "You are a strong woman who knows her mind. As long as I've had the pleasure of your acquaintance, you've known where life will take you. There is so much ahead of you. Open your heart. Clear the space around you of any negative energy. Walk in nature. Cleanse your spirit. Open yourself up to new and amazing possibilities."

She squeezes my wrist and opens her eyes. "Sleep well tonight, love. Restore yourself. Tomorrow, begin anew. Celebrate the birth of your beloved."

She turns and gathers her things and floats away in a cloud of lavender.

When I sleep, I dream of my beloved at the river, building a fire that smells of pine and snow.

Chapter Thirty-Three

GABE

WHEN I WAKE UP MONDAY MORNING, I'M EIGHTEEN.

The blink of an eye. The tick of the second hand.

Nothing feels different. Nothing feels the same.

Today, I tell myself, I'm not going to think about the mistakes I've made in the last year, the shithole I need to dig myself out of.

An impossible task.

I slept hard. Working at a farmers' market is more difficult than I thought it would be, especially because so many people wanted a piece of my time, a conversation, a shared laugh.

Chris is already in the kitchen when I go downstairs. He's not usually up this early. He pours me a cup of coffee and pulls me into a hug.

"Kid," he says. "If I haven't told you lately, I'm glad you were born."

"Thanks," I say into his shoulder, guilt rolling through me. "I'm glad you're my dad." I mean it, and I hope I haven't completely fucked everything up between us.

He pulls away in surprise. "Well, look at you, all mature and shit on your eighteenth birthday."

"Ah," I say. "That's more like it. Don't try to get all sentimental on me. I'm still an asshole."

He laughs. "Good. You're still in there. I was worried for a minute."

I sit down, and Chris slides a plate covered with foil across the table.

"Your timing is perfect. Still hot."

I lift the foil to find perfectly crispy bacon, hash browns, and an omelet. "Sausage or ham?" I ask.

"Ham and cheese. It's a special day. My kid gets ham *and* bacon on his eighteenth birthday."

The food's delicious, but I barely have time to shove the last of it in my mouth before I hear Juniper pull into the driveway. She's early.

"Reservations are at six at Seasons Tavern," Chris calls after I grab my backpack and walk toward the front door. "Let her know."

Juniper wishes me a happy birthday as soon as I open the passenger door and slide in next to her. Today, she looks like cotton candy. Or a birthday cake. She's wearing a poofy pink skirt with a fuzzy white sweater that looks like frosting and black high-tops. Her hair is down and wild with curls.

"How'd you sleep?" I ask, and she throws me a confused look as she backs into the turnaround.

"Ah, OK? How'd you sleep?"

"Great," I say happily.

"This is weird, Gabe. Don't you think it's weird? Like, to ask me how I slept?"

"I care about your well-being. Why are you so early?"

"Bunny and Bucky need a ride. Bucky hit a deer last night."

"Shit. Is everyone OK?"

"Luckily. This is his second one already, and he's only been driving a few months."

I straighten up and scan the road. "Tell me about your friends. Bunny and Youa and Amelia."

She turns her head and wrinkles her brow. "What do you want to know?"

"How you all got to be friends. How long you've known them. Things like that."

"Well, I've known Bunny since kindergarten and Youa since about third grade. Amelia moved here in seventh grade. You already know that Amelia and Youa are cousins."

"What's Bunny's real name?" I ask.

"Oh no. Nice try. I'm not going to be the one who lets that cat out of the bag." She shakes her head.

"Come on. It's my birthday!"

"That's getting real old, real fast."

"OK, fine. Your turn. You ask me something."

"Hmm." She taps her fingers against the steering wheel as she waits her turn at the four-way stop coming into town. "If you could do anything in the world *except* play music, what would you do?"

Her question stuns me into silence. I mean, she hit the nail on the head, didn't she? The root of my current existential crisis, and on my eighteenth birthday, no less. The day I become an adult in the eyes of the law. The day I inherit my grandmother's farm.

"That's easy," I say, trying—not very well, I think—to play it off lightly. "I'd be a farmer."

"Gabe," she says quietly, "I'm serious."

"So am I," I say. "Honestly, Juniper. I never thought I'd say this, but I'm happier here at the farm than I've been in months. Yesterday, working at the farmers' market and talking to all those people—well, it was exhausting. But it was also exhilarating. Have you ever felt like that? So tired that you could drop right where you are and sleep for days, but at the same time so jazzed up you can't sleep?"

She nods as she turns into the driveway of a little brick house next to the Tom Thumb gas station. She doesn't say a word. I wonder what has ever excited her so much that she would feel that way. Me, I was surprised when I got home from the market and my mind wouldn't settle down for all the ideas spinning around.

Ideas for new songs.

Ideas for our e-biz project.

Ideas for Stone & Wool, ways we could make it better.

Together.

Chapter Thirty-Four

JUNIPER

I HAVEN'T BEEN TO SEASONS TAVERN FOR MONTHS. AS FAR AS DIN-ing establishments go, this one's not the most modern or well-kept—the chairs date back to the sixties, many of the maroon leather cushions are worn or split, and a thick layer of dust has settled over the vast collection of Saint Patrick statues and leprechauns on shelves around the room—but the food can't be beat.

Mom had a few errands to run in town before dinner, so she and I meet Gabe and Chris at the restaurant. Gabe looks happy. In fact, I don't think I've seen him this content and at ease since he came to Harper's Mill.

"Elise called me after school," he says as he peruses the menu. "It was eight in the morning—well, tomorrow—but she said she didn't want to miss talking to me on my birthday."

"That's great," Chris says, his tone warm and genuine. "Did she say how the film's coming along?"

"Good," Gabe says, "although Ryan Ballard is acting like a complete diva. She said she's never met anyone as self-centered or demanding."

Chris laughs but my mouth drops open. Ryan Ballard

is well-known as one of Hollywood's most altruistic, generous stars.

"Hold on," I say. "Ryan Ballard. *The* Ryan Ballard who builds a Habitat for Humanity house, like, every other week and donated most of his salary from *Hunger Strike* to Feeding America?"

Gabe gawks at me. "Oh, come on. You don't actually believe all that, do you? It's called PR, Juniper."

Chris nods. "I've met the guy. He's a prick. You ready to order, Laurel?" He nudges Mom.

"You know what I'm going to order, Chris. How many times have we come here? And how many times have I not ordered the exact same thing?"

He laughs. "True enough. Tell the kids the story."

I roll my eyes. A thousand times, I've heard the revolting story of what happened the *one* time she didn't order her usual. "Can we at least wait until *after* we've eaten?"

"Wait," Gabe says. "Laurel, you order the same thing every time you eat here? Like Juniper at Pizza Ranch?" I'm glad he didn't call it Pizza Snatch in front of Mom.

"I do. Tenderloin tips with mushrooms and au gratin potatoes."

"And you order this every time you're here."

She nods. "Well, except the once . . ."

"Right!" I say. "We know. What's your point, Gabe?"

He turns to me. "What about you? Are you going to order the same thing?"

"I guess you'll have to wait and see," I say. I smile.

"She always gets the fettuccine Alfredo with shrimp and asparagus," Chris says. "Watch. I'm right."

I smile. That is what I usually order, yes. Tonight, though, for Gabe's birthday, I'm stepping out of my comfort zone and trying something new.

Our server, who happens to be Bunny's mom, Mel, steps up to the table. "Laurel, Chris, Juniper. How nice to see you." She turns her attention to Gabe. "And you must be Chris, junior."

"It's Gabe, actually," he says. Again, he's cheerful and friendly, holding out his hand to Mel like he did with Guinevere at the farmers' market yesterday.

"Well, you're an exact replica," Mel says.

"Nah," Chris chimes in. "He's a lot smarter than his old man."

"I don't doubt it. What can I get you folks?"

"Well," Gabe says, "we're here for a special occasion. My eighteenth birthday. Tell me, do you know what Laurel and Juniper plan to order?"

"Oh, of course. Everyone knows." Mel nods. "But if you're not sure what you'd like, I can make some recommendations. We've got a terrific Monday night special—shepherd's pie."

"I see. Thank you."

"You go ahead, hon," Mel says to Gabe, "since it's your birthday."

"Oh, hold on. You're *Bunny's* mom!"

"Yes, indeed I am."

"You know, I've been wondering something, and you're the perfect person to ask."

Mel shakes her head. "Don't even think about it. Bunny will murder me with her bare hands if I tell you her real name."

"Nice try, Gabe," Chris says.

"I'm sure it's absolutely lovely. I'd be honored to know it."

"You've got a smooth one here, Chris," Mel says. "He should come with a warning label."

I snort.

"Now, what'll you have?" Mel taps her pen against the order pad.

"I'll go with the Dublin Delight combo platter," Gabe says confidently.

"Our barbecue pork ribs are the finest around," Mel says. "How would you like your shrimp? Fried or broiled?"

"Broiled."

"Choice of potato?" Mel rattles off the options and then moves on to Chris, who orders the shepherd's pie. Mom orders her usual, and then it's down to me.

"And for you, Juniper?" Mel asks with a smile.

Everyone looks at me, waiting to see what I'll do. I square my shoulders. "I'll have Vivian's Variety, broiled, with steamed vegetables."

Mom's jaw drops, Chris swears under his breath, and Gabe leans over to hug me.

"Oh my God, Blue, this is the best birthday gift you

could give me. You're trying something new! What's Vivian's Variety, anyway?"

Mel chuckles. "Scallops, shrimp, and fish. Excellent choice, hon."

When she walks away, no one speaks for long seconds.

"I didn't think you had it in ya, kid," Chris finally says.

"I did," Gabe says softly. "I knew it all along."

❖ ❖ ❖

After we've all pushed our plates back, overfull and content, Chris reaches into his pocket and tosses a set of keys across the table at Gabe.

"I'm going to catch a ride back to the farm with Laurel and call it a night. But why don't you and Juniper go for a spin?"

Gabe's mouth falls open. "You're letting me drive the *Twister*?"

"That's the 1970 Ford Mustang Mach 1 Twister Special to you," Chris says. "Happy birthday. Don't fuck this up."

"It's about damn time," Gabe says, grinning.

I've only ridden in the Twister one time, right after Chris brought it home from the car show in Kansas. Gabe is quiet, almost reverent, as he runs his hand across the gleaming yellow-orange paint and the chrome door handle on the passenger side. He opens the door for me, and I slide in, hit with the unmistakable scent of old leather, oil, classic car. Seconds later, he's in the driver's seat, caressing the wide steering wheel.

"Finally," he says on an exhale, as though he's been holding his breath. He turns to look at me, blissful and disbelieving at the same time. "Blue, where should we go? California? The moon?"

I laugh as Gabe turns the key in the ignition and the car rumbles to life.

Chapter Thirty-Five

GABE

I'VE WAITED FOR THIS MOMENT FOR WHAT FEELS LIKE MY WHOLE life. Which is dramatic, I know. But ever since the BMW incident—I was sixteen and the ink was practically still wet on my license, but I insisted Chris let me take the car because (a) I was sixteen and thought I knew everything and (b) I wanted to impress a girl—Chris hasn't let me drive any of his vintage cars.

Not that I blame him.

Driving the Twister fills me with an undefinable joy. I've never felt this alive before behind the wheel of any vehicle. Not the BMW, for sure not the RAV4.

Driving the Twister with Juniper next to me? Even better.

I inhale deeply.

"This car," I say. "God, it's even better than I dreamed."

"You dreamed about this car?" Juniper says, scrunching her little nose up in that cute way she does when she's confused.

"Oh yeah, since the minute I found out Chris was going to that auction in Kansas. I had this feeling he was going to bring her home. I thought that meant LA, but for some reason, he wanted her here."

"Where are we going?" Juniper asks as I drive the car down Main Street and out toward the highway.

"The open road, Blue. The open road."

She laughs. I love hearing it.

"An adventure?" she asks.

"Are you kidding me? You ordered something new tonight. I'm going to take advantage of this adventurous spirit of yours while I can."

"Look out for deer," she says.

"Help me watch for them," I say.

"I take that job very seriously," she says. I can tell without looking at her that she's sincere.

"I know you do." Every day, I find there's something more I like about this girl.

We drive north, where the landscape changes into even more forest and hills. Eventually I'll need to stop for gas, but for now I want to feel the hum, the heartbeat of the vehicle beneath me. I turn on the radio and punch one of the preset buttons, a classic rock station. Not surprisingly, it's playing a Led Zeppelin song. More surprisingly, it's "When the Levee Breaks," not "Stairway to Heaven."

"This is my favorite Zeppelin song," I say.

"I'm not sure that I have a favorite Zeppelin song," she says.

"Oh, come on. Everyone has a favorite Zeppelin song. Even if you think you don't, you probably do."

"I don't know about that. I don't listen to a lot of music."

"Come on. Humor me. 'Whole Lotta Love'? 'Ramble On'? Oh, wait. 'Kashmir'?"

"No, none of those."

"Are you going to make me work through their entire catalog until I get it right?"

"Number one, I'm not sure. Number two, I don't know all the song titles if I did know."

"We'll have to work on this. It's *Zeppelin*, Blue."

"You're the famous rock star son of the famous rock star, not me."

"What's your favorite Dig Me Under song, then?"

"That one's easy. And no, it's not 'Juniper Blue,' even though, you know, it probably should be, for obvious reasons. It's 'The Spell of Memory and Imagination.'"

"See?" I ask. "Was that so hard? I'll bet you could do this for lots of artists, maybe even me. What's your favorite song of mine?"

"Oh, slow down," she says, "there's a scenic overlook coming up. We should go."

"It's dark," I say. "Will we still be able to see anything scenic?"

Out of the corner of my eye, I see Juniper shrug one shoulder. "I've never been there at night, but it's worth a shot, right? Where's your sense of adventure, Gabe?"

"Oh, very funny," I say. I hope she never stops joking around with me.

I watch for signs for the turnoff to the overlook. The narrow road—which I wouldn't call well lit—ends in a small gravel parking lot with about seven spaces. We're the only car. Juniper gets out first, and I follow her up a short, narrow path—unlit and scary as hell, branches hanging in our way that she holds back for me—to a broad, semicircular area with a stone wall, waist high, and a large boulder with a plaque. A light shines up from the ground and illuminates the raised letters:

STUART OVERLOOK, LONE WOLF RIVER

IN MEMORY OF MATHIAS ROBERT STUART, LIEUTENANT,

U.S.N.

BORN MAY 4, 1917

DULUTH, MINNESOTA

DIED IN ACTION OFF GUADALCANAL

FEBRUARY 4, 1943.

One small streetlamp casts a dim pool of light, but otherwise we're surrounded by the deep blue of the night sky, filled with countless stars and, in the far-off distance, a swath of vivid green and blue and purple. The colors rain down from the darkness, vertical streams reflected in the black water below. Sharply cut silhouettes of evergreens line the wavering glow. I want to frame it, capture it, carry it home.

"Holy shit, Blue, is that the northern lights?"

She steps up to the stone wall and leans against it, looking out into the night sky. "Yes. We can't always see them, but it's not uncommon this time of year."

"That's—holy shit," I say again. I'm not sure what else to say. In all the times I visited Gran for a couple of days or the weeks we spent at the cabin, I never saw the northern lights.

"This is incredible," I say quietly. "I've never seen anything like it."

"I agree, it's spectacular," she says. "But you live in LA. I mean, you have that view from Mulholland Drive and, oh, what about the Griffith Observatory?"

"Ah, so you've seen *La La Land*," I say. "It's not like I spend my time driving around town looking for spectacular views. Mostly I shut myself up in a soundproof room and play guitar."

"I'm lucky, I guess," she says. "I don't need to look very far to find the beauty around me. Up here, up north, it's always there, you know? I've been going to the park reserve since before I could walk. I've hiked every trail, I've explored every corner. It's all right in my backyard. A two-minute walk, and I'm in the park. The overlook—well, you know that's my favorite place in the world. It's not as grand or sweeping as the view here, but it's etched in my heart."

I know she's telling the truth—it's all over her face and it's in her every word every day, her every breath. How much she loves the farm, the fate of which essentially lies in my hands as of this morning when I officially turned eighteen. The farm that's worth enough to solve all my problems but holds much more value for Juniper.

"How do you know?" I ask gently. "I'm not trying to pick a fight, honestly. But how do you know there's not something better? Someplace even more amazing? Someplace else that could be your favorite in the whole world?"

"I don't," she says. "I'm not like you, Gabe. I haven't traveled the world. The only time I've flown on an airplane was the trip to LA. I've never been anywhere else except for a family

258

vacation to Mount Rushmore we took the summer after third grade. I'm a farm girl, Gabe. I'm going to be a farm girl my whole life. There aren't a lot of adventures to travel the world in my future. This is enough."

I'm silent for a moment, listening to the rustle of the trees around us, the faint rush of the river below us, Juniper's soft breathing.

"But what if you could come back? What if you could see the world and then come back to the place you love best?"

She doesn't answer right away. Finally, so quietly that I have to strain to hear her, she says, "That's not how I'm wired, Gabe. Even if I wanted to change, to try something new, I'd have a difficult time with it. Why is it so wrong that I want my world to stay the same as it's always been? What's wrong with being content where you are? Or knowing what you want to do with your life and working hard to get there? You of all people should understand that."

She sounds sad, worried, even a little nostalgic. Hurt. Her eyes, blue and bright like the glowing waves in the sky, glimmer with unshed tears.

It hits me then. Except for missing Leona, the farm is exactly the same as it was when Juniper's father was alive.

Her breath stutters as I take her hand, slowly, gently, tentatively. I caress the back of it with my thumb. She looks up from our joined hands to my face, and I tighten my grip.

"I think I see," I say, and I hope she understands what I'm saying. "I—I can understand that, a little, at least. But when you're content to stay where you are, you might miss out on someplace even more magical, more beautiful. If I'd stayed in LA, I would have missed this. I would have missed *you.*"

Shit, I can hardly look her in the eye. Maybe I'm talking about myself. Maybe I'm feeling something for Juniper Blue that I have no business feeling. But I don't fucking care. I don't want to ignore it anymore, that feeling I get when I'm with her, that sense of happiness, the sense that something is filling a hole, deep inside, that I've felt most of my life.

I lift our hands and kiss hers, then tug her into me. I let go, move my hands to cup her cheeks. Her eyes grow wide.

"Blue," I whisper, and then I lean in and do what I've wanted to do for weeks.

I kiss her, and the world shifts.

Chapter Thirty-Six

JUNIPER

WHEN GABE'S LIPS BRUSH AGAINST MINE, TENTATIVELY AT FIRST and then without hesitation, with confidence, the world lights up in a burst of color and sound and stars.

My hands clutch the lapels of his coat, I pull him in, closer, closer still, and I'm dizzy with the sensation of skin, of touch, of connection as my mouth opens to his and his tongue slips in, tangles with mine, fills me with something undefinable, unimaginable. I have never known a feeling like this, like I belong with him.

He pulls away, out of breath, but still I clutch him like he's air itself and I won't survive without him. Gabe Hudson is turning out to be so much more than I would have ever thought. To mean so much more to me. I swallow hard, swallow down these tangled emotions.

"I'm so glad I came to Minnesota," he whispers.

"Me, too," I whisper back. This time, I'm not pretending. I don't know that I ever was. "Happy birthday."

He laughs. "I thought that when Chris tossed me the keys to the Twister, nothing could make this day any better. Then I saw the fucking aurora borealis. And then—holy shit, Juniper. That kiss."

My cheeks heat. This is not the time or place to tell Gabe that before that—let's face it, life-altering kiss—I'd kissed exactly one other guy. I can't help it—a laugh bubbles out of me, partly from embarrassment, partly from this feeling of utter and complete happiness.

Gabe tugs me even closer when I do.

"Hey," he says. "What's funny about that?"

"No, not that," I say in a rush. "There was nothing funny about that kiss, Gabe." My face heats even more. "I was thinking how you're only the second person I've kissed."

"You're kidding," he says. "How is that even possible? And by the way, I don't think I want to know who the first person was. But please, for the love of God, tell me it wasn't Ted."

I laugh again. "No, not Ted. A guy I worked with at the nature center. He had a girlfriend the whole time, so I reamed him out and stomped on his foot for good measure."

He laughs. "That's my girl," he says.

I don't know that I've ever wanted anything to be true as much as that. He kisses me again, his hand reaching around to grasp the nape of my neck, and somehow we're even closer than before.

The kiss sends a charge through me that lifts me up on my toes, a feeling as powerful as the northern lights in the sky behind me. He deepens the kiss, moves his hand to my lower back, drags a finger along the waistband of my skirt.

"Be my girl," he says breathlessly as he breaks the kiss. "I don't know what's happening between us, Juniper, or where we'll go from here, but I need to find out. I need to follow through on this adventure."

Be my girl.

"I want that," I whisper. "So much."

He leans in, forehead against mine, closes his eyes. The sky glows behind us. I never want to leave this place, this moment.

He opens his eyes and locks his gaze with mine. "I'll never forget this night, Blue. Never."

Chapter Thirty-Seven

GABE

SHE IS EVERYTHING I COULD HAVE IMAGINED AND MORE.

She is every swath of vivid color, every glowing star, every light, every reflection.

She is every note I've ever played, every lyric I've yet to write.

With Juniper, my world is more blues than grays. More sun, less rain.

My heart is hers to do with as she pleases.

✧ ✧ ✧

I drop Juniper off and drive the Twister into its special parking space in the garage. Chris is waiting for me in the dining room, working on a crossword puzzle from the newspaper.

"Hey, old man."

He looks up at me, then back down to the paper. "Five across. Four-letter word for birthday boy with a shit-eating grin on his face. What's going on, Gabe?"

"Thanks for letting me drive the 1970 Ford Mustang Mach 1 Twister Special tonight," I say, ignoring his observation and question. I can't seem to wipe the so-called shit-eating grin off my face, though.

"Where did you go?"

"We drove up toward Eveleth and stopped at a scenic overlook."

"Yeah, nothing like a scenic overlook in the dark of night."

"We saw the northern lights. That was pretty amazing."

"Oh yeah? What else was amazing at the scenic overlook?" he asks. When I don't answer, he keeps digging. "Is there anything else you'd like to tell me? Anything at all."

"Nope. Long day, turning eighteen and all. I think I'll go to bed. Thanks for a good birthday." I toss the keys to him, but he tosses them right back.

"Happy birthday. She's yours."

My mouth drops open. "What did you say?"

"Happy birthday. I've already transferred the title. You're a good kid, Gabe. I knew the first time I saw her that she would be yours one day. I think today's as good a day as any."

"Holy shit," I say, my grin widening. "That's fucking awesome. I don't know what to say."

"Take good care of her," he says slowly, locking his eyes on mine. "And I'm not only talking about the car, Gabe."

As I climb the stairs, a thought knocks me back: The Twister's worth three times what I need. And selling a car would be so much simpler than having to deal with attorneys or complicated real estate transactions or tools like Eric Dunbar. I could make it happen within the week.

I could make it happen, and then *I* would be the complete tool in this scenario.

What would be worse, though? Facing Chris's rage if I sell his baby or having to tell him I screwed up and stole money from him?

I lie awake in bed, the brick of dread back and much, much bigger. My gut churns with guilt for even thinking about selling the Twister, and heavier guilt for taking the money in the first place. And for what? For a girl in trouble, a girl I thought I loved, who didn't love me back. Who never did, no matter how many times she said it.

What happened at the overlook—that moment, God, I'll never forget—is overshadowed by all the stupid shit I've done. And the one person I want to talk to about it is the very last person I should talk to about it.

My phone chimes with an incoming message.

Juniper: I've decided. My favorite of your songs is Imitation of Life.

I'd forgotten that I'd asked her that question.

Me: Really? Not Burden or everyone's favorite ballad Fonder?
Juniper: Hmm, is it rude of me to say that I usually skip Fonder?
Me: You're not the only one. 😂 Everyone seems to think that song is about a guy missing his girlfriend but really it's about her cheating on him. Considering I was fourteen when I wrote it, can you guess who it's about?
Juniper: Your parents?

Me: Yeah the day I wrote it there was this photo of Elise spending a lot of up close and personal time with her costar in Love on the Line.

Juniper: That's awful. I'm sorry.

Me: Awful song for an awful subject.

Juniper: He's a terrible actor, too.

Me: I'm glad I got to spend my birthday with you.

Juniper: I'm sorry I didn't get you a gift.

Me: Not to sound creepy or sappy but the time we spent together at the overlook was better than any gift anyone could have given me.

So much for not being sappy.

Me: And that's saying something because Chris GAVE ME the Twister.

Juniper: SHUT UP

The phone rings as I'm thumbing a response.

"SHUT UP, Gabe," Juniper says in greeting. "He gave you the 1970 Ford Mustang Mach 1 Twister Special?"

I laugh. "You've been paying attention, I see."

She's quiet for a moment, and then, "I'm always paying attention."

"I know," I say and then yawn. "It's not you, it's me. I'm exhausted."

"Did you have a good birthday?"

"The best." I yawn again. "Good night, Juniper. See you bright and early. But tomorrow, I'm driving *you* to school."

"I'll grab my parking permit."

"Very practical. But I'd bet I could talk my way out of a parking fine. I know a few people."

"See you bright and early. Good night, Gabe. Happy birthday."

Sleep doesn't come, so I get out of bed and take the Martin out of its case. My brain slows down after a few minutes as I work through my usual warm-up. Some Floyd, some Zeppelin, some Alice in Chains.

Then I play "Imitation of Life." Juniper's favorite. I don't sing, I only play the melody. Of my own songs, I've probably played this one more than any other.

I didn't know Juniper when I wrote this song, not like I know her now. She was the girl who lived on Chris's farm, the girl he took to the Grammys instead of me, the girl I wanted nothing to do with.

Now, after only a few weeks on the farm, I can't imagine life without her. Now, it feels like I wrote this song about her. *Until I met you, mine was an imitation of life.*

Tonight, there are other songs in my head, new songs, new melodies. I play around with something slow and ballady, working in lyrics, until I can barely keep my eyes open. *More blues than grays, more sun in my skies, these are my days, the light in your eyes.*

It's not perfect, but I'll get there.

◇ ◇ ◇

When Juniper climbs into the Twister the next morning, the smile on her face is contagious and telling.

"Hi," she says, a bit breathless. "This car smells good. Like a hot summer day. A carnival ride. Swimming in the river. Like we don't have a care in the world."

"Hey." I reach for her hand and her smile grows. "We don't."

Today, she's dressed like fall with her bulky orange sweater and jean skirt with crimson maple leaves stitched above the hem. Her hair is one long, loose braid, a dark burgundy ribbon twisted through.

"Did you make that skirt?" I ask.

"No, it was Mom's from high school. I embroidered the leaves."

I let go of her hand to trace one of the leaves and then move my hand down to circle one of her tiny kneecaps. Finally. I can touch her. Well, I think I can touch her. She doesn't seem to mind. I slip a finger under the hem, and she swats my hand away.

OK, maybe I can't touch her everywhere, not yet. I grab her hand again and trace my thumb across her knuckles. She sucks in a breath.

I've kissed a lot of girls. I've even slept with a couple. But nothing compares to holding hands with Juniper Bell in the Twister, thinking about that kiss last night at the scenic overlook.

"Blue, I—" I start, but stop myself before I pour out my entire heart, how everything's changed, how I want to spend every waking moment with her and probably every sleeping moment, too. Tell her about the song I was writing late into the night. Tell her about Marley and the money.

I've been so stupid is what I should say, but I don't say that, either.

"What?" she asks, and she must sense my apprehension. She turns toward me, giving me her full attention, and squeezes my hand, encouraging me.

"I missed you," I say quietly, and even though my eyes are on the road, I know she's still looking at me. I feel it. "I mean, I know it's only been a few hours since we saw each other, but I missed you."

"I missed you, too," she says. "So much. Deer on the left."

I slow down as the young fawn leaps across the road. It's good to have Juniper looking out for me.

Chapter Thirty-Eight

JUNIPER

I WAS NERVOUS TO SEE GABE THIS MORNING. BUT THEN HE HELD MY hand and was so sweet to me and said that he missed me, and I admitted that I missed him, too.

Is it strange to miss someone after being apart for only a few hours? Separated by only fifty-two Norway pines?

The drive to school doesn't take long enough. I tuck my parking permit into the corner of his dash as we pull into the lot. My phone buzzes before Gabe turns the engine off.

Amelia: Excuse me! UR in Chris's mustang? WTH
Me: Library in 3 minutes
Amelia: OMG u kissed him didn't u
Me: Be cool Amelia!

She is definitely *not* cool. She's practically bouncing up and down at our regular table in what's affectionately known as the Dictionary Room, where someone has usually opened up the large dictionary on the display stand to a page with one (or more) vulgar words. We'd met here yesterday, too, so that she could tell me all about her date with Ted: They argued most of the drive there, shared each other's meals (chicken tetrazzini for Amelia, walleye sandwich with onion rings for Ted), walked along the harbor after they ate even though it was drizzling, and kissed in the rain at the lighthouse on the end of the pier.

"So," she says, squealing, "was it as romantic as mine with Ted? Like, one day apart! What are the odds?"

I grin. "Yeah, I think it was." I tell her and she squeals again.

"Do you still think he'll want to sell the farm someday?"

"Not sure," I say. Honestly, even though yesterday was *the day* that it could potentially happen, I haven't thought about it. "I think the farm's growing on him."

"That's reassuring," she says and smiles. "You took the advice from *The Godfather: Part II* to heart, then? Keeping your enemies closer?"

I'm hit with a surge of guilt for that plan. But I tell myself that if I hadn't done it, we wouldn't be where we are today. Would we?

✧ ✧ ✧

Gabe and I skip lunch and take a walk through the horticulture gardens, almost all of which has been harvested except for a few pumpkins and winter squash. The rich, earthy fragrance of any garden centers me. I think about *The Secret Garden*, how it brought new life and energy to Colin and his father, brought them out of their grief, and healed Mary, too. I know the healing power of working in the earth with my hands, bringing things to life, and ultimately creating a feeling of pure joy. I want Gabe to feel that, too. I tell him as much.

"Well," he says, "I've got that big test coming up in Horticulture on Thursday. Maybe you can help me study? I'm sure acing that test will bring me joy."

I elbow him. "Since when are you so concerned about your grades?"

"There's this girl I'm trying to impress."

"Well, I know one way you can impress her," I say.

"Oh, reallllly?" he asks with a grin. "Do tell."

My cheeks flush. "That sounded dirty."

"I liked it."

"I meant by knocking that e-biz presentation out of the park tomorrow."

"With your brains and my inherent charm and stage presence, it's a done deal."

"And at the end of the week, we'll celebrate."

"Yes. With an adventure. Let's skip school on Friday and go on a hike up to Kawishiwi Falls," he says. "You up for it?"

Kawishiwi Falls is about an hour and a half north of Harper's Mill, just past Ely. I've never been there.

I grab his hand. "Life with you is always going to be an adventure, isn't it?" I say the words without thinking—*life, always.* So serious, so long-term.

"I hope so," he says. He backs me up against a maple tree at the edge of the garden and kisses me, sweetly and quickly. Then he gently caresses my face, trailing his fingers from my

ear to my jaw. He smiles, and in a moment when I think I
could lose myself in that smile, I realize that I can find myself
in it, too.

○ ○ ○

That night after dinner, Gabe and I move into the living room
to run through our presentation. Gabe has spent the last
couple of weeks capturing footage around the farm with his
phone camera. He put together a movie trailer—complete
with original score on acoustic guitar—while I worked on the
presentation deck. In class today, we connected his laptop to
the projection system in class. We've gathered props—mostly
items we sell at the farmers' market and a couple of Mom's
smaller felted wool projects.

We're so ready for this presentation, in fact, that we close
the laptop and turn on a movie instead.

"I don't want to hear one word about who you know in this
movie or which song on the soundtrack is yours," I tell him as
I snuggle in next to him, a blanket across my lap.

Gabe laughs. "I promise. I won't drop any names. And I
don't have a song on this soundtrack, so we're safe. Go ahead,
forget I'm a celebrity."

I smile and rest my head on his shoulder. I won't ever be
able to forget that wherever he goes, people will know his
name, his music. But tonight, I'll try.

Chapter Thirty-Nine

GABE

OUR PRESENTATION GOES OFF WITHOUT A HITCH. THE TRAILER plays without any technological glitches and gets a round of applause from our classmates before we even get to the meat of it. Juniper and I nail our lines, working together to illustrate how Field & Flock is profitable, engaging, and timeless. And it has a pretty cool name.

Everything I've learned about starting up Field & Flock I'm thinking about for Stone & Wool, too.

My Horticulture test does doesn't go quite as well, but who cares? I've convinced my girl to make the leap to skipping school—not that it took much convincing.

Since I'm eighteen, on Friday morning I call in my own absence. Juniper somehow convinces Laurel to call her in as well. Not long after, as Juniper and I are loading our cooler and first aid kit into the trunk of her car, I get a text message from Janie in the office at school: You're not fooling anyone, Gabe Hudson. Tell Juniper hi. ☺

We listen to Led Zeppelin on the drive to Kawishiwi Falls so that by the time we arrive at the small trail parking lot, Juniper can pick a favorite.

"This is a tough one," she says. "I liked a lot of them. But

I think, since you're basically forcing me to choose a favorite, I'll go with 'The Battle of Evermore.' I like the story. And the mandolin."

"Solid choice," I tell her. "1971, from the *Led Zeppelin IV* album. Fun fact: Ann and Nancy Wilson of Heart did a cover of this song for the *Singles* soundtrack as the Lovemongers." I play it for her next.

"Oh, I think I like that version better," she says, and I know she must be teasing me because she smiles broadly. Who in their right mind would chose a cover over the obviously flawless original?

"Very funny. Let's go."

Before we get across the parking lot, though, my phone buzzes three times in quick succession.

Rocky: Gabey boy it's Rocky. Haven't heard from you in a while.
Rocky: How's it going?
Rocky: I don't know about you but I'm starting to get a little nervous? Call me when you can.

Well, hell. Rocky's worried that I won't come through. Welcome to my world, Rock. I shove the phone deep in my jacket pocket. I take a long drink from my water bottle and hope that I can keep it—and my breakfast—down.

"Everything OK?" Juniper asks.

"Yeah, of course," I say, but I don't elaborate, and I don't try to make up some story that she probably wouldn't buy, anyway.

We have the trail mostly to ourselves. It's a cold Friday

morning at a tucked-away trail in far northern Minnesota. We're closer to Canada than we are to Harper's Mill. A couple of minutes into the trail, I reach for Juniper's hand and tug her close to me.

"Hard to hike holding hands," she says. I can see her puffs of breath in the chilly air.

"Oh, really? Have you ever tried?"

She laughs. "No."

"We'll be fine. And if it takes us a couple of minutes longer to make it to the falls, oh well. I plan to kiss you at the end of the trail no matter what."

"Is that right?"

"I will kiss you at the end of every trail, Blue. At the top of every hill we climb," I say, all teasing gone from my voice. "And again at the bottom and everywhere in between."

She smiles. "You're something of a poet, aren't you?"

"I prefer songwriter. Lyricist if you want to get fancy."

We hear the rushing of the falls before we see them. After less than fifteen minutes on the windy, woody trail, we reach the waterfall. It's broad and magnificent, and Juniper's face lights up at the sight. A few people climb the rocks down toward the rushing water, but Juniper tugs me in the opposite direction, to a higher elevation point.

"Follow me," she says.

We climb up for a couple of minutes. The roots of a large tree near the edge of the hill extend downward along the trail, winding and overlapping one another as if holding down the earth, making sure it doesn't slip away into the lake below.

At the top of the hill, we stand quietly together, watching the rush of the water, churning as it meets the lake below. I stand behind her, my arms wrapped around her, my chin on the top of her head. I'm holding on tight. I won't let her slip away. I breathe the crisp, clean air deeply and try to let go of the sick feeling I've had since Rocky texted. He's right. Time's running out. Today, I'll hold my girl in my arms. Tomorrow, I'll figure out what I'm going to do about the money.

"This is beautiful," Juniper says after we watch the falls for a few minutes. "Thank you."

"For what?"

"For bringing me here. For the adventure."

So of course, I have to kiss her. I turn her in my arms and kiss her like it matters. She matters. She's everything.

✧ ✧ ✧

Saturday, Chris and I drive down to the Twin Cities for a show at the Palace Theater in St. Paul. On the drive, Chris drills me about school, the farm, and Juniper ("You better treat her right or you will deal with me," he says, as if I haven't been dealing with him my whole life).

"You get that real estate agent off your back?" he asks.

"Yeah, it took a few more calls, but I think he finally got the picture." I pause, not sure that I'm ready to tell Chris my latest idea for the farm. Not until I can solidify a few more details. I decide that it can wait another week or so.

"You know, it might not hurt to maybe go through Gran's

things? See what you can donate or shit, I don't know, put in a museum? Or, uh, sell?"

"You're not saying this because you want to demo the farmhouse, are you?" He side-eyes me.

"No, no," I'm quick to reply. "Nothing like that."

"Mm-hmm," Chris murmurs. "I suppose it's time." He pauses, then says, "You know, I've always wanted to build right on the river. Maybe I should sell the house in Venice Beach and come home."

I look at him in surprise. "You'd leave LA?"

He shrugs. "I can always get an apartment and fly back if I need to. You, too."

I don't respond right away, considering this. What it would be like to live here full-time. "Yeah," I say quietly.

We grab a bite to eat at a nearby brewpub before the show. The band, Default to Deny, opened for Dig Me Under on the Midwestern leg of their last tour, so Chris promised them he'd come to the show, maybe join them onstage for a couple of songs.

The guys (and one woman, the drummer) are pretty cool. Not much older than me, actually. The five of them met at the University of Wisconsin in Milwaukee and dropped out junior year to take a shot at the big time. I was at a few of the shows that they opened on the DMU tour.

Chris and I hang out in the wings. This band is good. And it feels good to be back in a venue, around musicians and their fans. Toward the end of the set, Ini, the lead singer with a big Lenny Kravitz vibe, launches into the story of how Chris gave them a chance and has been their biggest supporter and mentor.

"Chris has been spending a lot of time up at his farm in northern Minnesota," Ini says, "and would you fucking believe that he's here tonight? What do you think? Should we get him out here to play something?"

The crowd goes nuts when Chris steps out onstage and somebody hands him a guitar. He launches into the opening riff from "Desolation," and Kels joins in on the drums. Then they transition seamlessly into "Miss You" by the Rolling Stones like they did on the tour. It still sounds awesome.

When the applause dies down, Ini grabs the mic again and says, "Yeah, it's killer that Chris Hudson is here tonight, but it gets better: Junior's here with him. What do you think, wanna hear something from Gabe Hudson?"

The roar of the crowd is deafening and completely unexpected. Holy shit. Are they seriously calling me out there? The Chris thing was planned, obviously, but this? Nobody looped me in. But it doesn't matter. What matters is, the crowd is happy to see me. I join Chris and Ini onstage and throw my hand up in a wave.

"Dude," Ini says, "the last time I saw you, you still had braces! How the fuck you been, little dude? What do you think, people? What should we play with the little dude?"

I grin. I'd forgotten how Ini and the rest of the band called me little dude. The crowd's chanting "Burden" and "Imitation of Life." God, I've missed all of this so much.

"What the hell?" I say into the mic. "Nothing from the new album?"

That gets a laugh from the band and Chris and a lot of people in the crowd.

"Good one," Chris mouths to me.

"'Burden' it is!" Ini yells, and the next thing I know, I've got a guitar and I'm playing with this band as if we've done it a hundred times before. It's easy and loud and like not one day has passed since the last time I was in front of a crowd.

How does it feel
Well, how does it feel
Now that you're the burden
You always knew you would be
I know how it feels
Yeah, I know how it feels
I am the burden
I always knew I would be

The final ear-splitting notes of "Burden" settle over the roaring crowd. Eventually, the crowd quiets down again and Ini says, "One more. One more. So here's a quick story from when we got our big break, when we toured with DMU a couple of years back. We were hanging out backstage, right, and it was a big fucking deal. Like, we were *hanging out with* Dig Me Under. That's some fucked-up shit, right? Here we are, not even old enough to drink, and we're hanging out with these rock legends. Yeah, so, we're somewhere backstage and all of a sudden, we hear this singing. These two voices harmonizing, and I swear, I thought maybe I'd died, and I was in heaven, like, grunge heaven? You know that place. Chris and little dude were singing some Alice in Chains, and I think we should play that for you all tonight."

I remember that night. I remember how Ini and the rest of Default to Deny stood in the green room, how Ini's mouth dropped open when he realized it was me singing with Chris.

"Little dude," Ini said when the song ended, "when are you going to put out a record?"

Rico kicks off the opening riff of "Heaven Beside You," and Kels comes in on the drums a few measures later, and it's like Chris and I are down at the campfire but it's so much better. We hit the harmonies and the band kills it and the crowd is loving every minute of it.

I'm loving every minute of it, too. My heart's racing, I'm sweating under the lights, I'm grinning and playing guitar and singing my heart out for people who love music, love seeing a live show and being with other people like them.

We finish the song and Ini thanks us. "Chris Hudson and little dude Gabe Hudson, thank you!" Ini yells. "We love you fucking guys, you know that, right?" and the crowd roars.

Chris lifts his hand in a wave, and I follow him off the stage. Someone hands us each a bottle of water, and Chris gulps his down in a couple of swallows.

"Hell, that felt good, didn't it?" he says. "There's nothing I'd rather do with my life."

Tonight, nobody seemed to care that I put out a shit

album. Tonight, all that mattered was the band, and the music, and the people.

"That's the first step, kid," Chris says. "You're on your way back."

I hope he's right.

Chapter Forty

JUNIPER

GABE'S TEXT DOESN'T COME UNTIL ALMOST ONE. I'M AWAKE, WAITING.

Gabe: Are you still up? Can I call you?
Me: Yes

The video call comes through seconds later. He's in a hotel room, his curls a mess, a huge grin on his face.

"Hey," he says. "Tonight was so fucking awesome."

I can't help smiling at how happy he looks. "Yeah? The band was good, then?"

"Well, yeah, but I went up onstage and played. And it rocked. I wish you could have been there."

"What did you play?"

"The crowd wanted 'Burden,' and then Chris and I sang 'Heaven Beside You.' It felt so good to be back in front of a crowd."

My smile falls a little. I don't mean for it to happen, but it does, and Gabe notices.

"What's wrong?"

"Nothing, I promise," I say quickly. "It's strange, though,

this feeling I have right now. Like I'm so incredibly happy for you, but sad for myself." I laugh a little.

"Aw, Blue," he says as he flops backward onto his pillows. "Why are you sad?"

I swallow hard, not sure if I want to tell him. He's *Gabe Hudson*. He's a musician. His entire career revolves around traveling the world and playing live for his fans. He's *not* a farmer. "Someday, you won't be here on the farm."

He sits up again and startles me with how intensely he looks into the camera. "Blue, let's not worry about someday, OK? Let's think about today. Well, tomorrow, because I come home tomorrow."

I smile again. "What time are you leaving St. Paul?"

"Checkout's at eleven. I doubt we'll leave before then. And Chris wants to grab breakfast at Mickey's Diner."

I yawn. "Are you exhausted?"

"Yeah," he says, "but I'm inspired, too, and I can't wait to get back to my guitars."

"That's so good," I say and yawn again.

"Hey, you should go to sleep. Means a lot that you waited up for me, though. I miss you, Blue." He laughs. "That's actually kind of new for me, missing someone as much as I miss you."

My insides flip-flop. No one has ever said the kinds of things to me that Gabe says.

"Miss you, too," I whisper.

"Get some sleep, sweet girl. I'll see you tomorrow."

We hang up and I turn out the light. But I can't sleep. I pick up my phone from where I set it on the nightstand and pull up Twitter. I search for @thegabehudson, and sure enough, he's tagged in countless videos along with @defaulttodeny. I watch the videos, most of them shaky or blurry, until I find one from someone up close to the stage.

I watch, transfixed, as the camera zooms in on him as he plays a guitar and sings "Burden." He's all there, so into it. I'm amazed by his talent, how he knows exactly what he wants to do and what he needs to do to get there, even if he screws up along the way.

He's bigger than the world of the farm. He's meant for something greater, meant to inspire and fill up others. Like Chris.

Maybe, like Chris, he can belong in both worlds. I hope that he wants to try.

I turn off the phone and lie awake in the dark, "Burden" on a constant loop in my head.

✿ ✿ ✿

It's an off week for the farmers' market, so I sleep in until eight and dress in layers for another hike up to the overlook. Mom's already out in the barns, so I make a cup of Irish Breakfast tea and head for the trail.

The ground is covered with the spiky white crystals of the first hard frost. Finally. I smile, thinking that I can't wait to tell Gabe, that I'm sorry he missed it.

I'm about to cut across the yard to the trail when I notice a car parked alongside the private road north of our driveway, a car I don't recognize.

I change course and walk toward the car, a Lexus. Not many of those around here. Then I see a guy with pale, freckled skin and rusty hair, dressed in ripped jeans and a leather jacket, in the field next to the road, holding a camera up to his face. This used to happen a lot more, usually when Dig Me Under released a new album or if word got out that Chris was in town. This guy, in his rock star clothes and Doc Martens, standing in a farm field? Total Dig Me Under fan.

"Hey!" I call as I make my way over to him. "You know you're on private property, right?"

He turns, lowers the camera, and walks toward me.

"I'll be damned. Juniper Blue, is it?" His British accent is thick but clear.

He knows who I am. My heart speeds up. "What are you doing on our property?"

"Our? I thought this farm belonged to Chris and Gabe Hudson. Stone & Wool Farm, Harper's Mill, Minnesota, United States. The sign out front says Stone & Wool, so I know I'm in the right place."

"How can I help you . . ."

"Graham. Graham Briggs. Not sure that you can, sweetheart, unless you can let me in that round barn to take a look around. I thought that Gabe would be here, but there was no answer down at the farmhouse. Do you know when he'll be back?"

"Why do you need to get into the round barn?" I ask. My voice shakes. Who is this guy? Why is he looking for Gabe?

"You know what? Maybe I can come back another time." He must sense my nervousness. "I'm sorry to have disturbed you, sweetheart. I'll give Gabe a call. He and I can discuss the future of that old round barn another time. You take care."

The few sips of tea I've taken sour and threaten to come back up.

Gabe called him, and they need to discuss the future of "that old round barn." This can only mean one thing. They're selling. How could Gabe do this? How could he betray me?

Before I even turn away from the field, I'm calling Gabe. I don't care that it's early. I don't care that he's probably still sleeping after his late night. He doesn't pick up and the call goes to voice mail, so I dial again.

"What's wrong?" he asks, groggy, when he finally answers on the fourth ring.

"Who is Graham Briggs?"

"What? Who?"

"Graham Briggs. British accent. Doc Martens."

There's a moment of quiet and then: "Shit, Blue."

"So you know this guy? You called him? He was telling the truth?"

"Where did you see Graham Briggs?"

"In the west field. Taking pictures of the round barn."

"Oh, hell."

"Gabe. Tell me the truth. Did you call this guy and ask him to come out and look at the property?"

"Blue, it's not what you think."

"Did you, or didn't you?" I'm surprised at how high-pitched and shrieky my voice has become.

"Well, yes, I called him—"

I cut him off. I don't want to hear his explanation, his excuses. I end the call. When he calls back seconds later, I hit the red X. Again. And again. Finally, I switch the phone off altogether.

I walk down to the round barn, where I run my hands across the rules and cry.

I trusted him. I let him in. I fell for him.

He's selling the farm. He's breaking my heart.

Chapter Forty-One

GABE

Fuck.

I throw my shit in a duffel and pound on the adjoining door to Chris's suite. He's still wearing glasses, a white T-shirt, and his boxers, so I know he hasn't been up long.

"What the hell, Gabe? What's wrong?" he asks.

"We have to get back home. Now."

"What happened?" He backs up into his room, grabs his jeans, and tugs them on.

"Fuck, fuck, fuck," I say. "I'm so stupid. I called an architect."

"What? You called an architect? And that's the fucking emergency?"

"No, no. I called an architect. Graham Briggs. You know him? He's the guy who designed the studio where Crackerjack recorded *Heartbreak Holiday*. You know, that old stone barn somewhere in England?"

"Vaguely. So what's the problem?"

"I called him to come out and take a look at the round barn. For a recording studio. And this magazine—*Architectural Influence*—we're in talks about them bankrolling the renovation for an exclusive series and documentary. But

Graham Briggs lives in *London*. I wasn't expecting him to just pop over on the weekend."

"You've been busy."

"Chris, focus!" Jesus. My heart is pounding.

"So. Graham Briggs is at the farm. Did you tell Laurel and Juniper?"

"No, and that's why I'm an idiot. Juniper found him taking pictures of the round barn and freaked out. He must not have explained who he was. She won't talk to me. We've got to get back so I can explain."

To my surprise, Chris laughs. "You are learning some hard lessons these days, Gabe. Welcome to adulthood."

"Fuck off and pack your shit." I slam the door.

☼ ☼ ☼

Juniper's not at the house. She's not at the round barn. Her car's in the driveway, though, so I hike up to the overlook. She's not there. I walk all over that fucking farm until I finally find her at the firepit at the riverside, sitting in a chair, wrapped up in a wool blanket. There's no fire.

"Blue," I say.

She looks up but doesn't say anything. Her eyes are swollen.

"Please talk to me. You have to let me explain."

She stands up and shakes her head. "No, I don't. I don't have to do anything."

"Please. I'm asking you to give me a chance to explain. The guy you saw—Graham Briggs? He's—"

She cuts me off. "I've given you so many chances," she says. I'm not sure what she means by it. "I'm tired of giving you chances. You'll only disappoint me again."

"What are you talking about?"

"I thought the farm meant something to you, Gabe. I thought I did. But all this time, you were still planning to sell, weren't you? Graham Briggs? He's a developer, isn't he?"

"No, Blue, he's an architect. From London."

She waves her hand like she's dismissing me. "I don't want to hear any more bullshit, Gabe. I never should have trusted you in the first place." She steps toward me. She's close enough that I could reach out and pull her into my arms.

"You can trust me," I say quietly. "I trust you."

"No. I can't. I knew it from day one. I never should have let myself get close to you, Gabe. I only did it to save the farm." She barks out a laugh. "I've got more in common with Marley Green than I ever would have imagined. I guess fake relationships are the only kind you're cut out for."

My mouth drops open. "What did you say?" I can barely get the words out.

"I said I only got close to you so you wouldn't sell the farm."

I take a step back—from Juniper, from the girl I fell hard for and the future I thought we had together. "Fuck," I say under my breath. I'm shaking. "Please—please tell me that you're kidding."

She shakes her head, her face completely devoid of any expression, and walks away.

Everything we had is a lie. She fucking lied to me. She made me believe that she cared about me. *To save the farm.*

Fucking hell.

Everything about her is a fraud. A sham. Our relationship. Every kiss. Every sweet word. Every lyric I've written for her, about her. All of it a lie.

I think I'm going to be sick. I walk over to the river's edge, take deep, gulping breaths, bent over at the waist, my hands on my knees. It can't be true. It can't. She can't be like the others.

She is exactly like the others.

The river rushes past me.

You can never step in the same river twice. It is not the same river, and you are not the same man.

I am not the same man I was when I left LA.

I am not the same man I was four hours ago.

I am not the same man.

Before this moment, I've never known what it's like to have a broken heart.

By the time I walk back up to the farmhouse, I can't feel my toes or my fingertips from the cold. It doesn't matter. I don't want to feel anything.

I pull up the Delta app on my phone and book a flight.

Chapter Forty-Two

JUNIPER

GABE IS GONE.

Chris comes over Sunday afternoon, and I overhear a conversation between him and Mom: Gabe grabbed his Martin and a duffel bag and took a Lyft to MSP for a flight back to LA.

"Who in their right mind takes a Lyft to the airport all the way from Harper's Mill?" Chris says. "Do you know what the hell is going on?"

I close my door. I don't want to hear their speculation.

I don't want to think about Gabe's face when I told him what I'd done.

I did it to save the farm.

That's the most important thing, right? The farm. To keep things exactly as they've always been.

Isn't it?

I'm beginning to think it might not be. Because now that Gabe's gone, now that he knows I was pretending to be his friend, I still stand to lose the farm. I've already lost Gabe.

I call Amelia.

"I can't understand what you're saying, sweetie," she says. "I'll be right over."

She's at my house in less than fifteen minutes with a bag of Haribo Happy Cola gummies and *Monty Python and the Holy Grail* on DVD.

"Gummy colas and Monty Python?" I ask. "Is this supposed to make me feel better?"

Amelia shrugs. "We didn't have any ice cream. And this film is consistently ranked as the number one comedy of all time. It's sure to make you feel better."

"Nothing will make me feel better," I cry. The tears come faster.

"Take a deep breath and tell me what happened."

It takes me a few minutes to get control of myself, and then I start from the beginning.

When I'm finished, when I've cried myself out, she wraps an arm around me and says, "Well, the first thing we have to do is find out who Graham Briggs is." She pulls out her phone. "Graham Briggs. Oh, look, he has his own Wikipedia page."

"What? He has a Wikipedia page?"

"Let me read this. I'll skip over the boring stuff. Born in London in 1969, Graham Briggs is a world-renowned architect who specializes in historical buildings and arts venues. He is best known for his renovation of NoTe Studios in Warwick, England, a stone barn built in the early seventeen hundreds, where bands such as Crackerjack and Hot for Teacher have recorded iconic albums. He also designed the art museum blah-de-blah-blah-blah and a performing arts center in yada yada."

She looks up from her phone. "He's an *architect*, Juniper.

Who designed a *recording studio* in a *stone barn*. Are any of these pieces coming together for you yet?"

I sit up. "Oh, shit."

"Yeah," she agrees. "Why didn't you google this guy *before* you called Gabe?"

"I didn't think of that! Heat of the moment!"

"OK, how about *after* you called Gabe?"

"Amelia!" I wail. "What should I do?"

"Call him? Tell him you screwed up?"

"It's too late. He's gone. And I told him what I'd done. I'm no better than Marley Green. How will he ever forgive me for that?"

"I don't know," she says. "I wish I did. Why don't you start with a text?"

I start and delete dozens of messages before I hit send.

Me: I'm sorry. I was wrong. I miss you. Please call me so we can talk about this.

Chapter Forty-Three

GABE

Ted: Well how'd you manage to fuck this up?

Me: At airport. Flight boards soon.

Ted: Nice try. I'm calling you.

Me: Nice try. I won't answer.

Ted: LeeLee says Juniper's a MESS. What's going on? Why are you at the airport?

Me: Going back to LA where I belong. Juniper can tell you what's going on. If she's a mess, it's her mess. Not my problem.

Ted: Harsh.

Me: That's life, I guess. Gotta go. They're calling my section.

They're not calling my section. I'm shaking and my heart's racing and *shit*, I can't have this happen in the middle of Concourse F. I close my eyes, take a deep breath, try to think of something that will work to get me past this, think of a time and place when I didn't feel this endless, relentless feeling. Something other than all those perfect moments with Juniper. Those perfect, pretend moments.

"Sir," someone's saying above me, "are you all right? Would you like some water?"

I take the bottle of water the Delta gate attendant is holding out to me. My hands are shaking so much, I can't twist open the cap, so she takes it back and does it for me.

"Is there someone I can call? Or I can call a paramedic if you think—"

"No." I cut her off. "I'll be fine. Thank you for the water."

She nods. I drink, scrub my hand across my face, take deep breaths until the moment passes. Satisfied that I'm OK, she walks back to the gate.

Before I board, another text notification comes through.

Juniper: I'm sorry. I was wrong. I miss you. Please call me so we can talk about this.

I power off my phone.

On the plane, I close my eyes and wish for sleep, but all I see is the ice blue of Juniper's eyes.

Chapter Forty-Four

JUNIPER

GABE DOESN'T RESPOND TO MY TEXT.

I'm in a funk, my stomach churning, alternating between the guilt of what I've done and obsessively thinking of how I can fix this.

I text him again. He doesn't respond. I try calling, but he sends me to voice mail.

Sunday night, Mom starts to dig as we wash the dishes after supper. Gabe's gone. Chris flew back to LA, too. It's just the two of us.

"How are you doing, Juniper?" she asks.

"I'm fine," I say.

"Are you fine? What happened between you and Gabe?"

I sniffle. I'm not sure that I'm ready to tell her the whole story. "I don't know where to begin," I admit. "Things have gotten so tangled up."

"They might not seem so tangled once you talk through it."

I swallow hard. "How do you deal with the possibility that someday, Gabe and Chris might sell the farm?"

"Oh, honey. I wake up every morning and I tackle my to-do list. I've got a farm to run *today*. The sheep don't care what's going to happen tomorrow. I can't worry about what I can't control, Juniper. If there's one thing I've learned in life, it's that."

"Easier said than done," I say, sniffling again.

She rinses the last plate and hands it to me to dry, then pulls the stopper out. "Let's go in the living room, and you can tell me what's going on."

We move to the living room sofa, and I rest my head on her shoulder. I'm so tired, so wrung out. "You know how you're always telling me that you can catch more flies with honey than you can with vinegar?"

"Yes, of course. In fact, I recall telling you that about Gabe when you wanted nothing to do with him."

I nod. "Well, I may have taken it a step too far."

"Oh, Juniper, what did you do?"

Now I can't stop the tears. I let them roll down my cheeks and splash onto my hands where they lay in my lap.

"Sweetheart," Mom says, "just say the words. You'll feel better after you say them, I promise."

Or I'll feel much, much worse.

"You might not like me very much after I say them," I sob. Mom wraps an arm around me and tucks me in close. I take a deep breath and I say it: "I broke the rules of the farm."

"You broke the rules of the farm? That's not . . ."

"I know!" I wail. "That's not how I was raised. Rule number one: Always tell the truth. I've always told the truth, even if it hurts, but something in me flipped when I found out Gabe could sell the farm. I needed to do whatever it took to keep everything the way it's supposed to be!"

"Honey, you can't always stop change from happening."

"I know!" I wail again. "But then, something else happened. The more time I spent with Gabe, the more I got to know him, I actually started to *like* him. I *wanted* to be his friend, truly. And then—" I sob, and more hot tears streak down my cheeks.

"Go on."

"I think . . . I think . . . that I'm in love with him, Mom. I think I love him."

She doesn't say anything. She simply holds me while I cry, and I let it all out.

"Does Gabe know that you . . . lied to him? Is that why he went back to Los Angeles?"

"Yes. I've tried to apologize. I've sent so many texts to tell him that I know now that the man in the field was an architect. Why didn't he tell me? We could have avoided this whole situation!"

"Or maybe you shouldn't act so impulsively," she says and pats my knee.

"He won't respond to my text messages."

"Have you called him?"

"Sent to voice mail."

"You know that you need to somehow tell him that you know. And you need to tell him how you feel," she says firmly. "That you love him."

I shake my head.

"Yes, Juniper. Life's too short to let a misunderstanding or whatever this is come between you. Don't let one more day pass by. Tell him the truth, what you've just told me. And then tell him that you love him if that's how you feel. Whatever happens, happens. But you have to tell him."

"How? If he doesn't take my calls or answer my texts?"

"You'll find a way," she says.

✿ ✿ ✿

Chloe Horrible corners me in the hallway by the library Monday morning before school. "Oh my God, Juniper, you look absolutely terrible."

"Thanks, Chlo." I roll my eyes.

"I have something for that under-eye puffiness. I'll text you the link."

"Chloe. What do you want?"

She glances down at her sparkly pink glitter nails and then slowly back up at me. "I wanted to say that I'm really sorry Gabe went back to LA and I hope he comes back soon. And not for me!" My eyebrows shoot up as her words rush out in a steady stream. "Don't get the wrong idea. I swear, I'm not after him anymore. For *you*. I hope he comes back for *you*. You two make such a cute couple. So, that's it. I hope you two can work it out."

She shrugs, turns quickly, and saunters down the hall.

"Wow," Amelia says as she walks up beside me. "Did that really happen?"

I nod. "It did."

She puts her arm around my shoulder and squeezes.

"Teddy wants to know if you want to come to the movies with us tonight. Five-dollar Monday."

I try to laugh, but it comes out as more of a puff. "No, thanks."

"Why not? The three of us used to go to the movies together all the time."

"That was before you two won Cutest Couple."

She scoffs. "The voting isn't until March."

"It'll be a landslide."

"The movie?" she prods.

I smile at my best friend. "I love you. You know that. But I think I'll stay home and wallow in my misery."

"Hey," she says. "I've known you for a long time, Juniper. You're super badass. I know it hurts and you miss him, but I know how strong you are. You're going to get through this."

The lyrics to "Juniper Blue" follow me wherever I go.

I muddle through another day at school, and during Marxen's class—without Gabe—I come up with a plan. It's not a sure thing, and it's not a rom-com-level grand gesture, but it's from my heart and that's the best I can do. I stay up late, sitting at my desk with a sketchbook and a pail of bright, cheerful markers.

After Mom's gone to bed, I snoop through her desk until I find Chris's Venice Beach address in her planner. I stop by the post office on my way to school Wednesday. I drop my heart in the mailbox.

Chapter Forty-Five

GABE

LA is LA.

Nothing has changed here since I left. It's as eclectic and electric as it's ever been. The city moves at its same brisk, determined pace.

I'm the one who's stopped moving forward.

In my short time in Minnesota, in the cold and the clouds, Juniper burst into my life, a vibrant kaleidoscope, and filled my days with sunshine and color. She made me want to be better.

This isn't better.

I didn't think this through.

Now that I'm back in LA and away from that place, maybe I can figure out a way to get that money. The clock's ticking.

Then again, fuck it. I'm tired. I'll figure it out tomorrow.

✿ ✿ ✿

Monday. I get up around noon, move to a lounger next to the pool, and fall asleep until midafternoon. I shuffle into the kitchen and sit down heavily on a stool at the breakfast bar. Chris, who I've avoided since he got back late last night, puts a plate of food in front of me. I eat a little, move the food around, and drink water to help alleviate the dehydration I feel after sleeping in the sun all day.

"Call her," Chris says. "Let her explain. She knows about the architect now. Tell her about the recording studio. Tell her your plans."

I shake my head. "The recording studio's off. All the plans for the farm. They're all off."

"Like hell they are. The only thing that's off around here is *you*. Snap out of it already and get your shit together, Gabe."

"So nurturing of you in my time of crisis," I mutter.

"I see your heartbreak is also messing with your head," he says. "Don't be stupid."

I go back to bed.

I wake up, sweating and twisted in the sheets, gasping for breath.

"You good?" Chris is standing in the doorway. "I heard you yelling all the way in my office."

"What—fuck. What did I say?"

"Couldn't make out the words. I'm starting to worry here, Gabe. What can I do to help you through this?"

God, there it is again, echoes of "Juniper Blue." I shake my head. "You can't help me with this one," I say.

But—could he?

"I'm good," I say. I look at the watch on the nightstand. It's 11:18, but the windows are dark so it must still be night. I switch off the lamp and turn over, my back to the doorway.

✧ ✧ ✧

Tuesday. I swim. I call the delivery service, send them to a nearby farmers' market, and charge it to Chris's account. "Bring me whatever's in season, whatever looks good," I say.

A couple of hours and a couple of hundred dollars later, the kitchen overflows with produce, most of which I don't recognize and will probably spoil before we can possibly eat it all. I call Chris's chef to take care of it. All afternoon, I hear him swearing and muttering about the young fool in love. That night, though, Chris and I are treated to salmon and an amazing array of vegetable side dishes. I try every single one.

Nothing tastes as good as Laurel's chili with cinnamon and honey. Nothing beats sitting at their homey farmhouse table, bickering with Juniper.

It's too hot here. The sun shines too much. There's no variety. No rain. No hard frost.

"Do you think it's snowed there yet?" I ask at dinner.

"Snowed where?" Chris asks.

"Back home."

He shrugs. "Why don't you call Juniper up and ask her?"

I push my plate away and go back out to the pool.

My neighbors, Genesis and Collins, come over to invite me to their upcoming party. They're twins, a year younger than me, named for, well, the band Genesis and Phil Collins. I try not to hold that against them. They're good people, even if their parents do have questionable taste in music. Their parents are *loaded*, both of them entertainment lawyers or something. Maybe they can help me out. We're friends, right?

"This party is going to be so fetch," Genesis says and giggles.

"Stop trying to make fetch a thing, Gretchen," her brother says, mimicking *Mean Girls*, their favorite movie. He doesn't get the line quite right, I think. They both dissolve into laughter.

"I've got plans that night."

Genesis pouts. "But we haven't even told you what night!" she says.

"Didn't you say Saturday?" I guess.

Genesis and Collins look at each other incredulously. "Did we?" Collins asks. "It *is* Saturday."

"I hate to miss it," I lie.

Always tell the truth.

Genesis sits down at the foot of my lounger and pats my foot. "Gabe, we're so, so sorry for all your troubles. Marley— she's so lovely. I'm sorry you're hurting."

"Thanks, Gen," I say. "That's nice of you to say."

"I heard she's out," Collins says. "Of *rehab*."

"Is she?" My stomach twists. She might be out of rehab, but she's not knocking down my door to pay me back. "I hadn't heard."

"KidCo canceled her contract," Gen says, shaking her head. "I probably shouldn't spread rumors, but I heard that she's planning to sue them. Poor thing."

Poor thing. Poor Marley. Poor me.

"You look terrible, you know," Gen says. "But let us know if you change your mind about the party."

"Or if you need a little something to help you through this," Collins adds. "You know what I mean."

Oh, fuck no. Fuck Gen and Collins and their designer drugs. I may be out of my head shattered, but I'm not going to mess with that shit.

I go inside. I wander around the house and mentally catalog things I could sell. All of it belongs to Chris. I'm chasing my own tail.

I think about Juniper. I try not to think about Juniper. I wonder if she's thinking about me.

✧ ✧ ✧

Wednesday. Graham Briggs calls to finalize dates for the spring.

"I'm still in Harper's Mill," he says, "and the photojournalist from *Architectural Inspiration* is flying in for the first photo shoot later this week. I was hoping you'd come back before I'm due back in London so I could show you what I have in mind. I think you'll love it. That's quite a building you've got there."

I almost call off the project, but this isn't only about me. This is Chris's farm, too. And Laurel's and Juniper's, even if their names aren't on the deed.

"I trust you," I tell him instead. The words sound hollow.

✧ ✧ ✧

Thursday morning, Chris yanks the sheet off my bed while I'm still sleeping.

"Get your lazy ass out of bed," he growls. He shoves his phone in my face. "You want to tell me what this is about?"

I rub sleep out of my eyes and look at the screen. He's got a text conversation pulled up. Rocky. Oh, fuck. I sit up, my hands shaking, an ocean of fear and adrenaline and despair rushing through every cell.

Rocky: Hey it's Rock. Any word on the cash? Mtg with Chris Jan 3. Shoot for at least a month before that so I can play around with shit.

Fucking Rocky. It's not every detail, but it's enough. I look up from the phone to Chris. His face is red, his jaw tight, his fists clenched. "Chris, I can explain—"

"Check your phone," he bites out as he takes his back.

"What?"

"Check your fucking phone, Gabe. I'll wait." His words are a blade of steel, even and cold and sharp.

I reach for my phone on the nightstand and swipe it open.

Shit. I can't believe I didn't hear it blowing up.

Rocky: This is Rocky. Answer your fucking phone kid we got an issue
Rocky: Not kidding here I fucked up big time
Rocky: Goddamn it we have a situation I sent a text to your goddamn dad and thought it was you

Rocky: We are in deep shit if you don't get to that text before Chris does

Everything goes cold, my blood freezes, the hard frost.

I look up at Chris, open my mouth, nothing comes out.

"Well?" he roars. "You want to tell me what the *fuck* Rocky's talking about?"

I rub a hand across my eyes. I'm between a rock and a fucking hard place, and I've got nowhere else to go.

I shake my head, not so much to tell him no as to clear it. This can't be happening. How could Rocky have been so stupid?

How could I have been so stupid?

"Tell me the goddamn truth, Gabe," Chris yells.

Always tell the truth.

I get out of bed, pull on dirty jeans and a T-shirt, and pace. There's no way around it now.

I tell him the truth. All of it. Marley and the drugs, Rocky, the money. All the shit that's happened since. I tell him about Juniper and how she lied to me, and I tell him about my stupid shattered heart.

"How much?" he asks when I'm out of words and out of breath. He's not yelling, but the lines of his face are drawn and tight. His jaw twitches. "How much did you take?"

I press the heels of my hands against my eyes, aching and raw. I can't look at him as I tell him the dollar amount. He whistles. "That's a lot of smack," he says. "Jesus, Gabe, what the hell were you thinking?"

"I fucked up," I say, my voice thick and rough. "I don't blame you if you want to call the cops or, shit, I don't know."

"Calm down. I'm not going to call the cops." He scrubs a hand across his eyes.

"Don't fire Rocky," I blurt out. "This isn't his fault. This is on me."

"This *is* on you," he agrees, "and you're going to figure out a way to pay me back, but Rocky needs to own up for his part, too."

"I begged him." My heart's pounding. I can't catch my breath.

"Calm down, OK? Focus on something else for a minute. Try to breathe."

I put my hand across my abdomen where the brick of dread lives, swallow hard, inhale and blow it out, long and heavy.

"Don't worry about Rocky," Chris says. "I'm not going to toss him aside for fucking up. His heart is always in the right place. Like yours."

I shake my head. "My heart is about as fucked up as my head."

"You've got a lot of shit to fix, I'll give you that, so first things first, we're going back to Minnesota."

"Go ahead," I mutter, "I'm not going."

"The hell you aren't, Gabe. We've got a meeting with Graham to talk about renovations."

"*You've* got a meeting with Graham. FaceTime me in. I'm not going."

"You're going. You owe me a shit ton of money, which you're going to pay back with interest, by the way. And if I say you're going back home, you're going back home."

"It's your home, not mine," I spit.

"It *is* your home," he says, and he sounds pissed again. "Don't argue with me about this."

"I'm *not* going." I can't see her. I can't see Juniper and own up to what I've done.

"You're miserable. Go back home and work things out with Juniper."

It's like he can read my mind. Yes, I'm miserable. I'm so fucking miserable I don't know what to do or how to move past the misery.

I walk to my bathroom and close the door. "I'm not going," I say loudly.

"Have it your way," Chris calls after me. "But know that I'm putting this house on the market. You have one week to get your shit together before my real estate agent starts showing it."

✧ ✧ ✧

Friday. Chris leaves for Minnesota. I stay in bed until two in the afternoon. The house is too empty, too quiet.

I text Rocky.

Me: Sorry for the mess. I'll fix it, I swear. Hope he wasn't too hard on you.
Rocky: Your dad's a *good* guy.

A good guy who's selling this house. I search for rental properties closer to the beach but close the app after five houses. I have no money to rent a place.

I watch the documentary about Graham Briggs and the stone barn recording studio. I listen to *Heartbreak Holiday,* the first album recorded there.

I go down to the basement studio and play guitar for the first time in days. I take Chris's Telecaster down from its place on the wall and play "Somebody to Shove."

I find a mandolin. I teach myself "The Battle of Evermore."

The weight of missing Juniper and the farm sits heavy on my chest.

I think about texting her back, calling her. I power off my phone and shove it under my pillow.

I grab my phone and power it back up. I type "therapists venice ca" in my search bar. I scroll through the results, click on a few. I change the city to "frederick lake mn." The results list is smaller. I read through them all until I find an anxiety guy whose bio says he's on a mission to hike in all fifty states and he likes to go to concerts. Odds are he likes country music. I take a chance and make an appointment.

I search for last-minute flights to Minnesota.

God, I miss her. I miss her eyes and her smile and her laugh. I miss arguing with her. I miss her stubborn streak. I miss that she's so stuck in her routines. I miss that she was willing to try new things because I encouraged her. I miss our adventures. I miss us.

I fall asleep on the living room sofa, my arm thrown over my eyes to block out the goddamn sun.

When I wake, it's late, dark.

When I wake, the hole in my chest from missing her has tripled in size.

Then I remember.

She betrayed me. She broke me.

I cancel my appointment.

I delete the Delta app.

I delete her contact.

Saturday. A letter arrives from Minnesota.

One word is written in the upper left corner where a return address should be.

Blue

Stare at the envelope for what feels like an hour.

Take a shower.

Check the refrigerator. Make scrambled eggs with tomatoes, spinach, even radishes. We still have so many vegetables.

Play "High Hopes" on the grand piano in a great room designed specifically for the instrument. The acoustics here are amazing, but still it doesn't sound nearly as good as Gran's out-of-tune, hundred-year-old upright.

Go for a run, the first time I've left the house in days.

Take another shower.

Stare at the envelope.

Dig through the cupboards to see if Chris has any tea. In luck. Find sealed plastic pouches with loose tea and labels in

Juniper's handwriting: *Bliss Blend, Serenitea Now!, Summer Sunshine.*

Google how to make tea.

Too fucking hot. Wait for it to cool down.

Open the envelope.

In the envelope, I find a single sheet of thick paper that looks like it's been torn from one of the journals in her greenhouse. The notebook where she jots down her ideas. The paper is bursting with color, like Juniper herself, a rainbow of words and doodles: clouds, flowers, a waterfall, headphones, a pizza, a ghost. Across the top, in a blue the color of her eyes, she has written *30 Days of Adventure.* Below is a numbered list:

1. Eat a slice of pepperoni pizza
2. Go out for Mexican instead of pizza after the football game
3. Listen to *Led Zeppelin IV* on vinyl
4. Watch *Singles*
5. Hike (part of) the Willard Munger Trail
6. Go to a haunted house
7. Drink a cup of coffee instead of tea
8. Adopt a rescue dog*
9. Visit a fire station
10. Visit an art museum
11. Make egg rolls with Youa
12. Drive a stick shift
13. Sleep in a tent (brrr)

14. Bake a pumpkin pie
15. Order ribs instead of chicken from Happy's
16. Play touch football with Ted and Frankie
17. Write lyrics to a song**
18. Shear a sheep***
19. Photograph the round barn
20. Make a candle
21. Finish a crossword puzzle
22. Deliver Meals on Wheels
23. Volunteer at the food shelf
24. Travel the entire Skyline Parkway in Duluth
25. Dye my hair
26. Eat peanut butter M&Ms
27. Fly a kite
28. Wear jeans (!!)
29. Go rock climbing at the Y
30. *Live in the sunshine, swim the sea, drink the wild air*
if Mom says it's OK
**with guidance from a professional (you)*
***this will have to wait until spring*

Beneath the list, there's a note.

Gabe, I want to live in the sunshine, swim the sea, and drink the wild air with you by my side. I want to try new things and go on adventures with you. Thank you for challenging me. Thank you for seeing me. I love you with all my heart. I've never meant anything more than I mean that. And I'm sorry for everything and anything that hurt you. Please forgive me. Please come home.

My heart fills with the magnitude of her words. All the stress, the heartache, the worry, the panic, everything I've felt for such a long time melts away. I don't know whether to laugh at her ridiculous aspirations or call her and ream her out for even thinking about dyeing her beautiful hair. I fold the letter and slip it back into the envelope, lift it to my nose. Somehow, it smells like her, like cherries and vanilla.

In less than three hours, I'm at LAX waiting to board a flight back home.

Chapter Forty-Six

JUNIPER

Sunday morning, I get up early to work the farmers' market, but Mom waves me off.

"Janie and Izzy are managing the booth today," she says. "I think you could use the break."

"What about you?" I ask. Mom hasn't missed a farmers' market since—well, ever.

She shrugs. "I don't mind a break once in a while."

I go back to bed for another hour. I drink cup after cup of tea. I research the Willard Munger State Trail and nearby haunted houses. I order *Singles* on Blu-ray and find an online candle-making tutorial. I search the basement for our old tent. Later, I'll set it up to air it out. This will have to be one of the first things I do, before it gets too cold or snows.

I take a long shower with one of Guinevere's aromatherapy tablets. I leave my curls wet and braid half around the crown. I pull on olive-green cargo pants and a long-sleeved T-shirt that reads, *Hike More, Worry Less*. I should do both of those things. I peek out the window. Sunshine, blue skies. Maybe after lunch, I'll hike to the overlook.

I've felt better since sending Gabe the list—and much, much worse. Worried that he'll toss it in the trash without even reading it. Send it back. Burn it.

Mom pops her head in a few minutes before noon. "Glad to see you're up and moving. Lunch is ready and we've got company."

I sigh. I'm not sure that I'm in the mood for company, but I follow a few minutes later. I walk downstairs into the kitchen, expecting to see Mom or Chris at the table. The kitchen's empty, Gabe's favorite chili bubbling on the stove. When I turn toward the window to see if they're in the back-yard, I see Gabe standing at the door. I gasp.

"Hey," he says as he takes a step toward me. I take one back and bump up against the counter. I blink. He's really here, standing in my kitchen. He looks exactly like he did the last time I saw him—wearing Chris's Army jacket and a pair of worn jeans. His T-shirt's different, though. Today, he's wearing Soul Asylum. His hair's still a mess of dark curls, the skin under his eyes still dark and shaded. He looks terrible, but so terribly good.

"What—what are you doing here?" I ask, clearing my ragged throat.

"I got your letter," he says. "How are you?"

That's it? I got your letter? *That's* his reaction to my adventure list, my apology, my heart on the page? I'm happy to see him, but I'm sad and worried and frustrated, too. And *pissed*.

"How am I? How do you think? I'm miserable! You didn't respond to my text messages or answer my calls. You haven't given me a chance to tell you that I'm sorry I jumped to conclusions and acted like a complete bitch. And I lied to you and the whole mess with the honey and the vinegar. And I miss you, Gabe. I miss you so incredibly much, I don't know up from down! I miss you so much I must have checked flights to LA three thousand times this week even though I hate to leave home!"

"I'm sorry you've been miserable. Would it help to know that I've been miserable, too?" he asks.

"No. Not even a little bit." Of course I don't want him to be miserable.

He smiles that wide grin I love so much. "You know," he says, "you were wearing that exact outfit the first day I was here. Do you remember?"

I shake my head. *This* is what he wants to talk about?

"You were rude to me that morning, Blue," he says.

"*You* were rude to *me*." He's closer now, so I can poke him in the chest when I speak.

"I was." He reaches up and grabs my finger. "I've missed arguing with you."

"You came back," I whisper.

"I came back." He clears his throat and takes my hand fully into his, holding it against the word *Soul* on his T-shirt, against his heart. I can feel its strong beats. "Blue. There's something I have to tell you, and it's not going to be easy."

My eyes go wide and my stomach sinks.

"No," he says quickly, tightening his grip. "We're not selling, I promise you. Don't even think that for a minute, OK? The architect, the round barn, the recording studio—all that is really happening. We're not going anywhere."

I nod.

He takes a deep breath before he continues. "This isn't about the farm. You know already that things were bad with me and Marley for a while. She was in rough shape and she—she needed money. She came to me for help."

He swallows hard and turns his head to look away from me, then turns back almost immediately. His green eyes lock with mine.

"I didn't have the money, Blue. I was broke—I'm still broke—but I had to help her."

He stops and I squeeze his hand. "Go on," I say.

He gives a short burst of a bitter laugh. "You might not like me very much when you hear what I have to say."

"Gabe," I murmur, "that's not possible. Tell me."

"I stole money. From Chris. Marley was going to pay me back—well, she said she was, anyway—but then the wedding happened and rehab and I ended up here, and this whole time I've been trying to figure out a way to pay the money back before Chris found out. But he found out. I really fucked things up."

I suck in a breath as he runs his free hand through his long curls. Of all the things he might say to me now, this is the last thing I could imagine. I'm stunned. That he would do this, yes, but that he's been dealing with this for so long, alone, in a strange place. And I treated him horribly.

"Say something," he says, his voice breaking. "If it's too much, if you can't be with me because of it, tell me now."

I blink and screw up my face in confusion. "If I can't be with you?" I echo. "Gabe, you're *human*. You're a good person. You wanted to help."

"I screwed up," he says, his words filled with anguish.

"We all screw up," I whisper. "When you love someone, though, there's enough room for mistakes and forgiveness and second chances."

He lets out a long breath. "When you love someone," he repeats as he leans in to kiss that sensitive part of my cheek close to my ear.

"What . . . what are you doing?"

"Kissing my girl," he says. "Please tell me that you'll give me another chance."

A tear pools in the corner of one eye and escapes. He kisses that, too.

"Don't cry, Blue," he whispers, his breath like a promise on my skin.

"You came back," I say again.

"We've already established that."

"Are you staying?"

"God, yes."

I swallow, relieved. "OK," I say as I nod. "Good."

"Good. We've got to get started on your list of adventures," he continues, his tone light and playful and *Gabe*. "I'm not sold on dyeing your hair, though, and we'd better find a campground ASAP because it's pretty fucking cold to be sleeping outside in a tent."

I laugh, and it's the best feeling, to be laughing with him again. "Tell me about the studio. You brought in some fancy British architect, then?"

He nods, then kisses me near the opposite eye. "We'll only do this if you think it's a good idea. Graham's still in town. We've invited him to lunch to go over the plans. Chris and I want you and Laurel to have a say, too."

"I don't know anything about recording studios. And it's your farm, Gabe."

"It's your farm, too. It always has been. It always will be, one way or another."

He kisses me again, this time at the corner of my mouth. I hum.

"When did you get my letter?"

"Yesterday."

"When did you fly back?"

"Last night. I got back to the farm around midnight, and I wanted to throw pebbles at your window to wake you up. It's been so hard to wait to see you."

"You read the letter and booked a flight? Just like that?"

"Just like that. Luckily, I've racked up some miles over the years."

"It seems so . . . too easy. I should have sent you that list days ago. Before you left. Before we fought."

He laughs at my ridiculous statement. "Easy is good. Life's too short for difficult, Blue." He drags his lips from my ear along my jaw. "I don't want to be apart anymore. I want to go to school here and graduate and learn more about farming. Learn how to be a steward for the animals, the earth, our livelihood. I'm glad you want to live in the sunshine with me. Because I want that, too."

He's quoting the rules and my list. The tears are streaming freely now. He wipes them away with his thumbs.

"I love you," I croak out between sobs.

"That's good, because I love you, too." He smiles. "See? Easy."

"Please don't go away again." I lean toward him, and finally, finally, he puts his arms around me. "I'm so sorry for everything I did. I've been miserable without you. I need you. The farm needs you."

"I need the farm," he says. "That's one thing that became crystal clear in LA. More than that, though, I need *you*. I want to be with you, here, if you'll let me."

My heart melts. I smile up at him as he takes my hand again, and I'm filled with a rush of contentment, anticipation, love. This must be what all the love songs are about.

He kisses me again, this time on my lips, a long, lingering kiss that hints of a future together.

"I've been thinking," he says after we move apart, with our foreheads still touching, "about all the ways we can make the farm better. Maybe some of the ideas we had for Field & Flock. The recording studio is just the beginning."

I nod. "The recording studio is perfect. I can't think of a better way for you and Chris to honor the farm."

"You smell good," he says. "Like cherries and vanilla. That's one of my favorite things about you."

I smile. "What are some of your other favorite things about me?"

"How long do you have?" He pulls me into a hug, his chin resting on top of my head, and inhales deeply. "I love that for your entire life, you always ordered the same thing at Seasons Tavern. I love that you tried something new there. I love your unique outfits and your fake glasses."

"My glasses are not fake! This is not LA!"

He ignores me. "By the way, we'll be going through Gran's closets soon. You're welcome to take any of her things."

"Are you serious?" I hold back a squeal.

"It's all yours. Whatever you'd like. Now, where was I? I love that you hike even when it's fucking freezing outside. I love that you aren't afraid of coyotes. I love your tea."

"Oh, you tried some, then?"

"Chris had some in his cabinet. I believe my favorite is Serenitea Now! Very clever. And calming."

"It took me forever to get that one right. What else?"

"I love *you*, Juniper. I love everything about you, even when you're extra salty. Especially when you're extra salty."

I relax into him, loving the feeling of his arms around me. "Next time we go to Seasons Tavern, I'm ordering the fettuccine with shrimp and asparagus. Vivian's Variety was good, but I missed my fettuccine."

He laughs. I love that laugh. I never again want to go one day without hearing it.

"Next time I build you a fire down at the river, I'm going to play you the song I wrote for you."

I look up at his bright, open face, his flashing green eyes. "You wrote a song for me?"

He nods. "A love song. I've never written one before. You make me want to write love songs, Blue." He kisses the side of my neck.

"What are you doing later?" I ask. "Want to go on a hike up to the overlook?"

"Oh yeah," he says, moving his lips from my neck to my jaw, "if it means we can make out up there."

I laugh and lean away so I can stare at his beautiful eyes. "I'm in for a lot of adventures with you, aren't I?"

He nods. "Every single day."

Acknowledgments

Writing a book while packing up and selling our home and moving to a new state—all during a global pandemic—was not easy. I owe so many people my thanks, beginning with my agent, Steven Chudney, and editors Erica Finkel and Bethany Strout. I'm grateful for your time, insight, and intuition. To everyone at Abrams who worked on this book—wow! You did it again. What a gorgeous book.

My Beez—my dear friends and closest writing companions—Liz Parker, Rebekah Faubion, and Tracey Neithercott, I couldn't have done this (or anything in 2020) without you by my virtual side. I'm so thankful for your friendship and encouragement. I can't wait until we can all be together again.

Thanks to Allison Benson, Casie Beldo, and Mel Brutger for your unique contributions and for cheering me on. As always, thanks to Linda Diaz, Maris Ehlers, Sara Naegle, and the UMD gang: Heather Green, Jacqueline Bonneville, Jana Oman, Jody Rittmiller, Katie O'Dell, LeeAnn Evans, and Teresa Robinson. Love you all!

I found inspiration for this book in many places, and it took many years to cultivate. I owe my thanks to my longtime neighbor Bob Dylan and his son Jakob Dylan for planting the tiny seed of an idea, and to Chris Cornell for helping that seed grow. Chris, no one sings like you anymore. This book would not exist without your gifts to the world. I'm forever grateful.

Very early on, I told my husband, Troy, that I needed a name for a '90s grunge band that had faded away but made a big comeback. "Dig Me Under," he said. "It's from an Alice in Chains song." I put it in the book. The next thing I knew, Troy was writing songs for Dig Me Under, including one called "The Last Thing You Said" for my first book. The band became a real thing, with a fictional lead singer. Troy and our friends Kendall, Debbie, and Mike recorded an album, released it on digital, vinyl, and CD, and played at the launch party for *The Last Thing You Said*. I love how our creative endeavors came together because of this book. Troy, you are my rock and my rock star. Thank you for everything. I love you.

And thanks, as always, to my kids, Jude and Halen, for your love and hugs. Dream big.

About the Author

Sara Biren is the author of *The Last Thing You Said* and *Cold Day in the Sun*. She earned an MFA in creative writing from Minnesota State University, Mankato. She lives in Wisconsin with her husband and two children. Visit her at sarabiren.com.